ADULT PUBLISHING FOR
MIDDLE-SCHOOL GIRLS

D1133533

ADULT PUBLISHING FOR MIDDLE-SCHOOL GIRLS

a novel

S. J. Coffey

LUMINARE PRESS
WWW.LUMINAREPRESS.COM

Printed in the United States of America

Luminare Press
442 Charnelton St.
Eugene, OR 97401
www.luminarepress.com

LCCN: 2021911315
ISBN: 978-1-64388-682-4

For my mother Sarah,
who taught me the power of grace and dignity

Chapter 1

CARSICKNESS AND BIG GAME HUNTING IN NORTHWEST ARIZONA

S aguaro cactus, barrel cactus (five of those), green road sign full of buckshot holes (the words "Kingman–28 Miles" visible between the pocks), prickly pear cactus with two pear-shaped pink fruits left on it, another saguaro cactus (this one with a broken arm, looks like a wounded soldier), burned-out yellow Volkswagen bus with no side door...

We pass a dirt-brown roadrunner bird. Sorry, bird, Wylie Coyote might feel differently, but you're just not as fast as a car. Ugh, my stomach feels weird again.

"Dad, how much longer?"

"About ten minutes less than the last time you asked, Melanie. We'll be home soon. See what else you can observe between now and then."

I don't want to observe. I want to go pee, eat a baloney sandwich and finish reading my new issue of *Tiger Beat* magazine. But I forgot it at the hotel in Phoenix and I couldn't read it right now anyways, because I'd throw up before we even hit the city limits. So much for finding out who "The Hottest Hunk of 1976" is. I blast a puff of hot breath on my window, draw a mushroom cloud with my finger and wish for the world to blow up. I am so bored. Bored, bored, bored.

I'm not supposed to curse. My mom says only women who buy their shoes at thrift stores and leave the house without lipstick on curse. But I don't think that's true. My Aunt Marnie buys all her shoes at the Ferragamo's in the Tri-City Mall down in Scottsdale, and I've heard that lady use the f-word in all eight parts of speech. And yes, there are eight parts of speech. Eight. I know this because English is the only class I ever get an A in, and someday, when I'm free of my insipid little town, I'm going to move to New York City and be a writer. Not a writer of novels, or for ladies' magazines or any of that crap. I'm going to write for *The New Yorker*. I have things to say, and my dad says that when one has things to say and wants to say them well, one writes for *The New Yorker*. He also listens to a lot of jazz and drinks beer from a tall, skinny glass. My mother says he looks pretentious but it is my theory that before one can *be* something, one must *behave* like that something, so I am supportive of my father's efforts to be cool.

I am not cool. I am a dork. I am aware of this and accept it as the lot of an above-average thinker. In addition, I am a girl. And I—like so many of my beleaguered gender—have been marginalized and underestimated by the male persons of my ridiculous community pretty much every day of my short, sunburned life. Having blond hair does not help. If one more zit-faced, pubescent boy tells me another blond joke, I'm going to murder him. I don't care if I go to jail. I'm a minor and it'll be the juvenile jail, for sure. Doesn't worry me one bit. Aunt Marnie spent her entire sophomore year in juvy and she's got more money than anybody in our family; clean criminal record too, and obviously, better shoes.

It is hot as *hell* today. There's a reason why most of the people who grow up in Arizona never make it past the ninth grade. This state is perfect for creatures with small, reptilian brains, and that includes the ingrates who call the trailer park on the outskirts of town home.

Butler is five miles of redneck. My dad keeps telling my mom that if we don't move to a more civilized place, like Flagstaff, and soon, I'll end up married to a cowboy and living in a Butler single-wide with five kids and a cookie jar full of pot. I myself have never tried marijuana, but I'm pretty sure my fifteen-year-old brother Steven has. Either that or he's just really fond of sandalwood incense.

My brother is a problem. Not because he is a bad person. He isn't. He has a fine sense of humor and more often than not he can be counted upon to retrieve our report cards from the mailbox before our parents can get them (so they can be altered more to our favor). On a day-to-day basis he is, however, impossibly annoying.

Look at him over there, passed out cold in his stupid Black Sabbath T-shirt, his stupid head bumping against the stupid window of our stupid Chevy Suburban wagon. And this afternoon—because it's September and still like the surface of the sun, and because my mother is "chilly" and refuses to turn up the air conditioner, and because I'm so prone to car sickness I can't even tie my shoes in a moving vehicle without tasting my own bile—he is especially annoying. And I am bored. And this is a dangerous combination.

Steven is asleep and therefore a vulnerable and entertaining target. A flap of oily, paper-bag-colored hair is obscuring the better part of his face, including his thick glasses and a good-sized pimple that's formed in the dangerous crease between his nose and his cheek. But his hair can't cover the punishable offense that's developing just above his chin. A drop of drool has traversed his chapped lower lip and is dropping on Ozzy Osborne's fabric face. Something must be done. Not just to assuage my boredom and my complaining bladder, but because common standards of decency and public health demand it. I surveil my environs and assess the situation for hazards.

In front of me, my parents sit on the wide, white vinyl bench seat as far apart from each other as space and automobile engineering will tolerate. My father hums a Charlie Parker tune and studies the road from behind his gold aviators. He's losing his hair but he's still handsome in a dad kind of way. Like my brother, my mother dozes against the passenger side window, her curly, permed head jiggling in rhythm with the road. She's very pretty for a mom. Everyone says so. I'm not sure she knows it, though. I think that makes her prettier.

I look over at my brother again and smile as a marvelously adventurous and entertaining scenario begins to percolate inside my thirteen-year-old brain. The rousing theme from television's most popular animal program, *Wild Kingdom* (Sunday nights at 7:00 p.m., check your listings) swells in my head, and I hear the voice of the show's venerable host, Marlin Perkins, "We've got to be cautious when approaching the adolescent boy. One wrong move and our girl could end up with a saliva coated finger in her ear, or perhaps even a serious wedgie."

I heed his advice and carefully slide my bare left foot across the seat. Just before my big toe is about to make contact with the back pocket of Steve's jeans, we hit a pothole. He groans and turns toward the door. I hold my breath and listen to Marlon, "That was a close call, but now the dozing animal has given us a perfect shot at his hindquarters. My brave assistant loads her rifle with a tranquilizer cartridge and takes aim…"

I inch my toe closer, give his behind a quick jab, then hastily retract my foot and tuck it back under my lime-green sun dress. I wait. Nothing. "It seems my assistant has just missed her target," Marlon concedes, "but another attempt could prove fruitful." I slip my foot across the seat and poke at Steve's right butt cheek again, then pull my foot back under my dress like an offended hermit crab pulling herself back into her hijacked shell. Steve doesn't open his eyes, but he does rub his backside and mumble something about kicking my butt. Marlon is elated. "We got him! But the glancing blow won't be enough to bring the big fellow down. My assistant reloads as I maneuver the jeep to a better location."

I have to take a moment to think here. Sure, I'm no longer bored, and the adrenaline buzz I've achieved by hassling my poor brother is helping to distract me from having to pee, but if I continue with this, there could be consequences. Serious ones. Steven's best buddy Larry just recently taught him the fine art of "The Frog." It's a punch that's delivered to the fattest part of a major muscle group, preferably the shoulder or the front of the victim's thigh, with the middle knuckle of the fist jutting slightly beyond the other digits. When executed correctly, this attack results in a concentration of force when it hits the flesh, producing an agonizing lump that if watched closely appears to throb, or "ribbit" as the victim moans in pain and plots revenge. This, and the accompanying threat, which usually involves telling Mom what I've been up to, is something I desperately want to avoid.

I look out the window. We're still a solid ten minutes from town and if I don't distract my brain from my bladder with another hit of mischief-related adrenaline, I'm going to pee my pants, for sure. I eye my brother again. He does look to be truly asleep. My pulse rate takes a welcome jump. I slip my foot over, and with a notable degree of force I shove my toes into the portion of my brother's pants that most likely covers his butt crack. "It's a direct hit!" Marlon exclaims. "And moments later the beast is fast asleep and ready for weighing and tagging."

But the beast is not asleep. He is wide awake, and before I can yank my foot back under my dress, his hand shoots out and clamps onto my ankle. Steve is silent and very, very mad. So my parents don't hear, I scream-whisper, "I'm sorry! I'm sorry! I'm sorry!" But it's too late. Riled and not at all sleepy from the tranquilizer dart dangling from his denim butt, the beast assesses his prey. Steven's glasses sit cockeyed on his face, and his hair sticks up on one side, but he does not look remotely silly. "You're dead meat," he snarls, pulling my leg to his side of the seat.

"I said I was sorry! I didn't mean it!" I whine. Suddenly, the lunacy of this statement strikes me. It simply does not make sense. "You were sleeping peacefully and bothering no one, and out of nowhere, I jabbed my foot into your butt. And I did this for no other reason than to entertain myself. But I didn't mean to do it, even though I planned it for ten minutes." What?

My brother raises his balled-up fist in front of my face and pushes the middle knuckle up into a dangerous triangle. I suddenly feel the error of my ways and repent by doing the only thing I know will save me. I scream. I scream like a starlet with a chainsaw murderer on her jiggling tail. My

S. J. Coffey

dad hits the brake pedal, bringing the three-thousand-pound family fun vehicle to a screeching stop on the dusty shoulder of the road.

"Dan!" my mother wails. She sits up, her dented hairdo head swiveling back and forth in confusion. "What was that awful noise? Did we hit a coyote?"

"It was *her* fault," my brother growls as he releases my ankle.

"Was not!" I squeal. "Mom, he was gonna give me a frog!"

At this, my mother gives a little jump, lifts her salad-plate-sized sunglasses from her nose, and begins nervously scanning the interior of the car. "Steven Joseph, I told you to quit carrying those things around in your pockets!"

"I was not gonna give you a frog, you spaz."

"Yes, you were! You had your knuckle out and everything!"

"Oh, good Lord. Dan, you've got to search the car. If that thing dies in here we'll never get the smell out."

"Keep your feet outta my butt, you little freak."

"I am not a freak! Mom, he called me a freak!

"You're not a freak, dear. Steven, stop calling your sister a freak. Dan, did you hear what I said?"

"You got in trouble, you got in trouble!" I chime, turning the ridiculous retort into a song.

"Shut up, freak."

"I'm not a freak! Mom, he's doing it again!"

"That's enough, Steven. Now get out of the car and help your father look for that thing."

"What thing? And why do I have to help?"

"The frog you brought in this car, young man."

"What frog?"

"Dan, why are you just sitting there staring at the road? Help me here."

"Are too a freak, you little spaz."

"I am not! Mom!"

"People who poke their feet in other people's butts are freaks, freak!"

"Mom!"

"KNOCK IT OFF!" My father shifts the Suburban into drive again and pulls back out onto the highway. "Everybody just…be quiet."

"Are you all right, dear?" my mother asks cautiously. "Shouldn't we look for the frog?"

My dad lets out long breath. "I'll take care of it when we get home." My mother looks like she's about to say something more, but then stops herself and pulls her feet up onto the seat. Behind my parents' heads, Steve flips me the bird and mouths the words "dead" and "meat" before rearranging his glasses on his nose and turning to look out his window.

My dad eyes my brother in the rearview mirror. "We've talked about you harassing your sister, Steve."

"When we get home, you'll go straight to your room, young man," my mom sentences.

Understandably, Steven is not okay with this punishment. "Unbelievable," he complains. "She sticks her foot in my butt and *I* get in trouble."

This is unacceptable to me, as clearly I am the affronted party. "Oh, sure," I defend. "He threatens me with bodily harm, and as penance he gets to go to his favorite place in the whole world and worship the devil with Blue Oyster Cult again. Lovely."

My mother turns and lowers her giant sunglasses. "And you can spend the evening in your room, as well, Melanie JoAnne."

"But I was gonna go to a sleepover at Anna's with Leslie!" I am in agony.

Steven gloats, "Halleluiah. Justice."

"You're such a Neanderthal." I'm nearly in tears. Leslie will most definitely have a copy of the coveted *Tiger Beat* I lost, and Anna's mom makes the best brownies on the planet. All is lost. My brother twists the knife.

"And you're a wuss who gets away with murder just because you're a girl."

I sulk and stare out the window at the dusty basin town in the distance. Okay, so maybe my bonehead brother's right. Girls do get away with a lot. But there's way more stuff we can't do, like cursing or doing anything else fun. Seems like only the cool chicks who do stuff they're not supposed to do get to go anywhere in this world or do anything important. Seems like girls have to spend an inordinate amount of time primping and protecting themselves. Seems like boys get all the marbles. Seems like it stinks to be a girl.

Chapter 2

BUS STOP, BUS STOP

The variegated-iron stop sign pole I lean against is jabbing directly into my third thoracic vertebrae. Then there are my books: *Introduction to Algebra*; *Journeys in Physical Science*; a paperback copy of Jane Austen's *Pride and Prejudice*; and four yellow Pee-Chee pocket folders that are seriously testing the limits of my biceps. But I can't move. I'm watching a journey of physical science right in front of me. It's 7:43 a.m. and not six feet away, pressed against the Robertson's putty-colored garage wall, seventh grader Diane Rimerez is getting a tonsil check from eighth grader Cliff Barret's tongue. Her hands are in the back pockets of his Levi 501s and his hands are all over the horseshoe seam on the back of her Dittos bell-bottoms. I'm pretty sure that when the Robertsons agreed to allow the Mohave County School District to designate their address as a sanctioned bus stop, they had no idea it would become a make-out spot. Their house, which is conveniently located on the edge of our housing development on Southwest Desert Shadows Drive and Third, is the fifteenth, and second to last, stop on bus twelve's route to Kingman Junior High School. It is also apparently a good place to start an unplanned pregnancy.

I'm just deciding Diane and Cliff are only a few minutes away from parenthood when a scabby white hand smacks my carefully stacked learning materials, sending the whole shebang cascading down into the powdery dirt.

"Dennis!" I don't need to look up to know it's him—Dennis Franklin, our school's self-appointed comedian and trouble-maker-in-chief.

"Hey, Chaffee, dropped your stuff."

Smirking Dennis is parked on the banana seat of his metal flake, cherry-red Schwinn. He's flanked on either side by his irritating (but far less problematic) flunkies, Sean Mendoza and Joe Thomasson, who are straddling a beat-up navy-blue Huffy single-speed and a women's powder-blue Free Spirit three-speed, respectively. Under another leader's rule, these two would both be nice kids. But Dennis's vile influence has made sweet, chubby Sean and wiry, shy Joe accomplices to every ill-conceived plot or prank that Dennis comes up with. I stoop down and gather my things and I notice, as usual, that the stooges are trying to see down my shirt.

"You know, Dennis, if you want to ogle some action, just look over there." I point to Diane and Cliff. "Those two are so close I feel like *I* need to go to the free clinic." I dust off my Jane Austen and shoot him a glare.

"Diane Rimerez is a slut," Dennis says.

Sean shakes his head. "We didn't see anything, Mel, honest."

Dennis laughs. "Yeah, cuz there's nothing to see!" Joe laughs too. Sean does not.

"My cousin Diane isn't a slut. She's nice," he says, frowning.

Dennis's assessment of my mammary situation, although cruel, is not incorrect. I should be used to his insults by now. I've been a favorite target of his since we moved here two years ago. I am odd. Dennis reviles the odd.

I'm wounded but I hide it, grateful for bus twelve's arrival. I follow Cliff and Diane, their hands still on each other's backsides, to the bus. For some reason, Dennis decides to button up our latest encounter with a characteristically witty quip.

"See you in science, flat Chaffee!" he shouts. I sigh, one foot on the bus's first step.

"Why don't you clowns skip the attempts at an actual education past the seventh grade and just get jobs at the Gas and Go now?"

Dennis looks confused, but Joe is pained. "Hey, my brother just made assistant manager there."

"Exactly." I say, as I escape into the safety of the bus.

<hr>

Dennis watches the bus pull away in a dusty cloud. "She's so weird," he pronounces, before attacking Sean. "Hey dufus, where is it?"

"Where's what?" Sean asks, just before a dim light flickers on behind his eye sockets. "Oh, *that!*" Grinning, he digs in his beat-up Spiderman bookbag, then produces several ragged catalog pages. Dennis grabs them, smoothing the wrinkles as if the glossy images of women in functional white brassieres might be some sort of ancient, adolescent-boy scripture. Frowning, he throws the papers on the ground and glowers at Sean.

"Is that it? You can't see anything in those! They got underwear on!"

Sean shrugs. "It's all I could get."

Joe bends and picks up the discarded pseudo porn. "You shouldn't litter."

Dennis gazes off into the distance. "I want, no, I *need*,

to see real women. Naked women." He turns his attention to Joe.

"You got three older brothers, Joe, don't any of them have a *Penthouse* layin' around?" Joe shakes his head. Dennis lets out an exaggerated sigh. "Not even a *Playboy?*"

"You've met my brothers. It's a blue-ribbon day if I don't get more than four wedgies—I mean the 'change your shorts' kind of wedgies. You think any of them are gonna give me their porn?" Joe's hands are out in a plaintive, palms up sign of submission as Sean nods in solidarity.

"I've met your brothers..."

Dennis lets out another dramatic sigh. "What is it with you guys? Do I gotta do everything in this outfit?" Joe and Sean exchange a look of shared pain and Dennis throws his bike around, hits the pedals and speeds off, spraying his two best buddies in gravel and dust. "C'mon, you idiots! We're gonna be late for science again!"

Joe brushes dirt off his shoulder. Sean puzzles, "Tell me again why we put up with that guy?" This is a challenging question for Joe but, being a philosophical sort, he ventures a surprisingly esoteric response.

"I think the fact that we even have to ask ourselves that question *is* the answer to that question." Sean nods thoughtfully, then the two turn their bikes around and head off after Dennis.

———◇———

I'm sitting at the very back of the bus. It's bumpy and I can feel my Cheerios rising in my throat. Even thinking about Leif Garrett in a sparkly button-down shirt opened to his navel isn't helping. We jerk to a stop on Riatta Park Street and Fifteenth. One kid gets on the bus. It's Alan Bomart, or "Fat Alan" as he has been (unfairly, I think) labeled by the genius think tank that is my school. He's scooching down the aisle toward me, his flanks barely clearing the seats as spitballs and chewed pencils arc to and fro over his head and across his path. Despite the onslaught from his peers, Alan is smiling sweetly. He's always smiling. I've never figured out why everyone calls him Fat Alan when his most obvious trait is that he's always inexplicably smiling. People see what they see first and don't look much further, sometimes, I guess.

Smiling Alan has made his way to me. There were seats available along his journey towards me, but none were very hospitable. As the bus lurches forward, he drops his gentle smile on me. It is a nice smile. "Hey, Alan, wanna sit here?" I say, and he nods and sits down delicately next to me. He does not lumber or plop into the seat, and he is careful not to allow his girth to touch me in any way. He smells delightful, like the cloudy pink ceramic bowl of potpourri that sits on the back of my grandma's toilet. I study his pale freckled arm. It's patched with a delicate, coppery fuzz that matches his curling short hair. He gives me another soft smile. His eyes are very blue and very big, with pale yellow lashes I can hardly see. "I'm Melanie," I say.

Alan puts out his hand. "Nice to meet you, Melanie," he says, and I take his padded palm in mine. It the softest, pillowiest thing I have ever felt, and warm and dry too. I like him immediately, and this is very rare. I generally do not like anyone immediately, choosing instead to reserve my opinions about a person for at least a day or two. First impressions cannot be trusted. I'm a writer and writers do their research.

Alan and I stare ahead for a moment as the bus jiggles along and I try to keep my breakfast down. Then he turns to me and says, "Thank you for letting me sit by you. I'm kind of large and, well, people don't usually want me to take up two-thirds of their sitting space." His voice is as soft as his smile and kind of lilting and tinkling.

I smile. "You're not even taking up half of our seat. And you smell just splendid." Smiling Alan's smile broadens.

"Thank you for saying that."

"You're very welcome but you don't have to thank me for everything. I should thank you. You're taking up space that could otherwise be occupied by a less agreeable person of your gender, like Dennis Franklin."

I shudder, and (like a rounder, pinker version of myself in a mirror) Alan shudders, too. "Oh, he is a very distasteful boy, isn't he?" This is fantastic. Someone of the male persuasion in our school thinks Dennis Franklin, who is unexplainably popular, is as repellant a human being as I do. This is comforting beyond words. I throw an arm around Smiling Alan's considerable shoulders. "You, sir, can sit beside me any time you like." Alan beams. His cheeks are almost matching his hair. Today is definitely improving.

Chapter 3

ANATOMY LESSONS

Draped in high quality, navy-blue slacks, Mr. Greely's round behind jiggles in time with his arm as he scribbles on the blackboard, which is green. It is the most amazing butt I've ever seen and quietly, under my breath, I say so. "It's absolutely *lofty*. I could have a tea party on that thing." I turn to my lab partner, Mavis Jackson, the only black girl in our entire school and by far the coolest chick, for sure.

In her smooth, low alto, Mavis concurs, "Uh huh. Mister Greely is F.I.N.E., fine." Mavis always looks more like a final round contestant on *Soul Train* than an eighth grader in a small desert town. She's got a huge afro, acres of gold jewelry, and she wears platform shoes that would give most girls a nosebleed. We met two years ago in Physical Science class. She was my first friend here. After three classes and two conversations, she pronounced me, "weird but cool" and asked to copy my homework. We have been friends ever since, but strangely have never seen each other's homes.

We are waiting for class to start as I work on an anatomical drawing of a woman I plan to use for a project we have to present soon. Mavis is grossed out. "Uh, guts."

"Too much?" I ask.

"Kinda. Nice titties though. Very accurate. Damn, you can draw. I can do algebra all day long but I can't draw for shit."

Mavis is not wrong. I can draw. I do not, however, plan to pursue a career in art. My father is an artist and rather than *create* art, he *teaches* art. This is a situation that makes both him and my mother unhappy. He oversees the sculpture department at the local community college, but since the dean of the department there is only 32 years old and has no intention of leaving the position for more profitable climes anytime soon, it is unlikely my dad will ever be promoted.

"Thanks," I tell Mavis. "I like anatomy. It's one of the few things I don't stink at."

At this, Mavis scoffs. "Hey, I don't copy just any ol' kid's homework, you know." Again, she isn't wrong. Mavis is the first person I've ever let co-opt my schoolwork. I don't know if this is because I like her, and she likes me, or because she is the only black girl in our school and I feel bad about it.

Mr. Greely is finishing up his novella on the green blackboard just as a spitball bounces off the back of my head. "Hey!" I complain and turn around to see Dennis and Joe and Sean all giggling wildly at the last table in the back of the room.

Mavis follows my gaze. "I think Dennis likes you."

"Gross! Dennis is the worst." I look down at my chest. "Besides, I lack the assets to garner even that creep's attention."

"Awe, you're not doin' too bad, there." She offers a warm smile and I look over at her hands. Each finger sports a large, dangerous-looking ring. Some even have two.

"Hey, Mavis, how come you wear so many rings?"

Mavis lets out a little chuckle. "Hurts more when you hit somebody."

"Oh. Gotcha. Do you have to hit people a lot?" I ask.

Mavis's face clouds. "More 'n most girls, I imagine."

"You mean white girls, huh?"

Mavis just shrugs and I'm not sure what to say. Thankfully, Mr. Greely turns and begins strolling down the center of the room. "This year's first exam will be next Monday. Bring paper. You'll need to draw your own diagrams." He stops in front of our table and looks down at my drawing. He picks it up. I want to crawl under the table. He lifts the paper and slowly—painfully slowly—pans it around the room so every kid can get a good look at it. Titters and snorts escape from the class. I want to die. Mr. Greely clearly does not care. "And I know we can't all draw like Melanie here, but just do your best, okay?" He looks a little more closely at the drawing and his eyebrows reach for his hairline. "Whoa. Um, just keep them G-rated, okay?" He slips the paper back onto the table in front of me. "Exceptional work, Ms. Chaffee, but put a shirt on her, okay?" He smiles kindly, but I am confused.

"She's a cadaver..." I offer lamely. But Greely hasn't even heard me. His magnificent backside is already making its way back up to the front of the room. I frown and look over at Mavis. "Cadavers don't wear *clothes*."

Mavis is no help. "Hey man, I ain't the teacher."

I hear boys whispering loudly and turn to look at the back of the room. Dennis and the other two stooges huddle. Joe feels me staring at them and looks back at me. His eyes are wide. And very guilty.

Chapter 4

LOCKER TALK AND BULLIES WITH GOOD HAIR

The bell rings and Mavis and I follow the stooges out of the science classroom. They are still whispering among themselves and now and then one of them turns and gives me a furtive glance. I am disturbed. "What're those three clowns up to?" I ask Mavis. She frowns and adjusts a giant hoop earring.

"Hell, if I know. White boys don't make any sense to me at all."

I sigh. "I don't think *any* boys make sense to me. They're all weird."

"Mmm hmm. You said it, sister." Mavis puts out her palm. I slap it soundly.

"See you at lunch?" I ask. She smiles and nods before peeling off and heading down the hall, hoops and hips swinging. I watch her go for a second, then turn and hurry to the other end of the hall where my locker is. As I walk, I recite the prayer I always offer on my way to my locker. "Please don't let her be there. Please don't let her be there…" But when I'm almost there, there she is: Stephanie Harris, the most dangerous girl in the school. She leans against the bank of lockers, her left platform-sandaled foot directly in front of my locker. Her back is to me, but I know it's her. On the outside she is perfect. Her hair, an exact replica of Farrah Fawcett Majors' hair, is perfect. Her face, enhanced by seriously disco-rific makeup, is perfect. And I won't even get started on her tall, slim body capped with solid C cups. The grooviness disparity here is utterly glaring. Why in the world would God bestow so much on someone so unworthy? Because, under her Charlie's (fourth) Angel exterior, there lurks the mind and soul of a demon. I'm not kidding here. This girl is terrifying. Her five-coats-of-mascara, baby-blue-eyed glare can whither the soul of even the most self-confident and emotionally secure person on the planet, boy or girl. And the universe, in all its perverse wisdom, has chosen to put her boyfriend's locker directly above mine.

As I kneel to open my locker, I inadvertently brush the leg of Stephanie's bell-bottom jean leg. And like an aphid that has tweaked the outer ring of a spider's web, I am doomed. I look up. Predictably, her arachnid highness in staring down at me. She gives me a slow, slimy smile. Stephanie is a transplant from Atlanta, Georgia and her voice is syrupy and black, like poisoned molasses. "Why, looky here, Ethan, it's your lil neighbor." Ethan Wilde is the Devil Queen's boyfriend and quite possibly the most beautiful boy I've ever seen. And now he's looking down at me, too. The universe hates me.

"I'm sorry. Excuse me." I apologize and try to work the combination on my lock.

"No excuse for you." Stephanie lets out a plastic giggle. "Just kidding," she says, smiling.

I fuss with my lock. It's a new lock and a new year and so far, neither one of the two is working very well.

"That silly ol' lock still givin' you troubles?" Stephanie drawls. She pulls her attention from her prey to address her intended. "Ethan, honey, you should help her." I pray for him to ignore her and just walk away and leave me to deal with my uncooperative lock in peace. My prayer is not answered. I'm about to try the whole danged combination again when he kneels down beside me. Ethan Wilde. I can smell him before I look over at him. He smells spicy and warm, like a Christmas dessert. I take a breath and look over. His pale green eyes—fringed by velvet black lashes— are on mine, and I'm having trouble letting out the breath I just sucked in.

"Here, let me give it a try," he says. I drop my hand from the lock and nod. His caramel-colored hands take the lock. "What's the combo?" he asks.

Speak, Melanie, speak! "Um, fifty-four, twenty-three, five." She spoke! Give that girl a gold star!

I watch as he tries the numbers. I can see the tendons and muscles moving under the so-smooth skin of his forearm. He has a hangnail on his index finger. Someone should trim that for him. It's going to tear. He is wearing a red and white baseball T-shirt and faded Levi's. And as he works the lock, his unkept, shiny black hair swings in front of his eyes, causing him to flip it away in the most intoxicating manner. He pulls on the lock and it pops open. His eyes are on mine again and he grins, lips so fluffy, teeth, so, white… This is the part where you thank him, idiot.

"Um, thank you. It's, it's been giving me trouble for like, three weeks."

"Maybe I can get you a new one. I'm in good with the janitor. I play cards with him sometimes and I always let him win. He's old so I figure why not, ya know?"

I nod numbly. "That's really nice of you."

Ethan just shrugs, and I open my locker and pull out books, pull out papers. He's still here, next to me, looking in my locker. I feel naked. He spots my battered copy of *Pride and Prejudice* and smiles. "You read Austen?"

"Oh, yeah. Jane's kinda my hero, or ya know, heroine." I laugh. In my head it sounds tinny and ridiculous. Ethan is about to answer but from above, like an omnipotent, deadly goddess, Stephanie interjects.

"Ethan, baby. You gonna be all day?"

I watch sadly as Ethan stands. "Well, see you around," he says, and then his back is to me and walking away, Stephanie by his side. She gives her hair a toss, giggles and whispers something in his ear. Ethan doesn't appear to be listening, and then for some reason he looks over his shoulder at me and, what? Is that a smile? Did he just smile at me? I'm more confused than flattered and not entirely comfortable in a world where Ethan Wilde smiles at me. It's as terrifying as it is exhilarating. What's next? Am I going to wake up tomorrow a 32DD? I look down at my chest and decided that while that would be lovely, it is obviously medically impossible.

I wonder if Ethan actually reads Jane Austen. If so, that would further confirm my belief that the world is an absurd and often unjust place. Someone who looks (not to mention smells) like that shouldn't also get to be intellectually well-rounded. If I find out he's good at math, too, I will become hopelessly jaded. I slam my locker shut and start off for home economics class because—without an adequate education in the particulars of managing a home and family—how will I ever survive? Ahead of me, Ethan and Stephanie turn to go into Mrs. Stein's advanced algebra class. Well, there it is. He's good at math. I am envisioning my life as a lonely New York writer with too many cats when—just before he follows the Evil Princess Stephanie into the room—he looks down the hall, fixes his emerald eyes on me and smiles, again.

Chapter 5

BEST FRIENDS, DUDS AND LUCKY CLOVERS

We are sitting on the grass in the far right corner of the Kingman Junior High School football field. I like to sit out here with my friends. When there are no games going on it's a quiet area and its proximity to athletic pursuits makes me feel ironic. To my left, Anna sits cross-legged. In her lap, opened to a horrific crime scene photograph of Annie Chapman, the second victim of Jack-the-Ripper, is a huge hard cover book. Anna has short, no nonsense hair and favors a neutral palette for everything, even her watchband is beige. To my right, my other best friend, Leslie is on her hands and knees picking through a patch of clover, her aquiline, tanned face inches from the ground. She is everything I am not—bouncy, outgoing, good-natured and totally at home in P.E. class. You should see this girl serve a volleyball.

"Oh!" she squeals, plucking a tiny plant from its peers. "I found one!" She drops onto her backside and shoves the clover under Anna's nose. "Look!" Anna dutifully examines the treasure and sniffs.

"Nope. It's a dud."

Leslie is undaunted. "No, it isn't. It's got a fourth leaf, right there." She points.

With the smugness of someone who already knows they're right, Anna looks at the clover again. "That's a mutated third leaf."

Disappointed, Leslie chucks the unworthy, tortured sprig back into the patch from which it came, so it can be mourned by its fellows. I look across the field to where Ethan Wilde and a few other boys toss a football back and forth and call each other names. I'm flummoxed. "Why would he smile at me?" I say. "I don't think he so much as looked at me last year."

"Maybe you had something in your teeth," Anna posits.

Leslie, not to be out-posited, weighs in. "Was Carl Higgins behind you? He's always pulling his pants down for no reason. That always makes me laugh."

"No, Leslie. Carl was not behind me. If he had been, I would have smelled him. And I definitely brushed my teeth this morning, see?" I offer a grimace and both girls nod in approval.

"Nice work. I admire your dedication to oral health," says Anna.

Leslie's eyes widen, and she gasps. "Oh! I forgot to brush mine!" she huffs a breath in Anna's direction. "Do I have stinky breath?"

"No more so than usual." If Anna were any more droll she would be English. Leslie frowns and goes back to foraging for clovers of fortune, and I stare at Ethan again. The way he lobs a football gives me goosebumps. I chide myself for my foolish submission to my own hormones and wonder again why this Grecian example of pubescent male perfection would even look at me, let alone give me a smile.

"He smiled at me. Twice. I'm sure of it." I am sure of it. Ever since I started getting periods this past summer, I'm rarely sure of anything, but I am very sure about this. Leslie murders another clover, thinks, and then springs a little, as if she's about to take off like a rocket.

"Oh! I bet he was gonna ask you to the Harvest Dance!"

"Oh, yeah, and maybe Carter will solve the mid-east crisis with cookies and milk. Sheesh." Other thirteen-year-old girls would probably roll their eyes here, but Anna detests eye-rolling and all other things hackneyed and over-used.

Leslie scoffs. "My dad says Carter's doing a great job."

"Your dad's a left-wing pinko," Anna replies, her deadpan voice never changing octaves.

"He is not." But Leslie drops the defense in favor of another brilliant and insane idea. "You should ask *him* to the dance!"

Anna lets out a little snort. "Dream on, goofy. He's going with Stephanie Harris."

"How do you know?" Leslie counters.

"Yeah, smarty-slacks, how do you know?" Predictably, I am with my more optimistic friend on this one. Anna lets out an irritated sigh. Being best friends with your intellectual inferiors can be terribly exhausting.

"Because," she explains, "I've studied human behavior, that's why."

"Yeah, deviant human behavior." I roll my eyes. I'm too young to concern myself with being hackneyed and over-used. Anna frowns. I've insulted her hobby, and possibly her doctoral dissertation as well.

"I don't study deviant human behavior," she defends.

"Anna, you alphabetize your books on Northern European serial killers." I'm right. I've seen them, two full shelves, A to Z. Again, from Anna, the exasperated sigh.

"The rippers are unique and don't represent standard deviant behavior. They're just an interesting anomaly. Anyway, that's how it works. The alpha male always chooses the alpha female." Anna rests her case.

Leslie is silent for a moment and her forehead crinkles and she cocks her head to the left and eyes Anna. "What's an anomaly?" she asks.

I don't wait for Anna to answer. I've got this one. "An anomaly is something odd, like me."

Chapter 6

DRESS SHOPPING AND THE INTERNATIONAL JEWEL THIEF ACROSS THE STREET

We just got a new neighbor and I think she's a criminal. I'm sitting in the front seat of the Suburban watching the house across the street while I wait for my mother. Usually she's waiting for me but today I was ready early. It's Saturday and sometimes on Saturdays, Shirley takes me out for a day of shopping and lunch. It is something she thinks I need. It is not. I hate shopping, but this week is different. I'm on the hunt for a special outfit for the dance next Friday, so I'm excited to get started on my mission. Also, I do like going out for lunch.

A long, gold Cadillac has just pulled into the driveway of the house directly across from ours. The driver side door swings open and a woman steps out. She is not at all like the other women in the neighborhood. She's very tall and very thin and very tanned, and aside from her slim gold lamé pants and short, chic, auburn hairdo, everything else she is wearing seems to float around her like a multi-colored cloud. With a proper tent pole, her caftan alone could shelter a family of four. Her sunglasses (which are also gold) are huge, and as I watch her pull shiny department store bags and parcels out of the rear trunk, I decide this lady's really got a thing for gold. She slams the trunk down with her elbow and clicks toward her front door on towering (yep, gold) heels. One of the bags swinging from her forearms is from Ferragamo's. She and my Aunt Marnie would have lots to talk about, I bet.

I wonder who she is and what in the world someone like her is doing in this weird little town. She belongs two hours north in Las Vegas. Maybe, I postulate, she's hiding out from the Nevada law. I watch her dig in her cavernous handbag for her keys, I assume, as I build her a lovely backstory. "The international jewel thief, weighed down by the spoils from her latest crime, heads inside to prepare dinner and relax with a languid bath before her lover's arrival…"

Our neighbor has finally located her keys, and she's opening her front door, and someone is knocking. From somewhere far away, I hear my mother. "Melanie, open the door." I'm busy. The jewel thief is turning sideways in an attempt to get herself and her packages into the house. Her keys are dangling from her snow-white teeth as she maneuvers. She's graceful and clumsy at the same time.

"Melanie, open the door, please!" My mother breaks into my reverie and I pull my eyes from our neighbor and I look across the car to the driver's side window, where Shirley is two inches from the glass and yelling at me. "Melanie JoAnne, open this door instantly!" I lean across the seat and pull up the lock. The door pops open and my mom drops into the seat with a huffing sound.

"Honestly, Mel. Why did you lock the door?"

"I didn't. It was already like that. My side was open, though," I say.

My mom stuffs the key into the ignition and pushes her giant sunglasses up. I have an idea. "Can we have the new neighbor lady over?" I ask.

"I suppose. Why?"

"Well, it would be neighborly, right?"

She lets out a little laugh. "Since when have you ever concerned yourself with being neighborly?"

"Since our new neighbor shops at Saks Fifth Avenue and is probably wanted by Interpol."

My mother gives me the look she usually gives me when she can't figure me out, and as we pull out of our driveway and onto the street, I catch a last glimpse of the jewel thief as she pushes her door closed and disappears into her house.

———⬦———

Babbitt's Department Store is the only department store in Kingman. It's like a shrunk down version of the big stores they have up in Vegas and down in Phoenix. My mother prefers to get most of our clothes at the JCPenney in Scottsdale, but occasionally she'll put aside her thrifty and sensible standards and splurge for something from Babbitt's, because, well, it's the only place in town.

In the junior department I flip through dresses on a rack. At another rack nearby, my mother is a satellite in my general orbit. I flip through the mini dresses. I flip through the long dresses. I flip through the midi dresses. How those are a thing, I have no idea. I think they are a kind of fashion suburb for the hopelessly indecisive. "A mini's too short, a maxi's too long, hey, I know, I'll go with something in between."

Flip, no. Flip, no. Ugly. Ugly. Really ugly. Flip. Might wear this one to Stephanie Harris's funeral. Several rounders away, somewhere near Jupiter, my mother pulls a long granny dress from a rack and holds it up. "How about this one? It's pretty." I look up and take in the *Little House on the Prairie* nightmare my mother has suggested.

"I know you miss college, Mom, but no." She frowns and puts the dress back.

"Don't be silly, Melanie. I wouldn't have been caught dead in that thing when I was in college."

"Then how come you want me to wear it?" I wander over to another rack and flip some more.

"I don't necessarily want you to get that one, dear. It just seems like that's what all the girls are wearing these days." I'm not like "all the girls". My mother knows this, but she chooses to behave as though she does not.

I weave through the rounders and racks, a python on a search for the tastiest, least furry mouse - maybe a baby one. My mind wanders and I think of Ethan. "In the battle for the noble, if not totally blind, Prince Ethan, I, the fairest and most powerful maiden in the land, know that I must acquire the perfect garment if I am to turn the prince's attention from the evil Princess Stephanie." I turn a corner and just as the junior department begins to merge with the women's department, I spot it. On a low riser, a headless mannequin sports a stylish, modern, polyblend skirt, vest and blazer combo in eye-searing lemon yellow. I stop breathing for a second and touch the hem of the skirt. The not-found-in-nature fabric is smooth and drapes beautifully. This is it. This is the one.

———————◇———————

The suit, my perfectly wonderful new suit, is encased safely inside a slick plastic garment bag and draped carefully over my arm. I follow my mom down the store's main aisle toward the exit. I look up at her and beam. "Thanks, Mom." She beams back at me. She's so pretty when she smiles. But then her eyebrows meet, and her smile disappears.

"It's a lovely suit, dear, but why would you want to wear it to a party?"

"It's not a party. It's a dance. And I don't want to wear any old dress. I want to make a statement. You know, say something."

"Well, that suit definitely makes a statement," she concedes.

We're ten feet from the exit when I see them. Tucked in amongst all the other ordinary platform sandals on a three-tiered display are THE shoes. The magic slippers, if you will, that could make my perfect ensemble complete. I stop and reverently pick one up. The walnut toe of the platform starts low, maybe an inch high, then rises gently to a daring three-inch heel. The straps are dark stained leather and crisscross over the toe. The buckles are bright, gold-toned brass. The jewel thief would approve. I'm about to announce that I must have them when my mother makes an entirely untrue statement. "Oh, good lord, Melanie, you'd break your ankle in those things."

"No, I wouldn't!" Given our proximity to the exit door, I skip bartering and badgering and go right to whining. It does not work. She's heading for the door. She pushes the glass door open. "You have a perfectly good pair of clogs at home."

Is she insane? "I hate those clogs!"

"Six months ago you *loved* those clogs. Said you'd *die* without them."

"But…" A pointless, last ditch effort, but I have to try.

"But nothing, dear. Put it back."

Bereft, I return the sandal to its partner on the rack. "They're perfect," I say as I follow my mom to the door. But before I walk out, I glance back at the shoes as if they are a lover I must leave. "Alas, I, the fairest maiden, could not acquire the magic slippers. I will have to attend the ball and try to win the heart of my beloved, wearing…clogs."

Chapter 7

ZEN, THE ART OF GRAVEL RAKING AND INDECENT PROPOSALS

My dad's aversion to yardwork is legendary in our neighborhood. Although gravel "lawns" are not uncom-
mon in Arizona, our green-free home is something to be
admired—we don't even have a cactus. While visitors to the
homes on the left and right of us are greeted by refreshing
islands of tiff green floating in rectangular oceans of bark
chips or sparkling white quartz rocks, guests to the Chaffee
Hacienda are required to ford an endless sea of pea gravel
by way of seven octagonal steppingstones stamped with
disturbing images of sleeping Mexican fellows wearing
oversized sombreros. And because our house is built on a
slight slope, said pea gravel is contained by a two-foot-high
beige slump block wall.

I'm sitting on the wall looking down at my sandaled
feet. Two weeks ago, during a sleepover at Leslie's, I painted
my toenails "All About That Red". It was a polish I selected
from Leslie's impressive nail color collection, and one that
my mother has deemed "garish". Even though I was, indeed,
"All About That Red" two weeks ago, today my mother has
demanded that I remove it, as it has become chipped and

"unladylike". My tanned, skinned and scabbed legs dangle from the front of the wall. It's warm on the of my backs of my thighs, but the cool afternoon air feels cold on the front of them so I keep getting waves of delicious goosebumps, as I stare at the house across the street. The living room drapes are open, but I don't see anyone moving around inside. There's a conspicuous long black sedan parked out front, though. It is impossibly shiny, and all the windows are covered in that dark plastic stuff that lets you see out but not in.

Behind me, wearing green plaid Bermuda shorts and doofy dad sandals, my father rakes his swimming pool of gravel. It's almost silent outside today, the only discernable sound is the rhythmic zinging of the metal rake over the tiny rocks. My warm thighs and the rake's hypnotic thwanging are making me a little sleepy. I'm thinking about boys. I'm thinking about Ethan Wilde.

"Dad?"

"Yup?" he answers, stepping up onto the wall next to me in an effort to better tidy those hard-to-reach edges of our "lawn".

"What do boys want?" This is not musing, or even an opening for small talk. I seriously need answers here.

The zinging sound stops and I look up at my dad, who leans on his rake, the corona of the vicious Arizona sun just behind his head. I've spent so much of my young life squinting, I'm betting I'll have a pair of impressive crow's feet by the time I graduate from high school. My dad takes a deep breath and swipes at the sweat collecting on his retreating hairline before bestowing his sage words on me.

"Food, sleep and girls," he states matter-of-factly. Then, looking very satisfied with his decisive, if not a little perfunctory, answer, he returns to rearranging rocks. This is unsatisfactory. I frown.

"In that order?" I press.

"In that order." He moves down the wall, reining in errant stones as he goes along. I need clarification.

"But what do they want from us—girls, I mean?" I fix my eyes on my dad, who suddenly looks uncomfortable.

"Didn't your mom cover all that with you last summer?"

Oh, darn it. My inquiry has taken an unintended, cringe-inducing detour. I correct course and steer away from the conversational cliff. "Not that! Ewww! I don't wanna talk about *that* with my dad!" Grown-ups can be so dumb. My father is clearly relieved.

"Whew. That's good." He deflates.

"I meant, how do I get one to *like* me?"

"Why would you want one to like you? They're noisy and they smell bad."

"You don't smell bad. And the only time Mom ever complains about you being noisy is when you turn up the volume on your Dave Brubeck albums."

"True. But what about your brother?"

"Ugh. His feet smell like dead animals," I concede.

"Well, there ya go." My father has raked his way back across the yard to the concrete walkway that goes from our front door and around to the driveway and the backyard which, coincidently, is enclosed with a taller—matching—block wall. He steps gingerly up onto the walkway, dragging the rake across his footprints and leaving the graveled expanse pristine.

"Dad, you really need to get a new hobby."

"I have other hobbies, dear daughter." He smiles, plucks a few devoted stones out of his rake and tosses them back into the yard.

"Like what? Name one," I challenge.

He thinks for a moment. "Well, I placate your mother *and* I look after you. That's two, smarty-pants."

"You could take up dancing. Mom loves dancing."

"Yeah, your mom does like to dance. 'Fraid I've got two left feet, though." He looks far away and a little sad. I decide I've put him through enough for one afternoon and watch as he heads down the walkway and disappears around the end of the garage.

I turn my attention back to the house across the street—her house—just in time to see the long black car's driver side door slam shut. The engine revs and the massive machine slides away from the curb and down the street. In the living room window, I can see her now. The tall woman with the short hair. She's wearing a long, satiny pink nightgown with a matching robe. I've heard my mom call those "peignoirs". I decide "peignoir" sounds way better than "nightgown" and am concluding that the French have better names for pretty much everything when the woman walks over to the window. She reaches up, grabs the edges of the drapes and pulls, disappearing behind the heavy, swinging fabric. It is a scene in desperate need of narration. Despite a lack of audience, I oblige. "The international jewel thief makes herself a gin martini with two olives, and retires to her boudoir to reflect on her afternoon with her mysterious lover…"

"My mom says that lady's a whore." It's Dennis Franklin, so reluctantly I dig myself out of my fantasy. On the street in front of me, Dennis, Sean and Joe roll up on their bikes.

"What do you want, Dennis? No, wait, let me guess. Your mom kicked you out of the double-wide again and you want to crash in my storage shed."

"Me and Sean and Joe got a job for you. I mean, if you want it."

"What sort of job?" I am instantly suspicious.

Looking almost nervous, Dennis shifts on his banana seat.

"Well, most kids think you're kind of a weirdo…"

"Thank you, Dennis. That information is *so* helpful," I deadpan.

"Well, ya gotta admit, your starship is seriously in need of a new onboard computer," he says.

"I'm getting annoyed, Dennis. And when I get annoyed, I get Steven." Surprisingly, Dennis manages to focus.

"Normally, I'd try to avoid being seen with you…"

"Steven!!!" I yell, as loud as I can, in the direction of our front door. Dennis gets to the point.

"…But you're still the best artist in the whole school, I swear!"

"I'm listening."

More shifting on banana seats and averted eyes. Dennis jumps in.

"We want you to draw us pictures."

"What kind of pictures?"

"Dirty ones. You know, naked ladies."

"What! Are you insane?" My voice is little too high, and cracks a bit. Dennis forges ahead.

"We'd pay you."

"How much?" I can't believe I'm even asking, but I can't stop myself.

"A dollar apiece."

"You want me to sell out my sisters—so you guys can get your pubescent jollies—for a *dollar?*"

"Pretty much, yeah." The other boys nod in fervent

agreement. I'm momentarily, and unusually, speechless. Is this what the males of my species have come to? Newly indignant, I stand and swipe at the dust on the back of my shorts.

"You guys need to get off of my lawn!"

Joe looks puzzled and a little scared. "But you don't have a lawn," he offers quietly.

"Go home!" I'm so angry and humiliated. I don't like Dennis Franklin. He is beyond icky. But he is popular. And I am disappointed in myself for even thinking for a second that any sort of association with this soon-to-be second-rate used car salesman could, or should, benefit me in any way. I am embarrassed. Tears threaten, and I need to flee.

"I said, go!"

Being made of more humane and considerate stuff, Sean and Joe turn their bikes and pedal away. I'm standing on the edge of the block wall glaring down at Dennis, who squints up at me, his face not entirely unkind.

"Just think about it, okay?" he pleads.

"Please, leave, *Dennis*." I spit out his name and, looking strangely humble, Dennis flips his Schwinn around, pushes off and pedals down the street after Sean and Joe.

"Perverts!" I yell, even though they can't hear me. And (eschewing the dozing Mexicans) I stomp across the yard to the front door, leaving at least a dozen deep divots in my dad's smooth, gravel Zen garden.

Chapter 8

THE ADOLESCENT GIRLS' COUNCIL ON HIGH CRIMES AND MISDEMEANORS

Anna's bedroom is not like other girls' bedrooms. Her full-sized bed has got a navy plaid spread that I'm pretty sure I saw in the boys' department of Babbitt's last week. The walls are lined with shelves and shelves of books (mostly hardbacks) and on her nightstand, next to a copy of the United States Constitution, is a framed picture of Barry Goldwater. The entire effect is less like a teenage girl's hangout and more like a Christian Science Reading Room.

I am in a quandary and Anna has graciously agreed to host a sleepover so that the two of us and Leslie can discuss the situation. It is also likely that over-consumption of products from Hostess, Frito-Lay and Mountain Dew will be on the docket. It's a chilly sixty degrees outside this evening, but Leslie has still elected to wear a pink halter top and shorts. She's sprawled on her belly, flipping through a copy of *Cosmopolitan* she pilfered from her older brother's girlfriend, Marla. Anna's in striped pajamas (also from the boys' department, I suspect) and leaning against the headboard biting her nails. Everything in Anna's world is utterly under control except her nails. What's left of them

S. J. Coffey

consists mostly of pathetic islands of nail bed surrounded by angry, abused flesh. She doesn't bring up this shortcoming. Neither does Leslie. And neither do I. It is hard enough to be a brainy adolescent girl growing up in a small town, without having your best friends berate you about a habit you clearly have no control over.

I'm on the bed, on my back, in my favorite *Charlie's Angels* T-shirt and jeans. I'm parallel to Anna and perpendicular to Leslie, my legs over hers. She keeps trying to kick my shins with the backs of her tennis shoes. It's only six p.m. and Leslie and I just got here. Generally when we arrive Anna is already in her pajamas. This is typical. She is academically gifted, overachieving, and has an eight-year-old brother named Toby whose main goal in life seems to be harassing his older sister. Her life is unusually stressful and after a long day of making her classmates feel inferior she likes to relax in her jammies. I get it and am without judgment on the matter. So is Leslie. It's a best friends thing.

Leslie shoves the *Cosmo* at me, now opened to a segment featuring a starved model posing in one of those high-legged swimsuits with the crisscross straps on the back. "Am I too fat for this?" she asks. This is an absurd question. Leslie is a star athlete on the girls track team. Her 400-meter race times often outpace those of the boys. I let out an annoyed breath and prop up on an elbow.

"Do we have to go over this again? No, you are not too fat for that, Leslie. You are not too fat for anything." I examine the photo in the magazine more closely. "You are, however, too young for that little number. Unless you're trying to give your dad a stroke."

"Yeah, he wouldn't let me wear it, I bet." Leslie flips the page to a quiz that claims to solve the burning question of whether or not your boss might have the hots for you. I go back to staring at the ceiling.

"Can you even believe it? Me, use my God-given talent to debauch my noble gender. I'm not that kind of a sellout."

"I'd pose nude." Leslie looks over at me and nods earnestly.

Anna glances up from her butchered fingertips. "You'd pose in a swimsuit made of beer cans."

"Well, I'm photogenic. Everybody says so." Leslie is correct. I hate having my picture taken with her. I could be wearing a designer dress made of nothing but diamonds and rubies, and she could stand next to me in a cardboard box and completely eclipse me. She really isn't conceited, though. To her, her appearance is just another part of who she is. Her mother died when she was three. She doesn't remember her, but she has four brothers and a father who all treat her like one of the pack. In their testosterone-soaked family, Leslie is just another puppy. She can wear danged near anything with ruffles AND shoot a rifle as well as any man. I fear for the first boy who tries to put his hand up her shirt if she doesn't want him to. She kicks my shin. "How come you're so quiet tonight? I thought we were all here cuz you wanna talk about something."

I prop up on both elbows and just throw it out there. "Okay, so, if you *draw* the pictures, is it still considered pornography?"

Anna frowns and attacks her pinky finger. "Depends on who you distribute it to."

"Thirteen-year-old boys?" I wince.

"Felony." Anna has drawn blood and reaches into her bedside drawer for a bandage.

"Boys are pigs," I pronounce.

Anna dabs ointment on her pinky. "Well, your favorite swine asked me about you today."

My heart skips and speeds up like I just saw a spider. "Ethan?"

"The very one. Wanted to copy my algebra homework—again—and he asked if you would be going to the dance. How's your ensemble for the evening coming along, anyway?"

I groan and drop back onto the bed. "I *need* those platforms!"

"So, buy them." Anna wraps the bandage around her finger a little too tightly. First it turns first pink, then purple. I give her stare.

"*I* don't have two grand in savings bonds and a compounding retirement plan like you do, Poindexter."

Leslie makes a face. "Ugh, clogs."

"I know!" At least she understands. Anna is blunter.

"Well, short of a new career in smut-peddling, you're screwed."

I pop a cheese puff into my mouth and glumly decide she's right.

Chapter 9

MONKEY SEE, MONKEY DO AND OTHER POOR DECISIONS

I t is Labor Day so there is no school. This is ideal because I am depressed—and not just because the dance *next* Friday and I may be forced to attend it in last year's clogs. I have also not been able, with any certainty, to turn down Dennis Franklin's insane offer. It should be a no-brainer. I am a feminist, a trail blazer, a defender of my oppressed gender, right?

I'm parked on the far end of the sofa in our sunken living room, pouting. Normally, this room is off limits during the day. Like many women of her generation, my mother feels strongly about having a room in the house dedicated solely to hosting company. But we don't have a family room. So in the afternoons, or sometimes when my mother is feeling sorry for me, she'll let me sit in here and watch her soap operas with her. I think she thinks we're bonding.

Today, because I don't have school (and because I've been moping and my mom is in a good mood) she's letting me sit in here with her and have lunch while we tune in to the goings on in *As the World Turns*' angsty fictional hamlet of Oakdale. She's also making my favorite—grill cheese sandwiches and tomato soup—and as she steps down into the room balancing a tray I grab the clicker and turn on the television.

"Chanel six, Mel," she says as she deftly sits down on the sofa next to me and slides the tray onto the coffee table. My mom is the most graceful person I know. Her posture is perfect and when she wears pumps she practically floats across the room. You can hardly hear the heels click on the floor. I always imagine her as a teenager in old-timey clothes, practicing her posture with a book on her head.

I give my mom a wan smile and then crunch into my sandwich as the soap opera begins.

"Would you like to play a few hands of Go Fish after we eat?" she asks. I nod and take a sip of hot soup and feel a little better.

---◇---

The program is almost over, and I look up over my cards at my mom as things wrap up for the day in Oakdale. "Go fish," I challenge. On the other end of the sofa my mother glares at me over her hand of at least fifteen cards.

"For goodness sake, Melanie, I've got half the deck here."

I just giggle a little and look over at the TV while she pulls another card from the stack on the table.

On the screen, a curvy actress in a cleavage-enhancing nightgown is cuddling a can of dark roast next to her powdered cheek. Her hair is definitely not her own and as she makes out with the can of coffee, a chisel-jawed actor with very shiny hair steps up behind her and kisses her neck. For some reason, this compels her to expound on the superior quality of this particular brand of coffee and she purrs,

"Gourmet House Coffee, perfect no matter how you like to wake up." Then she giggles and falls into a passionate kiss with the shiny-haired guy.

I'm frowning and studying the screen as an idea, a justification really, forms in my head. My mother reaches over and swipes her hand of cards across my nose, startling me.

"Honey, go fish." She smiles and laughs a little, and I smile back and draw a card.

"Mom, what's coffee got to do with women's breasts?" She looks taken aback but unruffled by the strange question and answers frankly.

"Very little, dear," she says, fussing with her voluminous collection of playing cards. "And that reminds me," she adds. "I invited the neighbor lady to dinner, per your ardent request."

"Really?" I'm intrigued and thankfully distracted. "What's her name?"

"Nina something. She seems nice." She looks happy and I ask a question that will make her even happier.

"What're you going make for dinner? Can I help?" My mother's eyes ignite at the thought of another opportunity to bond with her weird daughter.

"I was thinking a nice pot roast with those little potatoes. And maybe you could help me make a cheesecake? I'll save you an extra slice." She gives me a wink and I nod enthusiastically.

"Sure! I'd love that." I'm not lying. I love my mother's cheesecake. As long as I get to have an extra piece, I'm always happy to help. Steven can kiss my butt.

I return my attention to the television, where *The Guiding Light* and its associated intrigues and dramas are now commencing. My mom is rearranging her cards again.

"Move 'em around all you want there, Mom. You've still got like, five times more than me." I grin, and she laughs.

"You are a ruthless card shark, Miss Melanie JoAnne."

"So, how come they always show women like that on TV?" I ask.

"Because sex sells." She's so matter-of-fact, it's frightening.

"And you're alright with this?"

"Well, there's not much I can do about it, is there?"

"You could refuse to buy that brand." A reasonable solution, I think.

"I buy whatever coffee is on sale, dear," she says, flatly.

"So much for the power of the consumer," I mumble.

My mother frowns. "What's on your mind, Mel?"

I think for a moment. This is my mother I'm talking to here. And even though we're having a very nice afternoon, things can go very south, very quickly, with this lady. My self-esteem is on the line, so I choose my words carefully. "I just don't get it, is all."

"What, dear?"

"Why it's always just women half naked in those ads."

My mom takes a deep breath. "Because men make the ads and men like sex."

"And women don't?"

"Well, for us it's just…different."

"How?" I press. "What kind of women like sex like men do?"

My mom thinks and then, sensing a teachable moment, sits forward with an intensity and enthusiasm I haven't witnessed in her since the last time JCPenney had a blow-out white sale. She looks out the window at our neighbor's house across the street.

"Well, our new neighbor is obviously that kind of

woman." Looking satisfied, she settles back onto the couch and continues arranging her cards. I'm still confused.

"But we don't even know her yet," I counter.

My mom shrugs. "She just fits the type, that's all."

"What type?"

My mother is starting to look annoyed. "The type that likes sex the way men do and uses it to her advantage." Now I'm really confused.

"Then why are we having her over?"

"Because you asked me to."

I'm still befuddled by what my mother has just revealed, but a thought, an idea, a concession, is beginning to congeal beneath my sun-bleached hair. I ask one more, very pertinent, very important question. "So, it's *alright* to use women to make money, then?"

My mother takes another deep breath. I think this line of questioning is causing her to become under-oxygenated, but she answers anyway. "Well, honey, I don't know if it's alright or not, but it is the way of the world, isn't it?"

I hate it when grown-ups answer kids' questions with questions. I'm thirteen years old. I don't know things, so I ask adults and they answer me with more questions. How're kids supposed to figure out anything?

I return my attention to the television. On the screen, a guy about my dad's age is standing in a car lot barking something about deals so crazy they'll make your head explode. I'm deciding this is a dangerous way to purchase a motor vehicle when the camera pans over to a woman with huge breasts reined in by a very precarious bikini top. She's waving excitedly from the driver's side of a bright yellow convertible, her teeth blazing white and her lips slick and red. I look back at him, more shiny hair, fat tie, fat face. I look over at her, big hair, big boobs, she looks happy. The connection is made. It is the transactional nature of the universe—this for that, that for this, the planets turn. Who am I to refuse to participate in what is obviously a system that has worked for humankind for millennia?

"Melanie," my mother intrudes, "go fish."

I smile and take a card, comfortable now with the hand I've been dealt. My mother smiles too. "Pretty soon, you'll have more cards than me."

Unlikely. She's terrible at this game. She's clearly good at other games, though—the games that matter. She's better at them, but I'm learning. I'm learning and I'm going to play them even better than her, just watch.

Chapter 10

DIRTY PICTURES, DRIED YUCCA AND MASCULINE RESPONSIBILITIES

The late morning sun is warm on my left side and, as I draw the gentle swell of a woman's breast, it occurs to me that I always sit this way on the backyard wall, and that I should probably start sitting the other way, or only the left side of my face will tan and I'll eventually look like an albino zebra.

I bounce the backs of my calves against the brick, and draw. This one is almost done. I've elected to produce my publications on a small, note-sized pad of sketch paper. The paper itself is good quality, and the modest page size makes for stealthy transportation and distribution. It's also a better size for clandestine under-the-desk viewing, and storage (most likely in some gross boy's sock drawer).

I'm just adding the finishing touches to a delicate patch of pubic hair when my brother shuffles across the hard-packed desert earth of our yard and looks up at me. "What're you doin', fruit loop?" he asks. I'm busy and don't feel like answering but it has been my experience that if I don't answer, I will pay for it later.

"None of your beeswax." A conventional retort—beneath

my capabilities, I know, but like I said, I'm busy. Steven steps up onto an old chair that we pushed up next to the wall, and plops down next to me. The backyard wall is seven feet high and an excellent vantage place from which to see darned near everything in our neighborhood. Our house is at the top of a low hill at the edge of the housing development, and if I were to turn around on the wall and face the other direction (so as to better color the other side of my face), I would be looking at nothing but expanding desert, cacti and the table-like Cerbat Mountains.

Steven scoots over and tries to look at my sketchpad. "Lemme see," he says, reaching for my illicit handiwork.

"No!" I squeal and flip the pad closed and stuff it in my shorts pocket. Steve grabs my waist and is about to tickle me to get at the sketch pad (an obnoxious and dangerous move that, given the height of the wall, could prove fatal) when the Suburban backs up to the wide front gate. Thankfully, Steven takes his grubby mitts off me and focuses on the gate, where my dad is getting out of the driver's side of our behemoth car. I look over at Steve. "What's dad gonna do now?" I ask. He shoves his glasses up and sighs.

"I dunno. But whatever it is, I'm the one who's gonna have to help him do it."

Steven is right, and I actually feel bad for him. A bead of sweat is making its way through the maze of worry wrinkles on his forehead. Poor Steve. It's as if he was born with all the worries of a two-term, war-time president who is about to be impeached.

The gate swings open and we watch our father march into his coliseum and prepare to do battle. "Well," he says, sticking his gloved fists on his hips and looking up at us.

"Well, what?" I ask.

My dad nods at Steven. "I was talking to your brother."

Steve shoots me a fuming look. "See? Told you."

On the surface, my dad looks like a forward-thinking seventies guy. He reads *Ms.* magazine at the dentist's office, encourages my mother to learn new things and tells me I can do anything I want to do as long as I look cute doing it. But deep down, he's Archie Bunker on a big-game hunting safari. Outside jobs are his and my brother's territory, while I'm relegated to the indoors, where I can learn valuable skills (like casserole preparation and stubborn mildew removal). My mother's taciturn approval of this arrangement (how else would I have learned to do such marvelous things with cream cheese and pistachio Jell-O?) is doing little to bring our family out of the patriarchal dark ages. Honestly, she's not helping at all.

Steven drops to the ground while I continue to smack the backs of my calves against the wall and watch. "What's in the cart, Dad?"

My father puffs with pride. "Well, MellyBean," he announces, "that there...is yucca."

Appropriate name, I decide. "What's yucca?" I ask.

He puffs up more. "It's a plant that grows here in the Southwest."

It doesn't look like a plant. It looks more like something you might pull out of the underside of a sofa from the Goodwill.

"What're you gonna do with it?" At this, my father walks over to the trailer and grabs a fistful of yucca shreds as he hands Steven a pitchfork. He rubs the fibrous material between his fingers like it's gold thread he's purloined from Rumpelstiltskin himself.

"Kids, this is some of the best mulch on the planet. We're going to till it into the soil, here, and grow your mother some grass." My brother and I exchange looks of disbelief. My father wants to grow grass? There is only one thing my father finds more useless than grass, and that is a golf course (which by its very nature is all about grass).

"Why don't you just take her dancing?" I suggest.

My dad chuckles and takes up the remaining pitchfork. Then, with a nod to my brother that says, "Let's get going, son. Masculinity's not a given, you've got to earn it," he begins heaving great forkfuls of yucca onto the unforgiving ground. I drop down off the wall and walk over.

"I could help. I like yardwork."

Steven snorts. "Yeah, right. Sure ya do."

My dad waves me off. "Nah, your mom probably needs you in the house."

For what, I wonder? Today's Jell-O selection is setting up in the fridge as we speak, the crock-pot's been melting a chicken off its bones for more than two hours already, and yesterday I helped that lady bleach the grout on the bathroom floor for the third time this month. Sheesh, you'd think that house was her whole life or something.

I grab a stick from the Yucca Express and flick a scorpion off the wall. "How come Mom needs grass so bad?"

My dad leans on his pitchfork, American Gothic style. "Well, she says she wants to have barbeques and stuff, but she's embarrassed to have anyone over because we don't have grass in our yard like everyone else does."

"Who does she want to have over?" I ask.

"Oh, I don't know, ladies from the PTA or something. Waste of money if you ask me. This is a desert. It's not supposed to have grass." He goes back to flinging yucca shreds into the center of the yard.

"Then why are you doing it?" Clearly, a legit question on my part.

"Because when your mom's happy, we're all happy, right?"

"That is the smarter option, I guess," I say, shrugging.

Steven weighs in. "Not to mention the safest." The three of us share a conspiratorial laugh over this latest exchange. I know my father is right. When my mom's okay we're all more okay, but I don't know that I've actually ever seen her *happy*. She's always some degree of just fine. When we go through the checkout line at the grocery store, and the checker asks how we're doing, my mom consistently answers, "Just fine, thank you." Never "Great, gracias" or "Atrocious, merci." It's always "Just fine, thank you." Problem is, I'm never entirely certain just how "just fine" she is. And I don't think my father and my brother are, either.

But, I love my mom. And because I love her (and because I'm getting really hot and I'm thirsty) I toss my stick back onto the yucca cart and head inside. Maybe if she's done cleaning the oven again she'll make me lunch.

Chapter 11

RACISM, SLEEPOVER POLITICS AND SHASTA VS. COKE

Sometimes Mavis and I like to sit up on the top row of the bleachers and watch the members of the Kingman Junior High school track teams torture themselves. I do not understand sports and I don't like watching them, per se, but the repetitive background cacophony of shouting, talking, whistles and cheering makes for an excellent working environment. Creating in total silence can sometimes feel like too much pressure. And the boys' track shorts this year are very short, so I have something to look at while I wait for inspiration.

This afternoon, Mavis sits beside me. I'm drawing and she's working on her third Tootsie Pop. This one is grape, and her lips are purple. She's so pretty it looks as if she chose the color on purpose. It does go nicely with her eyeshadow. I look over at her. Her always-curly lashes are cast downward and she's looking at my sketchpad. She pulls the lollipop from her lips and frowns. "Damn. Is that even legal?" she asks.

"According to Anna, no." I close the pad and Mavis goes back to watching the field. Today the girls' team is working on their shotput skills.

"She doesn't like me, does she?" Mavis asks.

"Who, Anna?"

"Mmm hmm."

"It's not a question of like. Anna thinks she knows everything, and she doesn't know anything about you, which makes her suspicious."

We're quiet for a minute and Mavis studies the girls on the field. "Why don't you go out for track?" she asks.

I don't know why she's asking me this question. We've been in the same P.E. class for the past two years. "Do we really need to review my athletic shortcomings?" I answer.

She smiles and gives me a nudge. "Bet you'd make people laugh, though."

"Ha ha. Very funny. In addition to providing entertainment, I'd probably end up in the hospital. How come *you've* never tried out for the track team?"

Mavis's face clouds. "Why, cuz my people's such good runners?"

"Calm down, Kunta Kinte. You know that's not what I meant." I nudge her back and I feel her shoulder push back against mine.

"I know," she starts. "I just, ya know…"

"Just wish you lived someplace else?" I ask, already knowing the answer.

"Sometimes." She's quiet again and we watch the girls down on the field. There are skinny girls in shorts, fat girls in shorts, girls with red hair, brown hair, blond (like me), but there are no black girls. I try for a minute to imagine what it is like to never see yourself reflected in the world around you—to always be the most different person in the room. I am generally the oddest person in the room and that is hard enough.

I stand and stuff my sketchpad in my back pocket. "Come on," I offer, "I'll buy you a soda. That is, if you're not already sliding into a diabetic coma."

"Gonna have to be a Coke," Mavis says, as she stands and drops her sucker on the ground beneath the bleachers.

"Coke, Pepsi, whatever," I say, heading down the bleachers as she follows, easily balancing on her towering platforms.

"Cuz I don't go for that Shasta shit," she declares.

"What's wrong with Shasta? My mom buys it all the time."

"Exactly. Shasta is for white folks."

I hop down off the bleachers. "You're prejudiced against a *soda*!" I tease.

"No, I ain't. Just know what I like, is all."

I understand. My favorite color is lime green, a preference that has caused more than a few arguments with my mother.

Dodging sweaty girls with weapons disguised as sports equipment, we make our way across the dirt track and onto the relative safety of the open grass field, being careful to stay out of shotput range.

"Anna and Leslie and I are gonna have a sleepover at Leslie's Saturday," I say. "Her dad's really nice and two of her brothers are pretty cute. The other two are, well, a little challenged, but they're okay. You want to come?"

Mavis frowns, the skin between her eyes forming a lopsided W.

"That probably ain't a good idea, little buddy."

"How come?" I ask.

"You know how come." Her eyes drop on mine and I don't answer.

"You wanna come over to my house?" she asks. This is a milestone. Neither of us has ever been to the other's house. She has never accepted an offer from me and never asked me to come to her home. Until now. I don't waste time wondering why.

"Sure! When?"

"Do I look like I got my damn calendar on me? I'll let you know."

"I'm free Sunday," I say, dopey and over-eager.

"Maybe. I'll ask my mom," she says. "Now, come on. You owe me a damn Coke."

"Gonna have to be a Shasta cola. Can't afford Coke." I smile.

"What chu mean you can't afford a damned Coke."

"Hey, I only get five bucks a week allowance."

Mavis is incredulous. "Allowance? Your parents just *give* you money?"

We step off the grassy field and cross the track again. I bump my hip against hers. "Well, you know, they're white. Once a week, quarters just fall out of their butts."

Chapter 12

THAT MAGICAL FIRST TIME

At the entrance to our housing development, not far
from the bus stop that doubles as a make out spot,
there is a giant billboard that reads (in an uncomfortable,
purple-hued script), "Desert Shadows Homes". While not
misleading in its claim (this *is* a desert, there *are* shadows
and there are definitely houses) it is redundant, but makes
for an excellent rendezvous spot in which to meet the idiot,
Dennis Franklin. Firstly, I don't want that guy showing
up at my house again. And secondly, if I don't give him
an easily located place to meet me, he will most assuredly
become lost and die and the fortunate accident would
certainly be blamed on myself. This would derail both my
educational and my writing careers, for sure.

It's just after noon and my left shoulder is against one of the
thick posts supporting the sign. Its white paint is peeling, and
I'm bored and hot, so I lend a hand with the inevitable process
and pick at it. I pause to dig paint chips from under my nails
and look at my watch—a snappy digital number in an annoying hot pink color. My mother gave it to me last Christmas.
Somehow, after thirteen years of knowing me, she still thinks I
like pink. I'm pretty sure she believes I am an amalgam of who
she *thinks* I am and who I *actually* am. Maybe that's the only
way she can continue to see this strange girl as her daughter.

It's twelve fifteen. Dennis is fifteen minutes late and my scalp is on fire. On the ground, a few inches from the toes of my flip-flops, two shiny black beetles work at making more beetles. The smaller one's struggling to get a purchase on the slick shell of the bigger one. It appears to be a herculean and very un-romantic exercise. I assume the smaller one is the male. I'm wondering why this obviously correct arrangement is so prevalent in nature but not at all common in the upside-down realm of American humans when I hear the unmistakable sound of boy—a playing card clicking in the spokes of a bike wheel.

One hundred yards down the long road that leads from the main highway into our housing development, Dennis Franklin is peddling toward me. He is late and he's not hurrying one bit. He spots me, my arms crossed in hostility, and slows down more, even taking his hands off the handlebars and weaving along the road triumphantly in a "Look ma, no hands!" way. I hope he wipes out and eats dirt. He does not. Instead, he glides up to the sign, grabbing the bike's handlebars just in time to skid into a one-eighty and spray me with dirt and rocks.

"Hey!" I scream, brushing dust from my shorts. Dennis is nonplussed.

"Oh, sorry, lost control," he states.

"Yeah, looks like your bike's got some serious power there. Better be careful, Dennis, somebody could get beheaded by a flying nine of clubs."

"Yeah, yeah," he says, sticking his gross, dirty hand out to me. "Where're my pictures?"

I pull three pieces of paper from my back pocket and hand them to him.

"Pay me for the ones you want." I watch as he examines the drawings, the sickening grin on his face growing bigger with each one.

"Very nice, Chaffee…"

Barf. "Just pick one, okay?" I'm anxious to go back home. My mom's making olive loaf sandwiches for lunch. I love olive loaf. As a mysterious girl, I'm a big fan of mysterious things like olive loaf.

"I'll take all three," Dennis says, still grinning.

"Six bucks, then," I demand. Dennis digs in his jeans pocket and produces a wadded, damp five-dollar bill, three quarters, three nickels and a dime that appears to be covered in hardened, green goo.

"Seis dineros, senorita," he blunders, dumping the monetary mess into my reluctant hands.

"Stick to English, would ya, Dennis? You got enough challenges in life already. Where're your lackeys today?" Dennis is confused by the complicated vernacular, so I elaborate. "Sean and Joe?"

"Oh," he starts, the lightbulb hitting him over the head. "They're at softball practice."

"Well, when you give them their drawings, tell them to keep their traps shut about where they got them, okay? My reputation's precarious enough already."

"Oh"—Dennis smiles—"I'm not giving *any* of these to those guys. They can buy their own." He pats his pocket with a grubby hand. "These are just for me."

Between the relentless sun and Dennis's disgusting insinuation, I'm pretty sure I'm going to toss my cookies right here, right now. The addition of my Cheerio and orange juice vomit could only improve the Desert Shadows sign.

"That is definitely more information than I needed, Dennis."

With great fanfare, he plants a sneakered foot onto a bike peddle and prepares to depart. "Nice work, space cadet. See you at school." He gives me a smile, this one sincere (but still icky), and speeds off to go do God knows what with the masterpieces I just sold to him for six dollars. Is that what my soul is worth? Six dollars? I decide it might be worth less than that, but I am now six dollars closer to the coveted magic slippers. So, feeling lighter, I shove the unproductive, negative thoughts about my worth (both existential and fiscal) into the back of my mind with the rest of the accumulated garbage, and hope for the best.

I watch Dennis, now at the end of our road, dodge and zip across the highway, only narrowly averting a gruesome death by an orange pickup towing a double horse trailer. Safely across the highway, he continues on his way, unscathed. I exhale. Was I holding my breath? "Oh, God in heaven," I pray, "please don't tell me I care about that ingrate." What's next, flipping my hair and laughing at his stupid jokes?

I check in with the beetles on the ground. The smaller one is scurrying away from the larger one, who's slowly following. I address the big gal directly. "Lady, I hope you at least paid for your own dinner. Remember what my Aunt Marnie says, 'Dignity has no price'." The insect ignores me and like an idiot continues her pointless pursuit. I stuff Dennis's dirty money into the front pocket of my shorts and start back up the street to my house. I hope the olive loaf sandwiches are done. I'm starving, and I need to fuel up before the Christian-sanctioned abuse that is youth choir practice at my church. If my recent actions are any indication, I should probably spend as much time as possible in a house of God. Even if, at least in my observances of the way the world works, that God is most certainly a dude.

Chapter 13

THE WORLD ACCORDING TO MRS. MAGNUSSEN

I t is her most favorite place in all of God's miraculous world. It isn't just *the* sanctuary, it is *her* sanctuary, especially on Sunday afternoons at precisely four p.m., when the weekly youth choir practice sessions—*her* youth choir practice sessions—commence. It is a weekly endeavor that defines her, although she'd never say so. She would say that she guides and musically shepherds the young people of Kingman United Methodist Church the same way our Lord Jesus Christ of Nazareth guided and shepherded his disciples to God, almost two whole millennia ago. She would say she does it for His glory, for His majesty, for His grandeur. But in her zealous righteousness, she would be wrong.

Mrs. Patricia Elaine Magnussen is zipping, quite literally, up the center aisle of the church. Despite her efforts to find quieter hose, her chubby thighs constantly betray her. She is short, barely five feet, but she is round; adorably, deceptively round. She never wears trousers (her beloved husband of thirty-three years, Lyle, preferring his wife to always look like a lady, and ladies wear dresses). This evening's dress is smart, checkered pink and white, and a little too snug, causing her white pantyhose to complain even louder than usual as she makes her way through the silent sanctuary toward the choir loft just above the nave where Reverend Hussy delivers his inspiring (if not overly liberal) sermons every Sunday.

Just before she mounts the spiral staircase that will take her up to the choir loft and (she always hopes) closer to God, she makes a sharp left and takes a few steps over to the wide, white-washed lectern that faces the congregational pews. Reverently, cautiously, she stands behind the pulpit and looks out at the empty seats, allowing herself for a moment, just a moment, to imagine what it would be like to lead her own flock in worship. She does not think of herself as an arrogant woman, pride is after all a sin. But she knows, deep inside her soul, in the small space where she cuddles up to Jesus every night, that she could give a far more inspiring and convincing sermon than that young upstart minister from Phoenix. He only took up residence in the rectory six months ago, and already he's got the children thinking they can worship the Lord with guitars. *Guitars!* Patricia Magnussen isn't certain of many things in this world, but one thing she knows for sure is that The Lord Jesus Christ prefers to be lauded with God's intended musical instrument; a pipe organ with no less than sixty-five pipes. Like drums and synthesizers, guitars are for the Devil's music.

She closes her eyes and can hear them—the good, if not flawed, people of her congregation singing, their voices raised in glorious praise, to God, of course. Inside the cathedral of her mind, she is about to lead them in another chorus of the hymn she just wrote, when she hears heels on the soft carpet runner between the pews. She opens her eyes. Strolling up the aisle in a virginal white eyelet sundress is Stephanie Harris, her star pupil in both musical and scriptural instruction. Sheepishly, she steps from behind the pulpit.

"Well hello, Stephanie, dear. How are you today?"

Holding her white bible and swinging her white purse, Stephanie makes her way up the aisle.

"I'm *so* very well, Mrs. Magnussen, thank you. How're you? Gettin' a feel for the pulpit, there? I reckon you'd deliver just the most magical sermon." She gives a sweet smile to her mentor. Embarrassed, Mrs. Magnussen waves her off.

"Oh, now, you silly child. You know I could never inspire the congregation like our fine Reverend Hussy." She giggles for effect and the two start up the steps to the loft.

"Mrs. Magnussen, you don't give yourself enough credit. I know our congregation and, well, even our Lord Jesus would hang on just *every* word you said. I know *I* would." The saccharin syrup in her voice is missed by Mrs. Magnussen, whose true vice and sin is a dangerous love of flattery.

"Oh Stephanie, you're too much!" she squeals, not seeing as the teenaged nightmare behind her on the stairs rolls her eyes and sticks her finger in her mouth before answering sweetly, "Well, I'm not exaggeratin', I swear! You speak even better than you sing, if that's even possible."

"Oh my, you *do* flatter me," giggles Patty Magnussen.

Yes, she does.

"But Stephanie," Patty chides, "you mustn't swear! Especially in the house of the Lord." She waddles up into the choir loft. Stephanie follows and sits down on one of the three long, terraced pews that look down on the sanctuary below.

"Alright, I won't," says Stephanie, smiling innocently at her tiny tutor.

Mrs. Magnussen smiles back, then sets about digging through a stack of sheet music on her music stand, which is positioned a little too high for her, making her seem even more diminutive. "Alright, then. Let's get to work on that solo of yours. We have less than an hour before practice begins and it needs to be Jesus-ready by Sunday!"

Stephanie nods with as much enthusiasm as she can fake and when Mrs. Magnussen raises her baton, she dutifully begins to sing. It's a solo verse from "Nearer, My God, to Thee" and her soprano voice is as light and angelic as her heart is dark and empty.

Chapter 14

SONGBIRDS FOR CHRIST, A TRIP TO BUTLER WITH MAVIS AND ART THIEVERY

C hoir practice is bad enough, but having to sit behind Stephanie Harris makes it almost unbearable. Fortunately I brought paper with me and, utilizing the United Methodist Hymnal as a lap desk, I'm turning today's unwarranted punishment into a working trip. Using the back of Stephanie's hair-sprayed head for reference (and exercising my creative license), I'm rendering a long-haired, Titian masterpiece featuring the evil queen's popular 'do. True to Titian's voluptuous style, I've given Stephanie's nude doppelganger a pair of spectacularly chubby thighs, complete with cuddly dimples. Stephanie, hopefully, will never see this exemplary example of neo-seventies-Rococo art, and no one will even know it's modeled after her (especially my moronic customer base), but the simple act of creating it still gives me a validating feeling of justice served.

We're waiting for choir practice to start. Steven and I are always a little early because my mom heads up the women's Old Testament bible study group that convenes at the same time downstairs in the church's basement, and she likes to set up the refreshment table before her fellow lady

Christians arrive. Trying to find valuable information for women in the rape-happy, wife-stoning books of the first version of God's word can be a daunting task. And as such, sustenance is vital.

Other kids are filtering in and I'm sitting in the middle of the back pew as far from everyone else as I can get. I put the finishing touches on the fluffy Titian goddess version of my mortal foe, and smile. It's perfect. I pray that Stephanie never sees this thing, but then secretly kind of wish that she would. In Stephanie's world, fat thighs are the equivalent of being born with two heads and she would (hopefully) be scarred for life.

Steven's on the far right of my pew playing that ridiculous, and painful, hand slapping game with his buddy Warren Huchison. Warren is nice. He's cute, too, and when he comes over to the house to join Steven in his ardent devil worshipping sessions with Alice Cooper and Blue Oyster Cult, he always smiles at me and says, "Hi." And then my brother usually socks him in the arm and tells him not to look at his sister, as if I'm some sort of forbidden zoo animal or something.

Down front, Mrs. Magnussen taps her music stand with her baton.

"Bonjour, my little songbirds for Christ!" She hands a stack of sheet music copies to a kid in the front row, who takes one and hands the stack to a kid next to him and so on.

"We'll be learning a new hymn this evening. If anyone is interested in performing a solo, there will be two available, so see me after practice if you'd like to audition for one," she chirps.

The stack of papers has made its way to the middle row and since there's no one sitting to my left, Stephanie turns around and hands the papers to me. I quickly fold my masterpiece and stuff it in my back pocket, but she is instantly suspicious.

"Hey, Ethan's lil' neighbor. What cha been drawing?" she purrs.

"Something I doubt you're familiar with. It's called art." I take a page of music and skootch over and hand the stack down to Warren, who gives me an illegal smile.

"Thanks, Mel," he says warmly. To the right of him, Steven frowns and punches him in the arm. I scoot back over to my spot behind Stephanie, who's still looking at me. I am deeply uncomfortable.

"Wanna take a picture?" I ask. "It'll last longer."

"You are such a lil' weirdo," Stephanie condemns. Then she executes a perfect "turn around, hair flip" combo so as to better return to ignoring me.

The afterthought community of Butler curls loosely around the northeast edges of Kingman like a poorly executed refrigerator crescent roll. It is largely comprised of homes on wheels, but more permanent dwellings are beginning to pop up here and there. Most of those are properties enclosed with ranch-style fences and boasting two or three horses and an occasional hog.

"My house is just over there." Mavis points to a tidy, light-blue double-wide at the far left end of the street we're walking along. The homes on this street are small but most are well kept and have mini gravel front "lawns" like ours. Some even have little gardens in the back. We pass an old white lady in a shift covered with exploding orange flowers. She's sweeping her little covered car port, but she pauses to wave as we pass, her floppy upper arm waving too.

"Afternoon, Mavis. How're you today?" she asks.

"I'm cool, Miss Lydia. How're you doin'?" Mavis smiles and waves back.

"Oh, fair to middlin', I guess. Stove's on the fritz again and my arthritis is acting up, but other than that, I can't complain."

"You got aspirin over there?" Mavis asks, as we near her driveway.

"Naw. Hank used the last two for his damn back yesterday. We'll get more tomorrow when he gets his pension check, I imagine."

Mavis frowns, the little lopsided W appearing between her eyes again. "I'll bring you some, okay?" she says.

"Oh, thank you Mavis, that would be such a help. We'd sure appreciate it."

"And I'm gonna bring you some stew, too. Momma made some last night and it's real good. Don't be takin' that aspirin on an empty stomach, okay? It'll make your ulcer flare again."

"You are such a dear. Tell your momma thank you for me, would you?"

"I will. You take care now," Mavis says, digging in her purse for her keys.

She opens her front door. "Well, this is me," she says, and I follow her inside.

The choir loft is empty except for Stephanie Harris. In addition to often coming to practice early to work on her solos, which she performs nearly every Sunday, she stays late after practice to tidy up the loft while Mrs. Magnussen gathers her things. But tonight, Mrs. Magnussen had to hurry home to check the crock pot. Her sister and her favorite nephew, Benjamin are coming for dinner, and it seems Lyle Magnussen went out for a day of quail hunting and left the slow cooker unattended, putting the family's thrifty, sensible meal in jeopardy. Stephanie is relieved. Her period started an hour ago, the cramps are unbearable, and she's still expected to look like, well, what she always looks like—perfect. It's exhausting.

She makes her way between the pews, picking up errant sheets of music and straightening the crimson velvet cushions. She gives the top row a once over then, sighing with relief, sits down. The funny thing about period cramps is that during that first day, it often feels like everything south of your belly button is about to fall out from between your thighs. Consequently, sitting down feels amazing. In hindsight, she probably shouldn't have chosen this white dress today. But, she was in a gambling mood this morning and the dress is new, so she couldn't help but wear it. Thank goodness she had a super tampon and a bottle of Midol in her matching white purse or the whole day would have been an unmitigated disaster.

Stephanie fluffs her hair and leans her head back against the wall behind the pew and thinks about Ethan Wilde, who seems eternally out of reach. She knows she is the prettiest girl in the eighth grade, she knows her GPA rarely drops below 3.8 and she knows her father makes more money than anybody in this town. She has everything but Ethan. In the eyes of everyone at school, even the teachers (who all love her, who wouldn't?) she's Ethan's girlfriend. But she isn't, not really. Like a boyfriend, he sits with her at lunch, he talks to her at her locker and walks her to class and sometimes he'll even kiss her on the cheek. But he's not hers and she knows it. It's a kind of game they're playing but he just hasn't told her the rules, yet.

While she thinks and waits for the double dose of Midol she just took to work, she rubs her manicured hands over the velvet cushions, feeling the fuzzy nap of the fabric beneath her fingertips. It isn't as if there's someone else Ethan is really interested in. He seems protective of his weird little locker neighbor, Melanie What's-her-name, but that's obviously just a little sister–big brother thing, right? What would a guy like Ethan Wilde want with a strange little seventh grade ninny like her?

She runs her hands along the backs of the cushions, her knuckles against the cool, smooth wood of the pew, until her forefinger hits something. It is a piece of folded paper, good paper, like the kind in the sketch pad her mother gave her last Christmas. The one she's never unwrapped. She pulls the paper out from under the cushion and unfolds it. It is a drawing of a naked lady—a fat, naked lady. *Ugh, look at those thighs!* she thinks. *I'm glad that's not me.*

Despite her opinions to the contrary, Stephanie does not know art from a well-decorated hole in the ground. But her grandmother used to take her to the museums in Atlanta and she knows what art is *supposed* to look like, and this is definitely something akin to art. She also has a good memory, and she remembers in great detail the moment, barely two hours ago, when she turned around and saw Melanie What's-her-name folding up a piece of paper just like this one. And what was it she had said to Stephanie about art?

Like used motor oil on dirty concrete, a slow smile spreads across Stephanie's perfect, powdered face. She folds the now weaponized piece of paper back up and slides it into

S. J. Coffey

her dress pocket. Lil Miss Melanie Weirdo may not be any real competition for her but given the precarious nature of her and Ethan's "relationship," it would be best not to take chances. She doesn't know when and where she'll need this evidence, but she knows—the way a cat knows when a mouse will come out to search for food—that she'll need it. And when she does, she'll be ready.

The Midol is kicking in now. The awful cramps are abating, and Stephanie is feeling much better. In fact, she's feeling just great.

Chapter 15

GUESS WHO'S
COMING TO DINNER

Mavis just ran over to the floppy arm lady's house next door to take her aspirin and stew, and I am alone in her living room. Her house is the antithesis of mine. I pick up a tiny black statue of what I think is an African woman. The piece is carved from dense, heavy wood and the woman is topless. I carefully set the statue back down on the shelf it came from and turn and survey the room. The walls are covered in art. There's barely two inches of space between each painting, tapestry or macramé wall hanging. There are colors everywhere, but the predominating theme of the place is orange and red; cool tangerines, blazing cardinals and crimsons and warm persimmons are set off by the occasional surprise of an emerald-green hummingbird painting, or a bunch of glowing blue peacock feathers resting in an oversized burnt orange vase.

I sit down on the long, low avocado-green sofa. In the middle of the coffee table, next to a copy of *I Know Why the Caged Bird Sings* by someone named Maya Angelou, a long, skinny incense burner holds a tiny log of burned incense ash. The room smells warm and inviting and nothing like my house. I pick up the book and turn it over. I'm reading

74   *S. J. Coffey*

the short synopsis of the story when the front door opens and Mavis walks in.

"Sorry I took so long. Miss Lydia is sweet but she is a talker," she says, walking over to a huge stereo cabinet near the window that looks out onto the street.

"Can I borrow this book?" I ask. Mavis flips through the dozens of record albums housed in the three storage slots in the front of the cabinet.

"Sure," she says. "Prepare yourself, though. It's pretty rough."

"Rough how?"

"Just rough," she says. "It probably ain't like what you're used to readin'."

I only read the paragraph on the back cover, but I already believe her.

"This place is amazing," I tell her. Mavis gives me a sly smile.

"Not too black for ya?"

I let out a little nervous laugh and shake my head. "It's fantastic. Beautiful, really. Our house is so…pale."

"I can imagine. Lots of pastels?"

"How did you know? My mom *loves* ecru." I say, as I watch Mavis pull a record from the cabinet, tip it slightly and deftly catch the disc with her other hand.

"What the hell is *ecru?*" The little crooked W has formed between her eyes again and I laugh.

"Just another version of the color white, I guess."

Mavis chuckles and lifts the lid on the stereo cabinet. "Crackers. They even want their damned house to be white." She places the record on the turntable and sets the needle. "You into funk?"

"Oh," I explain, "I'm not supposed to say that word. That one makes the veins in my mom's temple pop out."

A thudding beat emanates from the stereo's speakers and suddenly Mavis is laughing so hard she looks like she can't breathe. "Aw, man, lil' buddy, you're killin' me," she says between gasps for air. "*Funk*. It's music, dopey."

"Oh!" I am relieved she's only referring to a music style and not a cult devoted to my mom's most hated word. "What's funk?" I ask.

Moving to the music, Mavis struts over and grabs my wrist, pulling me up. "Funk is only just the best music ever invented, that's what." She grabs my other hand and pulls my arms back and forth with hers. I feel awkward and silly. I've never danced with a girl before, let alone a black girl.

"You gotta loosen up. Feel the beat. Funk's all about the *groove*. Don't worry. I ain't judgin'." From atop her platforms, she smiles down on me and I relax a little and let myself feel the music.

"Who is this?" I ask. "The band, I mean."

"This is the Ohio Players. They're the funkiest." She releases my hands and moves around the room in perfect sync with the throbbing music. It's as if she's part of it. I am not part of it. I think I'm actually fighting it, but every few seconds I can feel the sound slip under me and move me the way it wants to. It feels amazing. I decide I'm definitely going to buy another ticket on the "Love Rollercoaster". In fact, the next time my mom demands another excursion down to Phoenix for new underwear for us and the restoration of sanity for her, I might just buy the album.

Mavis watches me dance and laughs. "There ya go! You got it. See, you can't think about it, you gotta just *feel* it, right?" I take a breath and attempt a spin like I just saw her do.

"I feel it!" I declare.

Now, I'm a good dancer. I've taken four years of ballet and one torturous year of tap. I've also been known to let loose and jump around like a complete idiot to The Captain and Tennille, and for my birthday this year, my mom gave me the new Shaun Cassidy album, but this is different. Shaun Cassidy's bouncing rendition of "Da Doo Run Run" made me dance on the outside. This music makes me dance from the inside. It is an unprecedented experience for me and I am lost to it. So much so that I have not heard the front door open. Mavis stops dancing and looks toward the door, so I stop too and turn around. A tall black woman dressed in a fitted beige dress suit with slacks is standing in the doorway holding a bag of groceries. Her hair is pulled back in a tight bun and tiny pearl earrings swing from her ears. She is pretty, like Mavis, and shares her tilted, almond shaped black eyes. The song stops, and the woman just stares at me. I look over at Mavis, who is frozen. She makes eye contact with the woman.

"Hi, Momma," she says quietly.

"What's going on here, Mavis?" the woman asks. Her voice is soft and low and a W frown, just like Mavis's, is forming between her brows. From behind her, a young black man bounds into the room, one arm holding a bag of groceries and from the opposite hand another bag of questionable integrity dangles. He lopes past his mother and heads for the kitchen but stops when he sees me and starts laughing. He is tall and older than Mavis, about Steven's age, and very handsome. He gives me a once over and laughs some more.

"Look, Momma, we're being robbed by Goldilocks!" He slips into a new round of giggles and snorts, and I decide he's not that handsome, after all. The woman looks at her son.

"That's enough, Jamal. Go on and put the groceries away and let me talk to your sister."

"Oooooh, you in for it now, Mavis!" he says, as he goes into the kitchen, leaving us alone with what appears to be Mavis's angry mom, who sets her bag down on the coffee table. The only sound in the room is the scratching of the needle at the end of the record, scrape, scrape, scrape. I try to fill the silence.

"Um, hi. You must be Mrs. Jackson. I'm sorry. We were going to do homework but, and, I was just about to leave," I stammer.

"Uh uh. You're not goin' anywhere," she says, her fists finding a home on her hips. I'm terrified.

"I'm not?" I manage to spit out.

It's so quiet. Scrape, scrape, scrape. I want to run. But then, Mrs. Jackson smiles and winks at her daughter, who claps her hands and busts up laughing.

"Good one, Momma!" She's laughing and I'm very confused. Mrs. Jackson puts her hand in front of me. I reach out cautiously and take it.

"Call me Amelia," she says, smiling.

"I'm Melanie. Melanie Chaffee," I say shyly.

"Oh, my lord, Mavis, where did you find this little church mouse?" Amelia takes off her jacket and tosses it on the couch.

"Trust me, Momma, Mel ain't no church mouse."

"How many times do I have to tell you not to say 'ain't'? It *isn't* a word."

"Sorry," Mavis starts, "I *ain't* gonna say it again. I promise." This exchange has me utterly flummoxed. What's happening here?

Amelia walks over to the stereo cabinet and sets the

needle back in the middle of the record. "Love Rollercoaster" thuds again. She takes Mavis's hands and begins dancing with her daughter. My mother has never danced with me, ever, not even to "The Theme from a Summer Place". I doubt Sandra Dee danced with her mother, either.

Amelia dances even better than Mavis. I feel like an interloping moron, but then Amelia reaches out and takes my hand, pulling me into their small, joyous, gyrating circle. Amelia gives me a smile.

"You dance well," she says.

"Yeah, for a white girl." Mavis laughs.

Amelia lifts my hand and spins me. "Mavis, that's enough. Melanie's our guest. Now turn the stereo up, would you? I had a *tough* day. I need to shake it off!"

Mavis complies, and the music fills the room as Jamal returns from the kitchen with an apple. He takes a bite and begins dancing along with us. It is the easiest, most synchronous moment I have ever experienced with people I hardly know, and I wonder if this is how the Jackson family always treats their guests. If so, in the hosting department, at least, my family has a lot of work to do.

———◇———

In her pink fuzzy robe, Stephanie Harris sits at her dressing table, brushing her hair. It is smooth and unnaturally shiny. She pulls it into a high ponytail that she secures with a pink elastic band, then picks up a jar of cold cream from the table. She opens it and smears cream on her cheeks, her forehead, her chin, her nose—and rubs, making sure to get every square inch of her perfect… no wait, oh, oh no! Is that a pimple? She plucks a tissue from the box covered by a discreet lavender crocheted cozy, and wipes. Under her makeup and just north of the tip of her nose, a small but angry pimple has formed. She leans into the mirror and lets out a little gasp. "No!" she hisses to the empty room. "No, no, no!" She grabs another tissue and wipes the rest of her makeup off, revealing a blotched face and tired, red-rimmed eyes. She does not feel beautiful and she suspects she does not look beautiful, either. She rubs her belly. The Midol has worn off and she lets out a whimper.

Stephanie pulls open the top drawer of her vanity and digs. Finally, she locates a bottle of Midol and dumps two out into her hand. Then, she drops the bottle back into the drawer, where it lands next to six bottles of lip gloss ranging in color from coral to deep red, three shades of liquid makeup and the folded piece of paper that holds Melanie Chaffee's fate.

I'm standing at the counter in Mavis's kitchen watching Amelia run a sponge around a dinner plate over a sink of sudsy water. I am on dish drying duty because Mavis has abandoned me, but I don't mind. I like her mother. She is quiet and funny at the same time. Most funny people are loud, like my Aunt Marnie.

"Thank you for letting me stay for dinner," I say, and take the plate she just handed me. It is still warm from the water and I dry it with a dish towel and carefully place it in the rack next to the others. Mrs. Jackson's kitchen is warm and still smells like the pork roast she cooked. It also has wallpaper covered in lime-green mushrooms with orange dots. I couldn't have chosen a better pattern if I'd picked it myself. Amelia smiles.

"Thank you for helping me dry the dishes. Mavis should be the one to help but it's funny, she *always* seems to feel the need to visit the ladies' just about dish doing time." She laughs, and I laugh too.

"It's okay. I don't mind doing them," I explain. "We have a dishwasher and my brother and I always have to load it. I like doing this better. It's more fun."

"Well, you can come over and have *fun* at my house any time." She rinses another dish and hands it to me to dry. "And thank you for being such a good friend to my Mavis. I appreciate that."

"She's been a good friend to me," I answer.

"It's been hard for her here. It hasn't been great for Jamal, either, but he's funny. Even white kids like funny." She looks a little far away.

"Mavis is funny," I say.

"Mavis is funny with her fists. Ever since she was little, things don't go her way, she goes right to hitting."

"I'd probably be the same if I was her," I say, looking up at Mavis's mother. "But I'm not, am I?"

"No, you are not. But you know that, don't you?" She gives me a serious look and I nod soberly.

"Mavis looks out for me," I confess.

"I imagine she does. She's good at that."

I look up into her dark eyes. They are watery. "I'll look out for her, too, Mrs. Jackson. I promise." I mean it. Amelia smiles and goes back to scrubbing a roasting pan.

"You know, little church mouse, I'm inclined to believe you will." She hands me the pan and I dry it and place it in the rack. Then she takes the dish towel from me and hangs it on a hook near the sink. "Now, you told your momma you'd be home by eight, right?" I nod, and she picks up her watch from a small plate beside the sink and looks at it. "Quarter til, we'd better get going, then, hadn't we?"

"Yeah, my mom's got a thing about punctuality," I say. In truth, my mom has a "thing" about a lot of things, but I keep that detail to myself.

Amelia buckles her watch. "Go on and find that Mavis, would you? Bang on the bathroom door if you have to. Now where did I put my pocketbook?" She leaves the kitchen to search for her purse and I head down the hall in search of my friend.

Chapter 16

ATTACK OF THE INTERNATIONAL JEWEL THIEF FROM ACROSS THE STREET

Our living room's long sofa is situated under our equally long front window. My knees are digging into its scratchy fabric and my right one hurts. Two days ago, I called Steven a butthead and he retaliated with a swift thwack to my bent knee with a hair comb. Not a regular, lady-sized comb. This was one of those big, heavy, handled jobs all the boys carry in their back pockets. And it hurt. It left a bizarre wound comprised of five bloody dots. My knee now looks like it was about to say something but then forgot what it was and trailed off at the end.

I'm watching for her. Across the street her house looks quiet, but the living room drapes are open, as they always are during the day.

"What do you think she'll wear?" I ask my mom as she steps down into the living room carrying a tray of wine glasses.

"Whatever they wear in Las Vegas, I imagine." She sets the tray down on the coffee table next to a platter of cheese and crackers. I'm wondering if this lady's feathered head-dress will fit though our door, when her front door opens and she steps out.

"There she is!" I gasp. My mom kneels on the couch next to me and we watch together as our neighbor clicks across the asphalt street on her soaring heals. Today they are strappy gold sandals with ankle buckles. Her toes are painted pale pink and her left big toe hangs over the tip of her sandal as if it's trying to hold the thing on her foot. The other toes are lazy and don't seem to be involved in the effort. Above her sandals, what looks like two feet of tanned, shimmery legs draw my eye up to her black leather mini skirt. My mother's eyes must be on the same trajectory as mine because her fingers float up to hover in front of her lips and she says, "Oh, dear. Her skirt is very…" Like my punctured knee, she is at a loss for words.

"What's her name again?" I ask.

My mom's fingers are still flirting with her mouth and for some reason she leans over and whispers, "Nina something."

"Nina," I repeat the mantra. Like its owner, the moniker is a magical thing filled with many possibilities and mysteries, and from what I can see so far, this lady is living up to her name.

She arrives in front of the brick retaining wall that surrounds our lithic lawn and stops. A long, thin cigarette sprouts from her long, thin fingers that are capped by long, thin (and very pointy) red nails, and in the other hand she grips a bottle of red wine like a weapon she's about to wield. Long, sparkly green earrings dangle from her tanned earlobes and over her teeny tiny black skirt, she's wearing a huge peach-colored sweater with voluminous sleeves. Leslie informed me not two days ago that those are called "dolman" sleeves and that they are all the rage right now. Nina shoves her giant sunglasses up to rest in the copper nest of her cropped hair and surveys the landscape. I can see her eyes now. They have tiny crinkles around them like my mom's, but she does not look *anything* like my mom. She turns to the left, where the concrete walkway begins down at the driveway and leads to our front door. The walkway is a solid thirty feet from where she stands, and she turns her attention back to the yard. She spots the sleepy-Mexican-guy stones, so she sticks the cigarette to her glossy pink lips and—grabbing the wall for support—pulls herself up onto the wall like a praying mantis scaling a tree limb. She is surprisingly agile and in only seconds she is standing atop the wall, atop her spindly sandals. She takes a drag of her cigarette, puts it back in its holder between her lips and, stretching a long leg out in front of her, plants a heel on the first stone.

"Your father and his damned gravel." My mother pushes herself from the sofa and hurries out of the room. I move to follow her, but then yelp in pain as I leave at least two of my ellipsis-dot scabs on the sofa cushion. I examine my knee, which has begun to bleed again, but, luckily there's no blood on my mother's couch.

At the open front door, I join my mother and watch as Nina hops from the last stone onto the walkway in front of our door. She's not even out of breath and, without removing her cigarette from her lips, she juts out her free hand to my mother and proclaims, "Nina Reynolds, Realtor."

My mother takes her hand. Nina shakes it vigorously, then reaches up, plucks the smoldering butt from her mouth and chucks it into the gravel yard behind her. "Nice yard!" she shout-says. "What did it run ya? Two, three grand?"

<hr />

I haven't finished my dinner because I can't eat and listen to this amazing woman at the same time. My parents and my brother and I are at the dining room table with her, Nina Reynolds, and she's finishing a story about her last trip to Pamplona, Spain, for the annual running of the bulls.

"...then he got himself gored, the poor guy!" she finishes, unsuccessfully holding back a snorting laugh. Steven's eyes are huge.

"Was there a lot of blood?" he asks, before dropping his eyes to her chest, where she is clearly braless.

"Oh, shit, yes!" she squeals.

Shirley flinches at the expletive but quickly recovers. "Did you manage to get out of Pamplona alive?" she asks.

"Oh, I was fine." Nina blots her mouth with a napkin. "Enrique wasn't so great, though. Lost an eye."

"Have you seen him since?" my dad asks.

"Naw, we went our separate ways, I'm afraid. Things just weren't the same after his accident." She looks over at me and winks. "He lost more than just an eye that day, know what I mean?" I'm not sure I do, and my mother looks ruffled and stands and begins picking up plates.

"You kids have got school tomorrow. Better start getting ready for bed."

Nina seems not to have heard her and continues. "Confidence, Melanie, that's what makes a man." Even though I'm not entirely sure I follow, I nod sincerely. "Once that's gone"—she sticks one pointy index finger in the air then whistles as she curls it down, like a deflating balloon—"that's all she wrote."

I smile and giggle a little with the sudden realization that Nina is talking about Enrique's unfortunate trauma-related hydraulic issues.

My mom gives me an icy look. "Melanie, help me clear the table, please."

I exchange another quick smile with Nina and get up to help. As usual, Steven just sits there. Oh, that's right, we're indoors so he doesn't have to lift a grimy finger.

"Where else have you been Ms. Reynolds?" he asks.

"Oh, just everywhere. And don't get all formal on me, kid. Call me Nina, okay?" She gives my brother a respectable slug in the arm then smiles up at me. "Hey, Melanie, why don't you come over for tea and we can have some girl time and discuss my other adventures?" She hands me her plate and I look over at Shirley.

"Can I, Mom?"

My mother catches my dad's gaze. "Would you like to take this one, dear?" she says as she makes her way towards the kitchen.

Sensing a possible marital minefield, my father treads lightly. "Well," he begins, feeling his way, "I don't see why not?" He watches my mother for some kind of indication of the correctness of his reply but comes up empty.

Nina is elated and claps her hands, then pops a fresh smoke between her lips and lights up. "Wonderful!" she exclaims through a puff of smoke. "How about Saturday at four o' clock? We'll have High Tea just like they do in London—cakes and cookies and everything!"

"That would be great!" I'm so excited I can barely breathe. Maybe it's the smoke. Nina takes another dramatic pull from her cigarette and stands.

"I'd better get home. I have a client coming over soon to sign some escrow papers."

"Really, this late?" I ask. It's past nine thirty, I'm supposed to be in bed by now. Nina shifts a little and seems suddenly uncomfortable.

"Well, can't just work nine-to-five if you want to get ahead, right?" She looks relieved as my mom walks back into the room.

Nina doesn't notice when Shirley looks at the cigarette like it's a flamethrower. "Oh!" she starts, "let me get you an ashtray!" She scoops one off a shelf nearby but Nina's already heading for the door.

"That's okay. I've got to get, really." Nina stops in front of the door. My mother eyes the growing ash on the end her cigarette.

"Are you sure you won't stay for dessert? Melanie made a wonderful cheesecake."

"Oh, no. I've got too much work to do." She gives me another quick wink. "But you can bring me some on Saturday, okay? It'll be just fabulous with tea, I bet." She jabs her cigarette, now sporting an impressive column of ash, in my direction to punctuate her point. In response, and with the grace and speed of a woman raised on Doris Day movies, my mother slips her ashtray under the burning thing just as its ash drops, catching the mess in the nick of time.

Nina opens the front door like there's a stage and an audience behind it. "I'm so sorry to have to run," she says, turning her attention to me, "but, nothing comes easy to us girls in this world and we've got to look out for our livelihoods, don't we?"

"You know, I've been thinking about that very thing," I say, smiling.

"Oh, do tell!" Nina snorts, before sweeping out the door in a cloud of cigarette smoke and Chanel No. 5.

Chapter 17

PRIDE AND PREJUDICE?

After having successfully survived P.E. class (today we practiced archery, which is both useless *and* dangerous so I'm pretty good at it) I'm crouched in front of my locker, pulling out books for my next class. Thankfully, it is advanced English with Ms. Shelley, which some would say is ironic, since obviously Mary Shelley wrote *Frankenstein,* and some other stuff, I think. But her name being the same as Mary Shelley's isn't irony, it's just a coincidence. Irony is a tricky thing to define.

I'm about to close my locker when a pair of Converse sneakers, nearly obscured by perfectly over-long bell-bottom cords, appears to my right. I stand. It's Ethan Wilde.

"Hi," he says.

"Hi," I say back. It's weird and silent for a second and Ethan's pale, grass-green eyes never leave mine. Then he speaks, thank God.

"Locker still giving you trouble?" he asks. It's a simple question but speaking when he's looking at me like that is so difficult. *Come on, Mel, just string a few words together,* I self-coach.

"Um, no. Seems to be working fine," I say, then pause and laugh moronically. "Must have been that magic touch of yours." *Red alert, danger Will Robinson! Nope, nope, nope!*

Went too far! Stop speaking, Melanie! But like a cat trying to barf up a hairball, I just let words keep spewing out.

"Not your *actual* touch, that would be weird"—insert more awkward laughing here—"I mean, ya know, what you did with my lock and all. You know, how you fixed it…" My brain hairballs are up and out in the open, where they lie on the floor at my feet (which I shuffle nervously). Ethan, who surprisingly has not fled, examines my stack of books.

"Where's your Austen?"

"Oh, we're not reading any Austen, I guess. Ms. Shelley's focusing on twentieth century writers this year."

Ethan nods. "Yeah, that's usually what she does in her advanced class. I had it last year. We read a lot of Hemingway and Steinbeck and Vonnegut and stuff."

I'm nervous but I still notice a discrepancy here. "No lady writers, huh?"

"No, you'll get to those. She spends most of the last term on Sylvia Plath, Woolf, Pearl Buck, even a little Maya Angelou."

"I'm reading one of her books now."

"Let me guess," he challenges, "I Know Why the Caged Bird Sings, right?"

I nod, impressed. "Mavis let me borrow it."

"Now that," he says, slamming my locker door closed for me, "is one impressive chick."

"That is a severe understatement, if I ever heard one," I say, stating the utter truth. The word impressive doesn't do justice to the magical mystery tour of purple glitter and platforms that is Mavis Jackson.

"How long have you guys been friends?" he asks.

"Pretty much since I moved here two years ago," I tell him. "We have a very mutually beneficial friendship. I let her copy my science homework, and in P.E. class she protects me from dodgeball-related injuries. It's a win, win."

Ethan laughs. "You're into literature *and* you're funny? Not many girls are like you, at least around here anyway."

"I've been more places than here, and trust me, there aren't many girls like me anywhere. It's honestly a little problematic."

Ethan's looking at me that way again. Darn it, just when I was getting comfortable and managing to not say anything stupid. I wish he'd stop looking at me like that. Well maybe I don't wish that, but how am I supposed to put two words together under these conditions?

"I don't think it's problematic," he says. "I think it's pretty great. Most of the girls I know just want to do their nails and read teen magazines."

"Oh, those are trash. I'd never buy those." Liar. "I mean, where do they get their facts? And who cares what Donny Osmond likes for breakfast, right?" I laugh and try to hide my guilt. I seem to be holding my own in an actual conversation with this Northern Arizona Adonis, so I decide to keep my attachment to adolescent yellow journalism to myself.

"You know," I say, "I don't think I've ever met a boy who likes to read Austen *and* plays football."

"Hey, guys can be into books and still do sports, too," he says.

"Contrary to my previously held beliefs, yeah, I guess they can," I admit.

Ethan looks down at his feet for a moment, then back at me. He almost seems shy. "You're different," he states.

"Tell me something I don't know." I let out another nervous laugh and try to act cool, but that's out the window when he locks his eyes on mine again.

"No, good different. I mean, other girls, they're pretty too." Hold up, here. He thinks I'm pretty? "But you're not like them," he continues. "You're pretty but you don't even know it, do you?"

I should answer but I can't. I'm still trying to wrap my head around his clearly inaccurate impression of me. I just watch as he looks away for a second then back at me, this time armed with that deadly half smile of his. "Modesty's not something you see much of these days. You're special."

I've got nothing. This kind of information is as foreign to me as Japanese. I'm speechless.

"Are you and your friends going to the dance on Friday?" he asks.

Finally, I manage to pull some words out of my flattery-fogged mind. "Um, yeah, we'll probably stop by for a bit," I manage.

"Do you have to go with them?" he asks.

"No, I don't think it's required. I mean, that's what we usually do, but we also usually spend most Saturdays eating corn chips and bean dip and analyzing adolescent boy behavior, but I doubt that's required either. Not like those two are gonna kick me out of the club or something," I joke.

Ethan laughs. "See, you're so different."

"Didn't we already cover that?" I ask, growing uncomfortable again.

"Oh, yeah. Sorry." He smiles. Yep, all is definitely forgiven. He shifts.

"So, do you want to…"

"Oooof!" I blurt out, as a force equal to a small truck hits me. Sean Mendoza bumps me in the shoulder again, then rubs his snuffily nose.

"Hey, Mel. Can I talk to you for a sec?" the filthy ingrate asks.

"Whatever unsavory thing it is you're wanting, Mendoza, can't it wait?" I look up at Ethan, who appears understandably confused by the situation.

"Sorry," I apologize.

Sean gets a clue. "Oh! Hey, I can see you're busy. But I just want to order one of—"

"Sean!" I cut him off.

Ethan smiles a little and shakes his head. "Listen, I'll catch up with you later, okay? I've got to get to class."

"Oh, yeah, sure. Catch you later," I say, trying to hide my disappointment as I watch Ethan stride away down the hall.

I want to wrap my hands around Sean Mendoza's chubby neck and strangle him, right here, in front of my locker, by the doorway to Mr. Ottopopy's eighth grade algebra classroom.

"Listen, Sean," I whisper, my voice low and scary, "don't ever bring up my *products* in front of anybody again, capeesh?"

Sean nods silently, his eyes wide. He capeeshes. I take a deep breath and try to relax.

"So, what do you want?"

"Well, um," Sean stammers, "can you make me some of those pictures too? Like the ones you made for Dennis? Those are awesome." He smiles so carefully and sweetly, I feel bad for getting angry with him.

"Okay, I can have some done for you by tomorrow." I pat him on his thick shoulder. He looks thrilled.

"That would be great! Can you make one of them with visible twat?" he asks, way too loudly. I don't feel bad for him anymore.

"Ew! Seriously! If you guys are so obsessed with the thing, can't you just call it by its proper name? It's called a vagina, you revolting imbecile!" I am beyond disgusted, but Sean just shrugs.

"Vagina, pussy, twat, what's the difference?" the idiot asks.

"Ugh. Just let me get to class, would you?"

Sean answers my question by turning around and bounding down the hall, whooping like a guy who just won the lottery. I turn, stalk the other way and wonder if Hefner has to put up with this crap.

S. J. Coffey

Chapter 18

CAFETERIA CONFESSIONS

Public school cafeterias should be deemed a health hazard. I don't care how many times a day our hairnet wearing lunch ladies clean ours, it's not enough. Every weekday from 9 a.m. to noon that cavernous hell hole, which is also the gymnasium, is filled with sweating boys. Lots of them. And I'm not saying boys are dirtier than girls, I'm just saying boys are grosser. Dirt and gross are not the same thing.

Me and Anna and Leslie are sitting at one of the long fold-up tables at the very edge of the dining area, near center court. Anna always brings her lunch, but Leslie and I are gamblers and like to take our chances with the gastrointestinal crapshoot that is hot lunch. Today's selection is beanie-weenie casserole. Despite its complex sounding title, beanie-weenie casserole is just beans and, well, sliced weenies. And a disproportionately small amount of weenies, in my opinion.

Anna crunches into a carrot stick and proclaims the obvious. "If Stephanie Harris finds out you talked to Ethan, you are so dead."

"Hey, he talked to me first." I am correct, here, and Leslie is very excited about that.

"Ethan Wilde talked to you!" she squeals, and I allow myself to get a little excited, too.

"And he reads Austen!" I say, but Leslie, holding a fork impaling three weenie chunks in front of her open mouth, looks confused.

"Steve Austin? I didn't know the Six Million Dollar Man wrote books!" she exclaims, squealing again. Poor thing, I better set her straight.

"*Jane* Austen, sweetie," I correct. "The Six Million Dollar Man does not write books.

"Oh," Leslie looks disappointed. "Well, if he did write books, I'd read them." Then she pops her forkful of weenies in her mouth.

I give her shoulder a reassuring bump with mine. "I know you would. And I'm sure he'd appreciate that."

With my fork, I push my two remaining weenies around in the rust-colored goo that keeps them wedded to the fifteen or so beans I have left on my tray.

"I think he was going to ask me to the dance," I ponder aloud.

"Really?" Leslie asks. "Why didn't he?"

I look across the lunchroom. At a table by the door, Dennis and Joe sit with Sean, who's stuffing peas up his nose and then shooting them out at his buddies.

"Sean Mendoza," I say, my nose wrinkling in disgust.

Leslie weighs in. "Ew! He's icky."

Anna bites into an apple. Along with conservatism and a marginally racist worldview, fiber is very important in her family. "What did he want?" she asks.

"Some of my art pieces."

"Oh, is that what you're calling your porn, now?" Anna's well on her way to a career in court room litigation. "You get caught," she continues, "you'll be expelled, for sure."

"Do you have enough money for the shoes, yet?" asks Leslie, whose career goals are a tad less lofty than Anna's.

"Not yet," I answer. "But I'm guessing there's enough male depravity in this school to buy me fifty pairs of shoes." I glance back over at the stooges' table. Joe has Dennis in a headlock so Sean can better fart in the poor kid's face.

"Yep, lots and lots of shoes," I conclude. I turn my attention to another table on the far side of the room where a huge hulk of a girl is sitting alone finishing her lunch. This is Nadine Melnick. She is terrifying. Nadine is a linebacker of an eighth grader with bleached, feathered hair and a poorly disguised case of acne. Leslie and Anna follow my gaze. Leslie's eyes are huge with awe and fear.

"My cousin's friend said that only a year after her mom died, her dad made her put down her *own* dog. Had to shoot it herself with a rifle. That's why she's so mean." This unsolicited information from Leslie concerns me.

"I saw her with Stephanie Harris the other day," I say, frowning. "I wonder what that means."

"It means you're in more trouble than I thought," Anna says, rolling her very clean apple core up in a napkin.

We watch as Nadine stands, picks up her tray and shuffles to the garbage can near the exit door. She roundhouses the tray and slams it against the inside of the can the way, say, Bigfoot might swing an unwitting camper into a tree. Then she tosses the tray, now cracked, into the bin for dirty trays and stalks out of the room. I feel a little sorry for her.

"She's always alone," I say.

"I know," Leslie affirms. "I feel so bad for her. We should ask her to sit with us." Anna does not share her viewpoint.

"Hey, do-gooder, I feel bad for endangered grizzly bears but I'm not gonna have a picnic with one."

I am about to come to Leslie's aid with the argument that it's our fault that bears are endangered and that as such we should probably provide them with all the picnics they want, when Mavis saunters up and slides onto the bench next to Anna.

"How you ladies doin'?" she asks.

"Ethan Wilde talked to Mel today!" Leslie blurts.

"Ooooh, Ethan Wilde *is* a fine young man," says Mavis.

"He's also a taken young man," Anna retorts, scooting a little away from Mavis (whose crinkly W is forming between her eyes).

"Says who?" she asks.

"Says Stephanie Harris, that's who," Anna defends.

"Hmm," says Mavis, "she is a nasty white bitch." She grabs Anna's lunch bag, extracting a leftover carrot stick.

"You mind?" she asks Anna.

"No, it's all yours," Anna replies with a curious look.

"Thanks. But see, it's like this. I never seen a ring on that boy's finger so I say he's fair game." She crunches on the carrot stick and gives me a wink.

"Yeah, well, Mister Fair Game is sitting with Stephanie Harris." Anna stabs a finger toward a table in the coveted center of the room, where Stephanie is parked next to Ethan, who—unless I'm imagining it—looks annoyed. Mavis whistles.

"That," she concludes, "is *definitely* one nasty white bitch."

Anna nods righteously. "See, joined at the hip."

Mavis shoots Anna a glare, then turns to me. "Listen, lil buddy, that girl ain't got nothin' on you." In response, Leslie bounces and nods fervently.

"Yeah, Melanie's a brick house, right Mavis?"

"Well," Mavis answers, laughing, "I don't know about that. But Mel here's got a quality that dudes like Ethan just kind of take to, ya know?" Anna is not impressed.

"Oh, yeah? And what kind of dude might that be?"

"A rich white one, that's what," Mavis says.

I sigh and try to turn the conversation in a more positive direction. "He reads Austen." At this, Mavis's little W returns.

"Who? Steve Austin?" she asks, causing Leslie to begin bouncing in her seat again.

"See! Mavis thought the same thing!"

I look over at Stephanie. And sensing my stare, she locks eyes with mine and smiles slyly. My stomach is suddenly queasy. I mean Space-Mountain-after-two-hot-dogs queasy. Mavis hears me suck in a breath and looks over at Stephanie too.

"Why's she lookin' at you like that? Like she knows something you don't?"

"I told you," Anna says, "she knows."

"What're you going to do, Mel?" Leslie asks, worried.

"She ain't gonna do nothin'," Mavis says. "She's too cool to get involved in that crap."

"Not going to be cool when Stephanie gets a hold of her," Anna says flatly.

"Don't be so negative!" Leslie interjects, "My dad says…"

But I'm not listening anymore. I drop my head on my arm and stare across the room again. Stephanie Harris has her arm looped through Ethan's now, and she's saying something in his ear. *In the battle for Prince Ethan, the maiden is probably toast*, I think. I frown and wish that that girl would choke on a weenie. I decide I'm not going to call her Evil Queen Stephanie anymore. I decide she needs a more fitting name. I watch as Stephanie tickles Ethan's sides. And then I say, under my breath and to no one but myself, "Nasty White Bitch."

Chapter 19

MOB JERKY

Having grown tired of just drawing pictures of naked female torsos, I'm branching out into film making. Well, a kind of film making, anyway. I finish a playing-card-sized image of a buxom lady with long, flowing hair, then put it on the bottom of a stack of similarly sized drawings. I get them all aligned and tidy then I staple them together on the left side, creating a small book. The first image in the book is of the same big-busted lady, but here she's wearing a cute nightie. I flip through the book and smile. In the course of the half-second it takes to flip the pages, the woman, in jerking fast-forward, appears to grab her nightie by the bottom hem and pull it off, revealing the naked woman, who is smiling broadly and clearly having a fabulous time marketing her assets.

The woven plastic straps of the lawn chair I'm sitting in are cutting into the backs of my thighs. It's evening but still warm and uncharacteristically sticky for the time of year. I peel my thighs from the chair straps, reposition myself on its seat and rub my eyes. For the past two hours, I've been sitting out here on the back porch working. And after a long day at school, I'm beat. Behind me I hear the back door open, so I slip my newest product into the front pocket of my shorts, as my dad steps out and turns on the little radio we keep out here. It's tuned to the local pop rock station since it's the only one we can get without a satellite-sized antenna mounted on the roof.

"How're you doin', MellyBean?" he asks, smiling down at me.

Heck, I'm great, I think. *I've just taken my talents into the cinematic realm and the profit prospects are excellent.* But I don't tell him this.

"I'm okay. How're you, dad?" is all I say.

"Oh, I'm alright, I guess," he answers. We're quiet for a moment and just watch the sun give up for the day. The sky beyond our brick wall is salmony pink and red, studded with the silhouettes of saguaros reaching to the heavens. It is beautiful. Our sunsets are always beautiful because the air is always full of dirt and crap. Great sunsets are impossible if the air's too clean, I guess.

"That's a nice one," I tell my dad, who's sipping on a beer with one hand while he rearranges the change in his pocket with the other.

"A real beauty," Dad says. I look out at the yard. The unforgiving desert earth has not been cooperative and has soundly rejected the yucca mulch my dad and my brother tried so diligently to get it to accept. Now, instead of a lush, green backyard lawn, we have a dried yucca farm. Parched tufts of the stuff lay all over the yard in an utterly rebellious and disorganized manner. I ask my dad a question I already know the answer to.

"Any grass yet?"

"Nope. Not a single goddamn blade." He laughs a little and continues sipping beer and jingling change. Jingle, sip, jingle. The sun surrenders and the deep blue sky grows black with zillions of stars. There are so many stars here. My dad lets out a sigh, then jolts slightly.

"Hey, cops found another mob body."

"Really?" I ask, excited. "Where?"

"Off of sixty-six again. About forty-five minutes out of town," he says.

Kingman is situated just two hours south of Las Vegas. This is convenient for several reasons: a) if desired, we could obtain fashionable school clothes at reasonable prices without the four-hour trek down to Phoenix, and b) according to my dad, our proximity to Elvisville makes us the perfect location for the disposal of human corpses.

If my father is to be believed, the organized crime lords (who run various branches of their businesses out of Vegas) are fond of having their henchmen wantonly toss squealers and other unsavory types into the desert just on the outskirts of our wholesome little burg. Apparently, this is something they do just as they leave the Kingman city limits, because bodies of the syndicated sort are always found between us and Phoenix. What I can't figure out is why a group of people as sophisticated, not to mention well-dressed, as the ones I've seen on *The Godfather* would be dopey enough to chuck their dirty laundry onto the cracked desert floor only minutes from the Tastee-Freez. Because, unlike the mobsters I've seen on television, the goodfellas to our north seem to be too lazy to even dump a shovelful of sand onto their dead.

Sip, jingle, sip. "Poor guy. They found him out there, still in his shiny suit. Just dumped him. You'd think they'd bury them," my dad says.

"I get the feeling that thinking is not really a big player in these guys' agendas," I offer. "Hey, maybe they want them to be found."

"You may be right, there, kiddo," he answers. "They might do it as some kind of warning or something."

"What do you suppose the guy did to end up like that, Dad?"

He strolls off the porch and I follow him as he jingles and sips his way out into the yucca farm. "You got me, hon. Maybe they said or did something they shouldn't have. Who knows?"

Bunches of desiccated, hostile yucca shreds stick to the hem of my dad's slacks, and he keeps having to pull his change-rearranging hand out of his pocket to pick them off. "Stupid stuff," he complains. "Your mother and her damned grass."

I would tell him my mother says the same thing about his damned gravel, but I'm having such a nice time I decide not to spoil things. My dad gives another little jolt, the way he does when something pops into his head. "Oh, hey, don't you go telling your mom I told you about the new mob jerky, okay? She'd have my hide."

I finger zip my lips. "She will not hear it from me. I promise." My dad smiles.

"Thank you," he says, gently bumping his forehead on the top of my head as the sound of a car's low idle emanates from somewhere beyond the gate. My dad frowns and peeks through the gap between the gate and the wall.

"What is it?" I ask. He moves aside a little and lets me peek too.

Across the street at Nina's house a large black sedan pulls up to the curb. The engine cuts off and then the driver's side door swings open and a man dressed in a dark suit gets out. He is tall and slim, and on the top of his head his slick dark hair reflects a thin strip of moonlight. He strides up Nina's walkway and presses the doorbell.

"Who's he?" my dad whispers as Nina, dressed in a ruffled nightgown and robe combo, opens her front door with two wine glasses swinging from her hand.

"I don't know," I answer. "But I don't think he's here to sign escrow papers."

"I think you need to stop watching your mother's soaps, kiddo," he says while we watch Nina let the man into her home before closing the front door behind him.

"Mom's shows aren't so bad," I tell him. "Besides, she's always nice to me when I watch them with her, and she lets me eat lunch in the living room." My dad turns to me and offers a slightly sad smile. "I'm glad you two can do something together you both enjoy."

I'm not sure I "enjoy" my mom's afternoon trips to Oakdale and Springfield but they sure are informative. But I don't tell him that.

"Hey, Dad?"

"Mmm hmm?" He's now staring straight up at the stars. He looks like he might fall backwards.

"How're you and Mom doing?" This is a serious question and my father's eyes quickly leave the sky and land on mine.

"We're okay. Why do you ask?"

"Oh, I don't know. Sometimes I think she watches those shows because she needs a little romance in her life or something. You'd never guess it, but I think she's actually pretty romantic."

"You think so, huh?" he asks, and I get the feeling he's actually very interested in my opinion.

"I do, yeah," I say.

"Well, how do you know?"

"I just know, you know? It's a girl thing."

"Ah, I see. And what do you suggest I do about the situation, Dr. Chaffee?"

I slip my arm through his change-jingling arm and we stroll back over to the patio.

"I prescribe dancing," I tell him. "Mom loves to dance."

"Dancing? I've told you, MellyBean, your ol' dad can't dance."

"Well, yeah, maybe not the fancy kind of dancing, like tango or waltz or whatever, but anybody can dance the way kids do."

"Oh, yeah?" His voice is teasing but he's still listening, so I ring my arms around his neck, middle-school style.

"It's basically just, you know, like a kind of spinning penguin hug," I say.

My dad puts his arms around me and smiles. "Okay, I guess penguins would know how to dance, they're certainly dressed for it."

"Very funny," I chide, laughing. "Now pay attention." I move my feet. He follows, and we slowly turn to the music on the tiny radio. My father is awkward and unsteady. It is sweet and strange. I never think of him as unsure about anything.

"See, it's easy," I say.

"Yeah, I think I can do this one without giving anybody a smashed toe," he says with a chuckle. "It's kind of nice."

"Bet Mom would think it's nice, too," I say and rest my head on his shoulder. I feel my dad nod against my head. I can't see his face but I know he's a little sad. I don't know how I know, I just do. And as we turn, I get another peek through the space between the wall and the gate, and I catch a glimpse of Nina at her living room window, just before she pulls the drapes closed.

Chapter 20

A DANGEROUS INVITATION AND AN ATTEMPTED HOSTILE TAKEOVER

The lines in Sean Mendoza's chubby left hand are filled with dirt, giving his palm a grimy, rural roadmap appearance.

"Ugh, jeez Sean, when was the last time you washed those mitts?" I ask.

We're standing in front of my locker exchanging money for illicit content. My locker has become a regular middle-school red-light district, and as I slap several drawings into Sean's grubby hand it occurs to me that perhaps this location is not the safest place to conduct my business, and that I should probably open up a new storefront elsewhere.

Sean examines the drawings, then hands the one depicting a tall, slim nude back to me. It seems he has chosen the other drawing, the one with the fluffier lady with her hair in a curly updo.

"I like this one," he says, running a thumb over the drawing. I am surprised by the choice and say so.

"So, you're a romantic, huh?"

"Oh, yeah," he says. "She's a beauty."

"Why, thank you," I reply. "I was going for a softer, more baroque look with that one. I'm glad you appreciate it."

"She's perfect," he says dreamily.

"Well, I'm sorry I misjudged you, Mendoza. You might just be a true gentleman," I pronounce.

But he opens his mouth again and ruins the whole thing. "Besides"—he grins—"she's got way bigger tatas."

"Okay, I guess not," I conclude.

Sean hands me a sticky one-dollar bill. I stuff it in my pocket and pull out my little film book prototype. "Here," I tell him, "give this to Dennis." I hand him the tiny "movie".

"Tell him it's three-fifty, okay?" I say as Sean flips the book and grins.

"Wow," he gasps, "this is amazing! Can I have it?"

"Sure, for three-fifty."

Sean digs in his pocket and hands me a five, so I give him back his single. "I don't have any quarters, so I'll have to owe you fifty cents."

"Oh, that's okay. This baby is worth four bucks, easy," he says, giving me an icky smile. "Thanks, Mel. You're the best." He turns to go.

"Don't forget to show that to Dennis, okay?"

"I won't! He's gonna want one for sure. Joe, too, I bet." I watch as he hurries down the hall like a plump hamster with a sunflower seed. Unlike Dennis, he's really a nice kid. I'm thinking that—paired with a nice woman possessing unsubstantial marital standards—he might just make a good husband and father one day, when I sense a presence behind me and turn around. It's Ethan.

"Hi," he says.

"Jeez, you're a stealthy one," I state.

"I'm sorry," he says, smiling. "I didn't mean to scare you."

"Oh, it's okay. I'm a girl so living with fear is kind of our thing. I'm used to it."

"Stealthy. Nice word choice. Don't hear that one too often," he says.

"A big vocabulary's kind of a dork prerequisite, and I am definitely that."

"I want to be a writer," he says, "so I notice good word usage."

"And here I am, surprised again," I say. Ethan just smiles and opens his locker.

"What do you want to be?" he asks.

"What? When I grow up?"

"Yeah, you know, someday," he needlessly clarifies.

"Someday isn't really on my agenda just yet. Right now, I'm just trying to survive junior high with my dignity intact. But, you know, it is very likely you and I will share the same profession," I say, smiling. "Someday."

Ethan closes his locker and looks at me thoughtfully. "You want to go to the dance with me?"

There it is and here I am, trying to put a decent response together in the beam of those green, green eyes.

"Um." *Excellent start, Mel.* "Yeah, I could do that," I manage.

When Ethan smiles, little crinkles form at the corners of his eyes, making him appear older. I didn't think kids our age could have wrinkles yet.

"Good," he says, pushing his locker closed. "I'll meet you there at seven."

"Okay," I say, feeling utterly numb and paralyzed in the moment. Ethan turns to go, then stops.

"You're really something special, you know? Not like other girls."

"No offense, but didn't we cover that already? My obvious singularity within our school has hopefully been addressed, hasn't it?" I'm concerned about the direction he's heading, but he laughs.

"No, it's just, you know, I'm talking about girls like Stephanie, I guess. They're always trying to be all sexy and make boys like them and stuff."

"I'd say that strategy's working for her pretty well so far, don't you think?"

Ethan shakes his head. "Not working on me. I like nice girls. It's like, you know, those pictures everyone has been talking about."

Oh dear. "What pictures?" I ask.

"Those drawings of the naked ladies. Haven't you seen them?" he asks.

"Um, no, I have not," I lie.

"Well, they're disgusting. Just terrible. How can a guy view a woman with respect if he looks at trash like that?"

"He can't?" My head feels like it's floating off my shoulders and I want to be somewhere else.

"No way!" Ethan says, continuing to torture me. "If I could find the guy who's drawing those pictures, I'd let him have it, for sure."

I gulp as much air as I can and ask, "What if a girl drew them?"

Ethan looks horrified. "Oh, wow, I just, God, that would be even worse, you know?" he stammers, his unknowing view of me impairing his ability to speak. "I really couldn't even look at a girl like that, honestly."

I wish I could reach up and pull my own head back down onto my neck where it belongs. It's feels disconnected, like I'm looking down on an unfolding disaster from above.

I feel like crying or running away or both.

"Wow," I say, trying to keep breathing, "you've got some strong opinions about us girls, huh?"

Oblivious to the damage, Ethan shrugs and smiles that deadly smile. "Yeah, I guess I do. I just think girls and women are better than us guys, you know? They should be revered and looked after. They're mothers, you know?"

No, I don't know, I think. So instead, I joke, "Well, yeah, I guess everybody's got one of those," I laugh stupidly. I must be hiding how I feel pretty well, because Ethan doesn't seem to notice anything different about me. Inexplicably, he steps closer and locks his eyes on mine, which are fighting to keep tears away.

"That's why I like you so much, you know? I bet you'll be a great mom." He touches my wrist lightly. Goosebumps zip up my arm like a column of fire ants.

"Motherhood. That's intense," I say, still trying to pull my head out of the air above me. "I'm not even thinking past lunchtime," I joke again. Ethan laughs and squeezes my wrist gently, sending the fire ants up into my scalp.

"Well, yeah, of course! That's a long way off, for sure," he says, smiling. "I should go, but I'll see you at the dance next Friday, okay? Seven sharp!" He drops my wrist and turns and heads down the hall away from me. I am a storm of feelings.

"Yup!" I spit out in his direction, "seven, sharp!"

Ethan waves and then disappears into the advanced algebra classroom four doors down. Bile and Cheerios rising in my throat, I bolt for the girls' room.

———————◇———————

Five minutes after the bell rang, I'm five minutes late for science. Worse, when I step out the restroom (my stomach empty and my head closer to my shoulders) I run into the stooges, who have, it seems, been waiting for me. Joe looks worried.

"Are you okay, Mel?" he asks. No, I am not okay but I'm not going tell these clowns.

"I'm fine," I say. "Shouldn't you three be ignoring your teachers somewhere?"

"We were on our way to gym class and Joe here saw you make a break for the can," Dennis explains delicately. "You got the Hershey squirts?"

"What? No! I don't have the, never mind," I try to say more, but Sean feels the need to integrate me, as well, and interrupts.

"Did you get your period? My sister gets the runs really bad when hers starts. She spends, like, three days a month in the crapper, I swear."

"No, Sean, I didn't start my period and I definitely don't have diarrhea."

"Whew, that's a relief," he says, wiping his dry brow dramatically. I'm annoyed, and sick, but a bit touched too.

"Were you guys really worried about me?" I ask.

"These idiots were," Dennis scoffs. "I knew you were okay, though. You're tough, right, Chaffee?"

"I don't know about that," I reply listlessly. "I sure don't feel very tough." I am not lying. I feel like a popped water balloon in the dirt on the day after the fourth of July.

"Listen guys," I say, "I appreciate your concern but I'm fine okay? I'm also late for science." I start to leave but Sean gently touches my shoulder.

"Hey, wait," he says. "We have to tell you something."

"What?" I ask, not really wanting to hear the answer.

Joe elbows Dennis. "Ask Mister Bigmouth here."

"What did you do, Dennis?" I grill. Dennis looks away then down at his feet.

"I sort of told a few more guys about your flippy movie book things."

"What!" I shriek. "How many guys, Dennis?"

"Just a few, I promise."

"How few?" My head is abandoning my body again.

Dennis tries unsuccessfully to suppress a grin and pulls a huge wad of cash out of his pocket. "This many," he says, letting his grin out as Sean bounces.

"We got you, like, twenty-five more orders!" he says, socking me in the arm.

"Ow!" I complain. It isn't that the playful punch hurt, it's just that all of me hurts right now.

"Sorry, Mel," Sean apologizes. "We're just so excited for you!" He begins bouncing again. Next to him, Joe nods silently in solidarity.

"You're like, a big-time business lady now, Mel!" Sean bubbles.

"It is exciting," Joe offers quietly.

Dennis hands me the cash and a small sheet of paper with names and numbers on it.

"I thought I told you guys not to tell anybody else," I protest, stuffing the money and order list into my pocket.

Dennis shrugs. "We knew you didn't mean it."

I am incredulous. "Why is it boys never believe girls? I hate to tell you fellas but when a girl says something, she generally means it."

On wobbly legs, I start off for the science room and the comfort of Mavis at my side. Whether I want them to or not, the stooges follow and Sean drops a protective arm around my shoulders.

"We'll walk you to class, okay, Mel?" he says.

"Trust me, guys. I can get to class just fine on my own."

"Hey, the period runs are no joke," Sean continues. "My sister fainted on the throne last month. Had to call an ambulance and everything."

Then Dennis interjects. "And being your business partners, we feel it's in our best interest to look out for you."

"I told you, I don't have my period and since when are we business partners?"

I'm not feeling like I'm going to throw up again, but I don't feel great either and I really want to sit down. Somehow sensing this, Joe reaches over and takes my books.

"May I carry these for you, Melanie?" he asks, so quietly I don't think the other two even heard him.

I smile and nod. "Thank you, Joe."

As we walk, Dennis blathers on about profit margins and production costs, but I can't stop thinking about what Ethan said. I tell myself that once he gets to know me, if he finds out about my secret, he'll understand and forgive me, won't he? After all, he does read Austen, right? Mr. Darcy forgave Lizzie Bennet and George Knightley forgot all about Emma's shallow manipulations once he realized he was in love with her, so surely Ethan will see past my infractions, too, won't he?

My head is settling back onto my shoulders and as I arrive in front of the science room door, Joe hands me back my books and Sean punches me in the arm again. "Take care, Mel," he says, as he and Joe and Dennis head off in the direction of the gymnasium.

Dennis gives me a mock salute. "Get better, then get to

work, weirdo," he orders as they turn and blunder down the hall, slamming into each other and snorting like idiots.

I watch them go for a moment. They are morons, but they are sweet. However, when I feel better we are going to have to have a conversation about company startups, partnerships and hostile takeovers. How did this all get so big, so out of hand? I never told them we were partners. I never told them I wanted them to bring me more orders. Why do boys never listen? And why do boys always take everything they can from girls?

Chapter 21

IF YOU WORK WHILE ATTENDING A SLUMBER PARTY, ARE THE SNACKS TAX DEDUCTIBLE?

It is Friday and I am at Anna's for a sleepover with her and Leslie. Usually, these Friday nights at Anna's are filled with nonsense and junk-food-induced nausea, but tonight, thanks to Dennis and his big mouth, it's a working sleepover. I'm sitting on the floor with my back against Anna's nightstand finishing the eighth flip-book for the order of twenty-five books. I've elected to do them assembly-line style, so when I finish one, I hand it up to Anna and Leslie for cover application and stapling. While they wait for me to hand up a product, they pore over a year-old issue of *Playboy* I pinched from the old file cabinet my dad keeps out in the garage.

"Doesn't your dad hide this stuff?" Anna asks.

"Yeah, but I know where to look." I hand her up the finished booklet and she tidies and staples it. Leslie is incensed. "Hey, I thought I was on staple duty!" she complains.

"The last one you did was crooked, so you've been reassigned," Anna tells her.

"Reassigned to what?" Leslie frowns.

"Reassigned to not doing any more damage. You're inhibiting production." Anna puts the little book into a paper bag with its seven carnal siblings.

Leslie flips through the porn magazine and pouts. "How'd you find out where your dad hides these, anyway?" she asks me.

"My dad's very predictable and my mom hates the garage and never goes in there except to do laundry. It was a no-brainer. I've known where he keeps them since the fifth grade. And I imagine my brother's known longer than that."

"Ew." Leslie makes a face. "I don't like to think of Steven that way."

"Trust me, Leslie, none of us do," I say. I'd could tell her that when I've found my dad's cast-off girly mags they usually look a little worn, indicating frequent viewing on the part of either my brother or my dad, or both. An unappealing prospect that would probably unsettle the poor girl even more, since I'm pretty sure she's got a rabid crush on my disgusting older brother.

"My dad keeps his out in the shed," Leslie says. "Sometimes my brothers are out there for *hours*."

Anna taps the top of my head with the stapler. "Think your dad knows you took this filth?"

"Ow," I say, rubbing my head, which really doesn't hurt. "And no, I don't think he knows. Besides, I took that one from the bottom of the pile. There are five of them out there. I'd save myself all this work and just cut out some of the pictures from those, and sell them, but my dad and my brother would definitely notice."

"There's a stack of them?" Anna asks.

"Well, yeah, I don't imagine you'd want to use the same one over and over." The information I've thrown into the room is lost on Leslie and not appreciated one bit by Anna.

"It's a good thing you don't have much in the way of a backyard over there," she states, "because I sure don't want to go to a barbecue at your place."

"What about sleepovers? We have sleepovers at Mel's," Leslie points out.

"Sleepovers rarely involve seeing her dad," Anna clarifies.

"Yeah, he kind of lives in the yard and the garage these days." The words are barely out of my mouth when it dawns on me that something might be up with my parents.

The more I think about it, the more I realize I haven't seen them actually together for months now. They used to sit out on the patio every night after dinner and watch the sunset with cups of decaf. But lately, after dinner my mom goes into their bedroom to read and my dad haunts the garage and the yard like a confused, change-jingling ghost. Have I been so wrapped up in my illegal enterprise that I haven't noticed my mom and dad are having marital problems? Thankfully, Leslie, who's closely examining a blond centerfold, interrupts the squirrel trapped in my brain wheel. "Do you think this is what our moms look like naked?"

Anna smacks herself in the forehead with the stapler. "Thanks a lot, dopey. There's a visual I'll never get rid of."

I start another booklet, and with spectacular obtuseness, Leslie muses, "It's weird to think of all the older ladies I know like that. I've only ever seen my aunt in pantsuits and flannel nightgowns."

"As God intended," Anna confirms.

Something floats by behind Leslie's big eyes and she frowns. "Hey, why are there no black ladies in these magazines?"

"Who wants to see that?" Anna says, her bias on full display.

"Um, black men, for one," Leslie rightly defends.

"And more than a few white ones, I bet." I look up at Anna. "I can't believe you. I should tell Mavis you said that."

"Please don't. I'd like to see high school," she pleads. How can someone so smart be so dumb?

"Sometimes, Anna, I'm not entirely sure why I'm even friends with you," I tell her as I start on the fifth page of this little book.

"I help you with your math homework?" she suggests.

She has a point there. As a solid member of the below-average math program, I'm very grateful to have a tutor who attends calculus classes over at the community college because she's already exhausted all the mathematical options available to her at the junior high. She does come in very handy, but she and I have got to have a talk about her worldview with regard to race, and soon. I turn and look at the clock radio behind me. It's after nine.

"Oh man," I say. "We have, like, sixteen more to go. Look what time it is."

"Gonna have to pull an all-nighter," Anna says, cracking open a Dr Pepper.

Leslie squeals again and bounces on the bed. "Yay! I love to stay up all night!" Anna holds up her soda like a sea captain with a cup of coffee in rough seas.

"Take it easy, spaz. My grandma just gave me this new quilt."

"Okay!" Leslie says, her glee subdued but undaunted.

Suddenly, it occurs to me that I've seen this before. Oh, yeah, Sean Mendoza. *I should really try and get those two together,* I think. But then Leslie rolls backwards off the bed, then pops up giggling and I decide it might be safer for everyone if I don't.

Anna sips her soda and looks down at my work. I finish the last page of the book and hand it up to her and she staples. "Mel, you are so gonna get busted," she begins. "And when you do, you'd better not tell anybody I let you work out of my house. Ivy Leaguers do not associate with pornographers."

"I think you might be wrong there," I tell her. "And when this order is finished, I'm closing up shop, anyway."

"You're quitting?" Leslie whines.

"Yep," I reply. "After these I'll have more than enough for the shoes. I can't get expelled, and I don't want to even think about what this would do to my mother." And of course, there is Ethan and his very clear view of my enterprise, but I don't feel like talking about that right now. Every time I allow myself to think of it, I get queasy again.

"Yeah, I guess you shouldn't risk it." Leslie looks disappointed at the impending end of her brief career as a felonious accessory.

"Well, I'm thrilled," Anna says. "I'm ready for things to go back to normal. For the past week every boy I've been dumb enough to make eye contact with has hit me up for one of your drawings. I feel like I'm your pimp."

I pick up the stack of tiny papers, I'm short five pages. "Okay, boss, you'd better tell your associate there to make with the scissors. I need more pages."

Anna tosses a stack of paper to Leslie, who grabs the scissors and begins cutting as she continues to bounce.

S. J. Coffey

Anna claps a hand on her friend's knee. "Hey, Little Miss Running-With-Scissors, slow down. I don't need you bleeding all over my grandma's quilt. I got enough liability problems already." Leslie giggles but complies and we get back to work. And with every page and every line I draw, I pray that Ethan Wilde never finds out who, and what, I really am.

Chapter 22

SHIRLEY CHAFFEE, MAVIS'S MOM, AND THE KINGMAN JUNIOR HIGH SCHOOL PTA MEETING AND REVIVAL

Her ankles crossed and her feet tucked demurely to the left under her cold, metal folding chair, Shirley sits in the second to last row of the Cerbat Mountain Meeting Room in the Kingman Parks and Recreation Facility. It's a new building. It went up just last year on the southern edge of Butler. The fact that the name of the building and its actual location don't agree bothers Shirley a little. Continuity is very important to her. It doesn't upset her, really, it just bothers her. She has noticed over the course of her life that people in charge of these sorts of things often throw caution to the wind when it comes to the important task of naming something. Names and labels are important. How in the world are people supposed to deal with something they can't properly identify?

Shirley smooths her herringbone skirt and pulls air into her lungs. Ten more minutes and she is out of here and back home to cheddar and crackers and a glass of reasonably-priced Riesling. She might need two glasses tonight because Mrs. Magnussen is leading the meeting this time. Between Sunday services, the kids' choir practices and her weekly women's bible study group, she sees more than enough of Patty Magnussen already. From what Shirley can surmise, Mrs. Magnussen is a pink, over-perfumed busybody with an unhealthy attachment to ruffles, dump cakes and everyone else's business. Still she has always been kind, if not subtly catty, to Shirley, who tries to keep her interactions with the tiny, civically obsessed woman to an absolute minimum.

"And finally," Mrs. Magnussen begins from the podium up front, "I feel it is my duty, as your Parent Teacher Association President, to address a, well, very sensitive topic." From behind her tiny wire glasses (Shirley wonders, *Does she have to buy them from the children's frame display at the optician's office?*) she casts a long look out over the room, allowing just enough time for an appropriately dramatic pause. While she waits for Patty to get on with it already, Shirley notices a lone black woman sitting in the second row from the front. She is pretty, with a tight bun at the back of her neck, and dressed in a smart, rust suit. Shirley approves of the woman's attire, although it is unlikely she will ever find herself with an opportunity to tell her so. Finally, back up at the podium, Patty Magnussen clasps her miniature, fluffy hands together and gets to the point.

"It has come to my attention, by way of a concerned mother of one of our seventh-grade boys, that some *lewd* drawings have been making their way through the deeply impressionable male population of our junior high school."

Murmurs and frowns trade places between the forty or so adults in the room, most of whom are women (as husbands have better things to do than concern themselves with their children's educations). Arizona State is facing off against U of A, so masculine representation at tonight's meeting is especially sparse.

"Needless to say," Mrs. Magnussen continues, "this information is deeply disturbing. The welfare of our young people is at stake here. Why, even their sparkling, young souls are in jeopardy!"

Church Patty Magnussen and local political activist Patty Magnussen often collide, a fact that Shirley Chaffee, a dedicated Methodist woman who holds a B.A. in Political Science from Eastern Illinois University, finds grating. And she winces, ever so discreetly, as Mrs. Magnussen lets Church Patty take the wheel.

"Our Lord will not suffer the presence of pornography in our educational institutions," she cries. "On behalf of our Lord Jesus Christ, I would greatly appreciate it if anyone having information regarding these filthy drawings would come speak to me directly."

By chance, or maybe because her eyes can't bear to rest on Patty Magnussen's screaming pink ruffles for one second more, Shirley looks over at the African American woman in the good suit and notices she has a fist to her mouth and is clearly trying to suppress giggles. Her usual decorum unchecked due to boredom and general irritation, Shirley smiles and has to fake a cough to keep from laughing too. And it takes all her strength, bolstered partly by fear of embarrassment and partly by her too tight tummy control pantyhose, to get through the remainder of Patty Magnussen's PTA sermon, which thankfully is wrapping up.

"Now," Patty announces, her cheeks growing a little less pink, "do we have any more motions to address?"

S. J. Coffey

Shirley looks down at her delicate gold wristwatch, the one Dan gave her for their anniversary last April. It's half past nine. If she leaves now she'll get home in time to take a quick shower and settle in for the ten o'clock news with those crackers and wine. She watches hopefully as Patty Magnussen waddles out from behind the podium, her demeanor completely changed from that of the fire-and-brimstone-spouting fuchsia munchkin, back to her more civic self.

"Alrighty then," she smiles sweetly and strangely, "refreshments are over in the vestibule. Oh! And Mrs. Branson has graced us this evening with one of her delicious, candied pecan Bundt cakes!" Clearly very excited about that last announcement, Patty hurries over to the refreshment table and begins cutting Mrs. Branson's hard work into small, equal slices.

Shirley watches as at least five women, most about her own age (save one in tight bellbottoms who must have had her junior high schooler when she was in middle school herself), hurry over to Mrs. Magnussen.

Shirley gathers her things and makes her way down the row to the center aisle, where she slips into the mass of women chatting and laughing as they move slowly toward the door. Ahead of her by at least two people is the black woman. Like Shirley, it appears no amount of delicious, candied pecan cake can keep her here one second longer, and she is moving intently in the direction of the exit as well. For a moment, Shirley has an opportunity to take in this woman.

The word lovely comes to her mind as she watches the woman gracefully slip through the pack of white women. As the throng clears the rows of chairs and turns right (in the direction of refreshments and more Christian fellow-shipping with the self-appointed Reverend Magnussen), the woman glides free and clacks to the front door on black leather platform boots. Buttoning her camel coat and adjusting her handbag, Shirley follows her to the door. The woman pushes the door, then turns and, seeing Shirley, she smiles warmly and holds the door open for her.

Chapter 23

HIGH TEA AND MAKEUP TIPS WITH NINA REYNOLDS, REALTOR

Nina looks younger in this photo, much younger. In a green sequined gown that shows at least two solid inches of tanned cleavage, and flanked by two very handsome men dressed in tuxedos, she is smiling up from a burgundy leather horseshoe booth into the camera. I decide the picture must be important because it is matted in white and framed in brass. A long, red dagger-fingernail taps one of the men behind the glass.

"And that's Frank Sinatra's manager," Nina explains from behind my shoulder. Her perfume is heavy and dark, but it hasn't given me a headache the way other ladies' perfumes usually do. We are walking down her hallway looking at pictures. There are dozens of them, some hung two and three high.

"He's a sweet guy," she continues. "Kind of pushy sometimes, though. Loud too."

"My mom hates Frank Sinatra," I tell her. "She says he cheated on his wife with Ava..." I can't remember the actress's name, but Nina does.

"Ava Gardner," she says. "Really beautiful woman, very sophisticated, and kind, too. She got a bad rap, that one."

I follow her down the hall and back into her living room. It is magical, even more magical than Mavis's house. The drapes are open wide, and the afternoon sun bounces off every intoxicating surface in the room. Nina has stuff from all over the world. Most of her furniture is big and puffy and red, but in the corners and in between the larger pieces there are old, handmade-looking things. I run my fingers over a weird-looking little chair with three legs and handles on the sides.

"What's this for?" I ask.

"That," Nina says, "is a Spanish birthing chair."

"For having babies?" I clarify.

"Yep. Got it in Barcelona. You sit on it backwards, hold on to the handles and hope for the best."

This is fascinating. I need more information. "What happens to the baby?"

Nina shrugs and laughs. "Guess somebody has to catch it."

Despite my new concerns for the infants of Spain, I laugh too and move my attention to a Japanese doll in a glass case. It is the most detailed, delicate doll I have ever seen. The woman in the case is tall and thin, with smooth black hair rolled up with pins and dangling bits of gold. She's dressed in a flowered kimono and even has those funny white socks on, so she can wear her wooden flip-flop platform sandals and still have toasty toes.

Nina steps up next to me and tugs on a little metal pull on the front of the case. The glass door opens, and she reaches in and carefully takes out the doll. She holds it out to me. "Do you want to hold her?" she asks. I nod and take the doll from her, being mindful to hold it by the lacquered black base, the way she did.

"She's so beautiful," I say, stating the obvious. "Is she made of silk?"

Nina nods. "Every bit of her. She's a geisha, from Japan."

"What's a geisha?" I ask.

Nina, who's enveloped in a floaty, orange satin caftan this afternoon, smiles a little sadly (if I'm not imagining it).

"Geishas were consorts. Companions for men—mostly powerful, wealthy men."

"Consorts as in prostitutes?" I ask, wishing I hadn't when Nina blinks and looks pained.

"Not entirely. There was sex involved, and payment, but geishas were highly trained and cultured. They weren't just hookers, they were entertainers for men who wanted to spend time with intelligent, beautiful women. They were actually very respected in Tokyo."

"Really?" I had no idea there were respectable hookers in the world. "Did you ever meet one?" I ask.

"I saw them while I was there. There aren't many left now, I don't think. But the ones I did see were just gorgeous. And they always traveled in style, you know? All decked out in their finest, a servant boy running alongside of them holding a parasol to protect their skin from the sun."

"Wow," I say, handing the doll back to Nina who puts her back into her case and closes the door. "That doesn't sound like too bad a life."

Nina smiles down at me. "I don't imagine it is too bad," she says, turning quickly and heading back down the hall in a cloud of orange satin. "Come on, I have something you might like."

———⋄———

Nina's bedroom looks like it belongs to another house. It's nothing like her living room. Her curtains are open, and the room is warm and sunny, but it seems that for a boudoir she prefers cool pastels. Her bed is a king-sized square of powder blue topped with a veritable colony of stuffed animals. As grown-up as her living room is, her bedroom looks much more like mine, although I have a penchant for lime-green checks and ruffles aren't really my thing. There's only one picture on the wall—a large painting of an ocean with a small, imperiled schooner fighting for survival on very rough seas.

I'm sitting on the edge of Nina's giant bed looking at a framed picture on her bedside table. Except for a box of tissues, it is the only thing on the table. And inside the frame there's a black-and-white photo of a pretty woman my mom's age, with her arm around a girl about as old as me. I pick up the picture and examine it further as Nina digs in the top drawer of her dressing table, which is older and also powder blue.

"Now, where is that damned thing?" she says, her head nearly inside the drawer.

"Is this you?" I ask. Nina pauses her search and looks over.

"That's me with my mother," she says. "Must have been about your age."

"She's pretty," I say, putting the picture back on the nightstand as Nina goes back to rummaging.

"She was. At least until she got sick." Nina looks sad. I've said the wrong thing again.

"I'm sorry," I say, but she laughs and waves me off, preferring the shelter of her makeup drawer. "Don't be. It couldn't be helped. I miss her, though."

"What did she die of?" I ask dangerously.

"Breast cancer, it's funny a woman can die from two of the very things men seem to want from us."

"I'm sorry," I say.

Nina stops digging and looks over at me. "Listen kid," she says, "if we're going to be friends you've got to stop apologizing. You're thirteen years old. You haven't been alive long enough to have anything to apologize for. Besides, women do enough apologizing. 'Sorry for this', 'Sorry for that', I don't know what we feel like we have to apologize for, considering we're not the ones who do most of the damage in this world."

I nod. Nina is right, but I don't feel like, given my current occupation, I should elaborate on my feelings about men and boys and their faults. A block of sun from the window is warming the square of light blue carpet along with my feet. I am barefooted. Nina asked that I remove my sandals when I came in her front door. She likes to keep her floors clean, she says.

"Your bedroom is so warm and sunny. I like it," I pronounce.

"I love the sun," Nina explains, sifting through a handful of lipsticks. "I lived in Seattle for a year once. Ugh, what a god-awful, gloomy place. Ever since, if the sun's out, I can't bring myself to close the drapes. Have to open them up and let in all that good vitamin D, right?"

She selects a tiny bottle of lip gloss and dumps the rest of the pile back into the drawer.

"Here it is!" she exclaims. She gets up and floats over, parking herself next to me on the bed.

"It's one of those fruit-flavored glosses," she says. "Not really my style but it would just be perfect on you, I think." She hands the gloss to me.

"I can keep it?"

"It's all yours, kid. Give it try! You can use my vanity. It was my mother's."

I walk over and sit down on the tiny stool in front of the vanity. Its light-blue velvet cushion is soft. Nina watches as I unscrew the lid on the gloss and slide some of the fruity goo on my bottom lip. I think it is watermelon and the color really is nice.

"How long have you lived here?" she asks.

"In Kingman? Just over two years. Which is some kind of record because up until now, we moved, like, every other year."

"Really? Why?" It is a funny thing to have an adult actually interested in what you have to say. It is gratifying and unsettling at the same time.

"My dad's job," I tell her. "He's always on the lookout for a better position. And I think he thinks that if he keeps moving, he'll hate the job less. But the job never really changes, just the location."

"Well," Nina replies, "I can tell you from experience that that never works."

"Do you like your job?" I ask. At this, Nina brightens.

"Oh, I just love selling properties. For me, it's all about the deal, you know? The excitement, going in for the kill." Her eyes are sparkly.

"Wow," I say. "I never knew real estate could be so violent."

Behind me, in Nina's reflection in the mirror, something dark zips behind her eyes, but when I turn around and pucker my slick, fruit-flavored lips, it is gone.

"Beautiful!" she giggles.

"Really?" I ask.

"Now, do I look like the kind of woman who would lie about makeup?" she says, letting out a snort and busting into husky peals of laughter.

Nina says that if you're going to have an English High Tea, you need to have the proper accoutrements—one of which is a three-tiered tower for cakes and sandwiches. Nina's is pale-peach china and on the bottom level there are two kinds of little crustless sandwich triangles. On the top, there's an array of tiny, frosted cakes and the five or so varieties of cookies she's offering have been appropriately relegated to the mezzanine.

"One lump or two?" Nina asks, pouring tea into a delicate china cup the same color as the tower of goodies.

"Is three an option?"

"Certainly," she says. "I'm a sugar nut, myself." She tongs cubes and plops them gently into my cup, places a tiny spoon on the saucer and hands it to me.

"Thank you," I say, and stir the sugar into my tea. "My mom thinks my sugar problem is why mosquitos like me so much."

"No," says Nina, "mosquitos go after you for your blood type. Do you know what yours is?"

I shake my head and take a tiny sandwich from the tower.

"Ask your mom," she suggests. "Bet it's B positive. Mosquitos love B positive." She stirs her tea and sips. I watch and try to copy her.

"I think I scare your mom a little," she says, smiling over the rim of her cup.

"Kosher delis scare my mom. She's afraid of everything different, including me."

"I'm not afraid of you," says Nina. "I think you're fabulous."

I shrug and raid the top of the tower. There are three kinds of cakes. I take a chocolate one. "Thanks for the sentiment," I say, "but according to a large segment of my peers, you should be. I'm pretty much the weirdest girl in school."

Nina watches me intently as I take another sip of the tea. It is delicious.

"This tea is amazing," I tell her.

"It's Darjeeling. I brought it back from Bombay last month. Can't find this blend anywhere else in the world."

"I thought tea was just for sore throats," I admit.

Nina laughs and refills my cup, then hers. "Tea is for everything," she says. "Except when it isn't. Then you need vodka." She gives me a wink and hands me the sugar tongs. "We're friends, right?" she asks.

"I think so, yeah."

"Then will you take a little advice from a friend?"

I nod, and Nina locks her eyes on mine. I am not uncomfortable, but I am very aware that she means to tell me something important, so I set my cup back onto its saucer.

"Don't allow other people to define you—ever," she says, her eyes never leaving mine. "They'll take everything from you, but only if you let them." She looks as though she might cry any second. I can't decide if I want to hug her or run out the door, but then Nina pulls her eyes from me and goes back to breezily stirring her tea. I take a bite of sandwich and think for a moment as I watch her slide her spoon onto her saucer, lift her cup and sip.

"Hey, Nina, can I ask you something?"

"Of course, kid, anything."

S. J. Coffey

"Who are all those men who keep showing up over here? I mean, so late at night." I regret asking but I couldn't help it. Nina seems flustered and I feel stupid.

"Oh," she says, waving her hand in the air at a nonexistent fly, "those guys are just clients. You know, lots of properties I handle are commercial and with the exception of myself, it's mostly a man's world, and they do business at all kinds of crazy hours."

"Ohhhhh," I say, sighing with relief.

"Why do you ask?" she says.

"No reason. Just curious, I guess." I decide not to tell her my mother thinks she's a call girl. Seems impolite to accuse someone nice enough to invite you to tea of trafficking in sexual favors.

"Have you ever been married?" I ask her. She is a far away for a second, then smiles.

"Once, a long time ago."

"What happened?"

"Oh, we were very young," she answers.

"Got divorced, huh?" I offer.

"Something like that, yes."

"My Aunt Marnie's divorced. Thought my grandma was going to have a stroke over that one."

Nina smiles, remembering, "He was sweet. I couldn't be what he wanted, though."

"What did you do after that?" I ask.

Nina nibbles absently on a sandwich. "Anything I had to."

"Aunt Marnie's in college now, but she gets alimony money, I guess."

"He couldn't do that for me, I'm afraid. I had to look out for myself." She smiles and brushes a strand of hair out of my face. "He was a good man, though. You've got to look out for the good ones, Melanie. There aren't many out there, I'm afraid, but there are a few." Then suddenly, the veil—the one I saw when I met her, one I've rarely seen this afternoon—slips up over her and she is jovial again. "Any young men on your horizon, kid?" she asks, plucking a cookie from the mezzanine.

"Maybe. I'm not sure. Can I ask you another question?"

"Of course," she answers, but I hesitate for a second, not knowing if I can trust her with my secret. I decide a vague approach is the best way to go, and cage my inquiry in supposition.

"If you do something you like, but a boy, or a man, doesn't like it, should you stop doing it?" I ask, my voice's rising octave its own curlicued form of punctuation.

Nina thinks for a moment. "Is this thing a good thing?"

"Kind of depends on who you ask," I say, frowning.

Nina snaps her fingers, startling me. "Ah!" she nearly shouts, stabbing a pointy nail into the air. "A relativity situation. I am *very* familiar with those."

"Relativity?" I ask, confused.

Nina pours us both more tea and settles herself back into her voluminous crimson sofa. "Tell you what," she says, slipping back out of her realtor persona, "why don't you have yourself another couple of treats, there, and tell me all about this *thing* of yours that boys don't like, okay?"

"Okay," I agree, "but you can't tell my parents, or anybody, promise?" I give her my most serious, "I mean business" stare. In response, she somberly zips her own lips. So, feeling that I'm in the company of a discreet (and certainly better-dressed) kindred spirit, I take a breath and a tiny cake and tell Nina Reynolds all about my new career.

Chapter 24

JUST ASK STEVEN AND FARRAH

S hirley Chaffee stands outside her son Steven's bedroom with her hand on the door. She can feel the wood vibrate with every beat from the rock music that's emanating from inside the room. The music's rhythmic thumping is almost exactly in time with the rhythmic pounding behind her left eye. It is five thirty, early evening, and Shirley's got a migraine. She's had it all day. Melanie has thankfully been across the street all afternoon having tea with the new neighbor lady, a woman Shirley is sometimes fearful of, and sometimes envious toward. Nina Reynolds, alone in her three-bedroom ranch, is not a sort of woman Shirley is familiar with. But for some reason she would like to know her better. She wonders why Nina invited Melanie, a thirteen-year-old girl, over for tea. She wonders why Nina did not invite her.

The music behind Steven's door stops. Shirley takes a breath and places a hand on the doorknob, just as something from inside the room thuds against a wall and the music, louder than before, starts back up. She knocks on the door, no answer. She knocks again—this time harder, the sound reverberating through her skull like broken glass inside an empty jar. Her head hurts and although she loves her son, she does not want to talk to him right now. She does not want to talk to anyone right now. She knocks again. "Steven?" From inside the room, faint against the thumping music, she hears her son.

"Yeah?" he calls out from behind the door.

"May I come in?" Shirley yells, angering her pulsing temple again.

"At your own risk," Steven says, his voice muffled, then punctuated by another thud against the wall.

Shirley opens the door. On his very unmade bed, Steven lounges on his back. He's staring up at the ceiling, where a Farrah Fawcett poster has been tacked up for more intimate viewing. He chucks a rubber Superball at the opposite wall, where it hits and returns to him, ka-thump, ka-thump.

"Steven, stop it please," Shirley says.

"Oh, sorry Mom," Steven apologizes, pocketing the rubber ball. He reaches over to his stereo and turns his music off.

Rubbing her temple, Shirley nods and gingerly sits down on the edge of her son's bed. Steven rubs his mom's arm. "You got a migraine again?" he asks.

"Yes," she answers, "I've had it all day." She pats her son's hand and gives the room a once over. The walls are covered with posters of women, most in very sparse swimsuits, some with very visible nipples.

"They're practically naked," Shirley says, frowning. "If I'd worn swimsuits like that when I was young, my father would have killed me."

"You're still young. And Grandpa's a good guy. He wouldn't have killed you," Steven points out.

"Yeah, well, you didn't know him then," Shirley says.

"So, what's up? What brings you to my humble abode?" Steven jokes.

Shirley rubs her temples again. "Honey, do you know anything about a bunch of drawings of naked women going around at school?"

"No, why?"

"Must just be the junior high school, then," Shirley muses.

Steven thinks for a moment then pushes himself up on his bed, half of his back resting on an AC/DC band poster, and the other half resting on Suzanne Somers' right breast.

"I did hear something about Nathan Willis getting grounded for, like, two months over some drawing he got from his little brother."

"Oh dear." Shirley kneads her temple again.

"How come?" Steven asks. "I didn't do anything, I swear."

Shirley laughs and pats her son's knee. "I know, hon. I was just asking. There was some talk at the last PTA meeting."

"There's always talk at those stupid meetings, Mom. Why do you even go? You're too smart for that shit," Steven says.

"Language, dear," Shirley warns.

"Sorry. You're too smart for that 'stuff.' Seriously, how come you go?"

Shirley looks up at Farrah on the ceiling. "Oh, I don't know. Seems like something I'm supposed to do."

"Well, that seems like reason enough *not* to go."

Shirley drops her gaze down onto her son. "Oh, you think so, wise guy?" she says, teasing.

"Why don't you ask Mel what she's heard. Maybe she knows something," Steven suggests.

"I will. It's just hard to talk to her now. It used to be so easy when she was little. She was so sweet and good-natured. She's different, now. Secretive and…"

"Odd?" Steven answers for her.

"Well, yes," Shirley answers. "I feel like she never tells me anything anymore."

"Mom," Steven counsels, "she's thirteen. You're lucky she tells you who her friends are and where she's going all the time. Melanie loves you. She's weird but she'd never do anything to hurt you. She's a good kid."

"That's not what you said last week when she told your friend Ben about your underwear." Shirley laughs, and Steven is suddenly embarrassed.

"Look," he says, "I had an upset stomach, okay? Accidents happen."

"I know, I'm just teasing," Shirley admits. "Your sister shouldn't have said anything to your friend, but I think that's kind of what little sisters do."

"I still haven't come up with a proper form of revenge for that one yet," Steven grumbles.

Shirley stands. She's nauseous now. "I think I'm going to go lie down before dinner," she says. "There's a roast in the crockpot and your sister should be home soon." She opens the door. Behind her, Steven launches his rubber ball at the wall again. It hits, bounces and—like lightning—Shirley puts her arm out and snatches the ball right out of the air.

"Whoa!" Steven exclaims. "Nice catch, Mom! I didn't know you could do that."

"There are a lot of things you guys don't know about me," she answers, tossing the ball back to her son, who catches it handily. She offers him a soft smile. "No more throwing things in the house," she orders. "And wake me up in half an hour if I fall asleep, okay?"

"Okay." Steven places the ball on his nightstand and watches as his mom closes the door behind her, revealing a poster of Cheryl Tiegs in a string bikini.

On the other side of Cheryl Tiegs, Shirley makes her way down the hall and into her and Dan's darkened bedroom. She stretches out on the smooth bedspread, a sensible yellow number she got on sale at Sears last year. Her down pillow, the only real home luxury accessory she's ever splurged on, is cool beneath her neck and the pain behind her eye edges down to a gentler ache and her stomach settles. Behind her closed eyelids, Shirley is remembering the day—during the summer before her senior year of high school—that she went to the lake with her friends Donna McBride and Bunny Lawson. Bunny (a nickname) was very beautiful and very fashionable. Shirley had never seen her without false eyelashes and perfect lipstick on. Donna wore her usual modest one-piece suit, but (feeling daring on that July after-noon) Shirley had borrowed one of Bunny's many bikini swimsuits. The three girls had had a picnic lunch and then sunned themselves for hours at the pebbly edge of the lake.

Alone now, in the quiet of her marriage bedroom, Shir-ley can still feel the warm heat of the sun on her exposed belly. It was a sensation she had never felt before. Her mother and father were moderate Methodists, but they still had insisted that she wear a proper one-piece when she went swimming. But that day, with most of her skin exposed to the sun, she had felt so free and so light.

Shirley was a diligent student and her father's favorite among his four daughters, and she rarely disobeyed him or came home with anything less than straight As on her report cards. She lived in fear of his and her mother's disapproval and worked hard to make them proud of her. That afternoon at the lake with Donna and Bunny had been the first, and the last, time she had crossed her parents. When she had returned home that evening, sunburned and twenty minutes late for dinner, her mother had chastised her for her tardiness but that had not been the end of it. At dinner that night, she made the mistake of wearing a too-small blouse, and when she stood and bent to help her mother and sisters clear the table, her father had spotted her lobster-red lower back and frowned.

Her dad had never said anything to her about the matter, but her mother had. At the sink, drying plates next to her, she had been told in no uncertain terms that immodest girls—in addition to buying a one-way ticket to Hades—always ended up shunned failures without decent husbands. Her mother's words were cutting and painful, but it was the silence from her father that hurt the most. He had softened eventually, and Shirley was sure he had forgiven her for her transgression. But for months after that glorious summer day, he had avoided his favorite, middle daughter. After that, Shirley's memory of the warm sun on her skin and the camaraderie of her two best friends had become hidden under the blanket of guilt and shame her parents used to tuck her into bed every night, and she had honestly not allowed herself to think of that day again until now. And dozing finally, the pain in Shirley's head gives way to the memory of her two friends' laughter, the rocks under her beach towel and the warm, warm sun on her exposed back.

Chapter 25

GIRLS' SOFTBALL AND OTHER FORMS OF VIOLENCE

I'm crouched in front of my locker looking for my science book. I know it's in here somewhere underneath all the wadded sheets of notebook paper, outdated copies of both *Tiger Beat* and *Teen Beat*, two pairs of dirty gym shorts and a half-eaten box of Jujubes. It was still fairly warm out this morning, so against my mother's protests I wore my favorite lime-green sundress and sandals today. To placate my mom's need to parent, I also brought a sweater. Although when I got to school I threw it into my locker on top of the cuvee of garbage I'm now digging through.

I spot the corner of my science book, pull it from the chaos and—being careful to prop up the pile, in hopes of preventing a locker garbage avalanche—I quickly slam the door closed. I'm relieved I've found my errant book and am thinking the day is going okay so far, when I realize that I've thought too soon. Because when I stand up, there she is. Stephanie.

"We need to talk," she says. I don't want to talk. I want to run away, but I don't.

"Talk about what?" I ask, trying to look defiant and confident.

"You know about what," Stephanie says. Her hands are on her high-waisted jeans, her right hip popped, and her hair blond-bitch perfect. She stares at me and tosses her head a little in an attempt to flip her unmovable, lacquered 'do. With growing alarm, I notice that Nadine and her immobile hair are behind my inquisitor, as well. I know exactly what they're here to talk about, but I feign ignorance and stall.

"I'm sorry but you're going to have to help me out here," I say casually.

Stephanie shifts, popping her left hip out like a weapon. "If you think for one second that you're going to the dance with Ethan, you can just forget it," she says, punctuating her statement with a frosty pink fingernail in my sternum.

"Hey," I say, "he's the one who asked me." In an effort to relieve what feels like fifteen pounds per square inch drilling into my chest, I take a step back. But Stephanie's forefinger just hangs there in the air in front of me, like a perfectly manicured pistol.

"I don't care who asked who," she sneers, repositioning her hand-gun, this time in my left shoulder. "I'm just telling you that if you show up at that dance on Friday, you'll have us to deal with."

Then, using her finger for emphasis, she leans in to properly button up our cozy encounter. "You'd—better—listen—and—do—what—I—tell—you."

My shoulder hurts. I'm sure it's going to bruise and I'm hoping my nemesis has not drawn blood. If so, it's a good thing I brought a sweater, I guess.

"What happens if I don't—do—what—you—tell—me—to?" I taunt, like a masochistic idiot.

Stephanie slowly withdraws her finger from my shoulder and smiles smugly, as she leans against the lockers and crosses one sky high platform over the other. And then, in a moment that I'm sure will be scorched into my brain until the day I die, Stephanie reaches into her jeans pocket and pulls out a small, folded piece of good quality drawing paper. Before she even starts to unfold it, I know what it is.

"This happens. That's what," she says, torturing me as she slowly unfolds the paper, revealing the chubby nude I'd drawn in choir practice. I had been so busy with my new live action "films" that I had all but forgotten about my still life drawings. An oversight that, I realize too late, could cost me everything.

Without my consent, my whole body starts to shake, and tears threaten.

"Please don't," I beg. "I won't go. I promise."

Stephanie refolds the paper and slides it back into her pocket.

"We have an understanding, then?" she extorts. I nod, unable to form words, and in response Stephanie pats my head the way one would pet a small dog. "That's a good little weirdo," she faux-pouts. Then she turns and elbows her silent, terrifying henchwoman.

"Come on, Nadine," she commands. After staring me down for ten very long seconds, Nadine obeys, and turns and follows her tyrannical, hair-sprayed leader down the hall.

I squat down and re-open my locker, my hands so unsteady I can barely work the lock. I don't need anything from my locker, but I open it anyway and act as though I'm looking for something while I cry and blot my eyes with a pair of my rancid gym shorts.

Wearing the same funky shorts I used to dry my eyes only hours ago, I lean against the chain-link barrier behind home plate, waiting for my turn to bat—which seems fitting since today is all about humiliation. Mavis is in my P.E. class and, thankfully, leans against the fence next to me, filing her long purple fingernails. I push my forehead into the thick wire of the fence and squeeze my eyes closed, hoping that when I open them today will be over. But when I do, it isn't, and the line has moved me one person closer to athletic degradation.

"Ugh, Nadine Melnick. She's like a huge, blond sasquatch," I groan. "And Stephanie…" I've run out of adjectives for the young woman who now holds my very future in the front pocket of her Jordache jeans.

I look over at Mavis. While the other girls' uniforms are regulation, Mavis has seen fit to alter her outfit to suit her style. Her grey T-shirt, emblazoned with the words "Kingman Jr. High School Phys Ed," is knotted above her belly button and its sleeves are rolled up over her shoulders. And despite the physically demanding nature of today's activity, she is wearing every piece of her signature jewelry. "I can't stand that cracker bitch," she states.

"I'm a cracker," I mumble pitifully.

"Yeah, but you're a different kind of cracker," she says. Looking out at the baseball diamond, she switches subjects. "I hate this honky shit."

"I've seen black baseball players on TV," I counter, grateful for the distraction.

"Naw!" Mavis corrects. "Baseball is the *man's* game. Now, basketball, that's where it's *at*."

I'm about to ask her who "the man" is and how he could take claim over an entire sport, when I look up into the bleachers behind us. Up on the highest bench, Stephanie lounges next to a sullen Nadine. I let out another groan.

"I can't go to the dance," I confess.

"What?" Mavis is incredulous. "You've got to go! I spent an entire afternoon teaching your dorky white butt how to dance proper-like."

"But I can't go," I whine, "I just can't."

Mavis stabs her nail file into her afro and gives me the little W between her eyes. "Why can't you go? What happened?"

"She found one," I tell her. She follows my gaze up into the bleachers, where Stephanie is flipping me the bird and smiling.

"Who? Stephanie Harris?" she asks. "What'd she find?"

I can barely get the heavy, doom-filled words out of my head, let alone my mouth. "She found one of my drawings. I think it fell out of my pocket during choir practice."

"Whoa," Mavis says, the W disappearing and giving way to three long lines across her smooth forehead. "Damn"— she whistles—"that is cold-blooded."

"If Ethan finds out he won't like me anymore," I complain.

"Who cares what he don't like. It's your mamma I'd be worried about."

"Oh God! I know!" I say, tears threatening again.

Mavis looks back up into the bleachers, where Stephanie is still staring down at us. "I'll take care of Stephanie Harris and her blackmail horse crap," she tells me.

"You will? How?"

"Real easy," she explains. "We're just going to have a little conversation, that's all."

I feel a little lighter and swipe at my uncooperative eyes. "So I can go to the dance?"

Mavis, who is still in a staring contest with Stephanie, just nods.

"But what if she shows up there?" I ask, already feeling anxious again.

Mavis pulls her eyes from the bleachers and looks down at me. "She won't. And if she does, don't worry. I'll be there, too."

I pull in the first real breath I've taken since Stephanie sucked all the air out of me two class periods ago. "Thank you, Mavis," I say gratefully.

"No problem," she says. "Gonna owe me a Coke, though. A real Coke." She nudges me as the line moves forward again and I am, unfortunately, next.

Up at home plate, I grip the shaft of the bat like Ms. Fitzmaker (our sturdy, no nonsense P.E. teacher) has shown me more than two dozen times. Dana Youngblood is pitching, a fact that would be appreciated by someone who actually cared about this stupid game. Dana is stout and strong, with legs like telephone poles and a fresh, suntanned face. She is always kind to me in the halls, and even lent me a pencil in health class once. But on the mound, Dana becomes a softball-throwing demon. The batter's physical wellbeing is inconsequential to her when she is on the job, and while this may be a desirable trait in a first-class pitcher, it is downright dangerous for someone like me.

Dana squints in the sun, then spins her arm and sends the ball flying at me like a torpedo. I flinch and hide behind the bat as the catcher yells, "Strike one!" At the fence, next to Mavis, Ms. Fitzmaker looks up from her clipboard. "Remember what we talked about, Melanie. Keep your eyes on the ball and remember your stance."

The eyes on the ball thing I might be able to manage, but how am I supposed to think about how I'm standing when I'm busy trying to make the stick in my hands connect with the harmful object hurtling at me?

I raise the bat and wait for Dana to launch her projectile at me again. "Strike two!" the catcher calls out.

Thank God, I think. *One more strike and I'm back behind the fence where I belong.*

But Fitzmaker isn't giving up. "Melanie, I know you can do this. Just try, okay?"

I nod earnestly. I really want to please her. Despite my repeated attempts to worm my way out of her class, she is always patient and hopeful that I will one day see the light of organized sports and join the ranks of the coordinated and physically fit. I know her faith is unfounded, but still I decide I'll give it the ol' college try. I scowl and twist my fists on the neck of the bat the way I have seen the other girls do, and I even stick out my elbows and swipe at the dusty ground with my Keds. I tell myself I am a focused, softball hitting machine, and that for once I am not going to make an idiot of myself. I have suffered enough today and desperately need a win.

Perhaps it was my little self-delivered pep talk, or maybe I just don't care anymore, but when Dana winds up and the ball comes flying at me, I am fearless. I watch that ball like it is a three-pack of Hostess Cupcakes. I don't take my eyes off it for a millisecond. Unfortunately, this strategy will prove problematic.

By the time I finally decide it is time to swing, I am so focused on the ball that I could tell Ms. Fitzmaker who had manufactured the thing, and exactly how many stitches are on it. And when my arms fling the bat at the ball (which is now directly in front of my face), they sort of wrap around my left shoulder. This puts the head of the bat, which is traveling at a serious speed (due to my Stephanie-induced frustration and fear both being released at once) in the perfect position to tag me on the back of the head, which it does. And at the same time—in a physics moment that probably ranks right up there with the mystery of how bumble bees can fly even though their wings are too small—the softball (which is in no way soft), makes fifty mile an hour contact with my right eye. I drop the bat, clap one hand over my eye and the other on the back of my head, then begin jumping around home plate.

In seconds, Ms. Fitzmaker is at my side with an ice pack, and as she tries to discern which part of my battered skull is most in need of refrigeration, Mavis runs up. "You're something else, little buddy," she says. "I've never seen anybody get hit with a bat *and* a ball! And at the same time!" She doubles over and begins laughing hysterically. Up in the bleachers, Stephanie leads the rest of the class in a slow clap that is, without a doubt, the icing on the poop cake that has been my day. Mavis stops laughing and jabs a middle finger at Stephanie.

"That's enough, Mavis," Ms. Fitzmaker scolds, "now, would you please take Melanie to the nurse's office?"

This is an arrangement that we both find satisfactory since it means that neither one of us will have to finish out the rest of class. "Mavis," I ask, as I alternate the ice pack between my eye and the occipital part of my head while we walk across the field, "how come you're friends with me?"

S. J. Coffey

She chuckles and drapes an arm around my shoulders. "'Cause you do stupid shit like that and make laugh. And there ain't many white people around here that make me want to laugh."

There have been few people, of any color, who have made me want to laugh today either. I don't tell her that, though, because somehow I know we are not talking about the same thing.

Chapter 26

HOW TO HIDE A SHINER AND AVOID PLATFORM-SHOE-RELATED ACCIDENTS

I t's bad, really bad. The entire lower half of my right eye socket, as well as a portion of my cheek, is purple. Not fun, Mavis-disco-glitter purple. Just gross, mottled-bruise purple. In a mirror in the juniors' department of Babbitts, I examine the mess further.

"Do you think Ethan will mind if I bleed on him when we dance?" I ask Anna, who is behind me flipping through a rack of polyester suit pants. She walks over and studies my reflection.

"It's a bruise. Bruises don't bleed," she states flatly.

"Well, that's good, I guess." I turn and follow her through the maze of rounders and racks.

"If you want to come over to my place before the dance, I can help you camouflage that thing," she offers. "My mom practically owns stock in Estee Lauder."

"Thanks," I answer, "that would be very helpful."

"Are you sure you still want to go to the dance? I imagine Stephanie and Nadine would love to make your left eye match the right one," Anna says.

"I think it'll be okay. Mavis said she'd take care of it." I'm hoping that assuring Anna I'll survive the dance unscathed will make it so.

Anna stops in front of a rounder of earth-toned cardigans. "If I were you, I'd be glad that girl is on *your* side."

"How come you don't like Mavis?" I ask, knowing full well why.

"She's got a decidedly criminal air about her," Anna says.

"Criminal?" I ask, my voice rising with my anger. "Seriously?"

Anna fusses with the collar of a particularly bland beige sweater. "Where are the sizes on these things?" she wonders aloud, ignoring my question.

"You really think Mavis is a criminal?" I say, crossing my arms over my Abba T-shirt. Anna gives up her size search and actually looks at me.

"Do you know how many fights she's been in, Mel? I mean, she's suspended half the year, for Chrissakes."

"That's not her fault," I defend.

Anna returns to her quest for the perfect inoffensive sweater. "I'm just worried some of her criminality might rub off on you, that's all."

I follow her into the shoe department. "Her criminality or her blackness?" I press. Anna picks up a tennis shoe and thinks.

"Listen, Mel, it's not a race thing. It's a socioeconomic thing."

"Socio-what?" I say. "And you know it's a race thing, Anna. I've heard your parents. They talk like it's the eighteen-fifties or something."

"Mavis lives in Butler. It's all just trailers and shacks over there," she says.

I've known Anna for over two years. She is a challenging

friend, but I give her a pass because she's the most interesting adolescent girl I know. She knows so much, but I can't figure out how somebody so smart can be so dumb.

"So what you're saying is, you don't like Mavis because she's black *and* you think she's poor, is that it?"

"It's not like that," she says, looking guilty near the penny loafers. I walk over and look her in the eyes.

"It *is* like that, and you know it," I tell her. "And I've been to Mavis's house. It's amazing."

"She lives in *Butler*, Mel." Anna doubles down.

I am disappointed by my friend. I wish I could say she is a political outlier in our community, but I know she's a member of the narrow-minded, hate-filled majority. "You're just like everyone else in this backward town," I say, walking away from her.

I'm looking through a display of leather shoulder bags when Anna walks up behind me and rests her head on my shoulder. "I'm sorry, Mel." She sounds genuinely contrite and I try to remember that—just like most people—she is a product of her environment. "It's not like Mavis isn't... intriguing," she continues. "I'm just afraid for your safety, that's all."

I sigh and loop an arm through hers as we make our way to the sandal section. "My safety?" I answer. "Jeez, Anna, Mavis isn't a ten-gallon drum of plutonium, she's a girl, just like us."

"That is true," Anna concedes.

"Can you please just try and look at things from her point of view for once?" I plead. Anna stops walking and frowns. Behind her eyes, I can almost see her internal computer, reels spinning, lights blinking, as she processes the input I just gave her.

S. J. Coffey

"That's a logical argument," she announces. "It is important to study all the angles of a given situation."

Sensing a crack in her worldview, I push on. "I mean, how would you feel if you were one of three white people in a town full of black folks? You'd get into a lot of fights, too, I bet."

Anna frown-thinks again. "An unlikely scenario, given the racial demographics in this part of the country, but point taken," she admits.

"Thank you, Spock," I say, nudging her as we walk up to a display of platform sandals. "Besides, there's cool stuff we can learn from Mavis."

"Like what?" Anna asks.

I pick up a platform sandal, the very one my mother refused to buy for me. "Well for one," I tell her, "she can teach me how to walk in these."

<hr>

I feel like I'm standing on two blocks of two-by-four. My arms out like a circus tightrope walker, I take an unsteady baby step and teeter. If teenagers came with cartoon sound effects, mine would currently be, 'whoop, whoop, whoop.' Mavis takes my arm and steadies me. "If you're gonna wear those shoes, you gotta walk like you mean it."

"Like I mean it?" I ask, confused.

"Yeah. Here, sit down," she commands, and parks me on the bottom row of the bleachers. We're in the gymnasium. The second lunch period is over and, other than a few hairnetted lunch ladies, the cavernous room is empty.

Mavis saunters out to the middle of the floor and demonstrates. It's as if her platforms (five-inch, see-through acrylic ones with embedded rhinestones today, a Tuesday favorite) are an extension of her legs. Sole to Afro, she's got to be almost six feet, I'm sure of it.

"I can see that you mean it," I tell her as I watch, mentally taking notes.

"You've got to plant your heel down first," she explains, "then roll through to your toes, see?"

I nod, and she continues. "*You're* wearing the shoes, not the other way around." Mavis strolls back over and helps me up off the bleacher. "Hold on to me, now." I do as I'm instructed and let her lead me out onto the floor, heel, toe, heel, toe. I am improving and Mavis grins, "See? You got it!" she encourages. "You rule the shoes. They do *not* rule you." She lets go of my hand and I walk, unassisted, all the way back to the bleachers. I turn and sit down carefully and Mavis drops onto the bench next to me. "You're gonna do fine on Friday," she tells me.

"You'll be there, right?" I ask, my eyes pleading, and thankfully she nods.

"Mmm hmm. I will."

"What about Stephanie and Nadine? What do I do if you're not there?"

"I told you I'd take care of it, didn't I?" she insists, smiling. "Besides, even if I didn't, you'd be okay. You're tougher than you think, you know?" She may be right, but I sure don't feel very tough.

"You think I'm tough?" I ask.

"I do," she says, then stands and pulls me up again. "Now come on. Let's practice a little more so you don't go and break any of Ethan Wilde's pretty toes."

I laugh and wonder what Ethan's toes do look like. Then, as I practice, heel, toe, heel, toe, I decide he could have feet like a medieval peasant and I wouldn't care. The rest of him is pretty enough for me.

That afternoon, as the last bell rings, I'm walking down the hall to get my stuff and go home when I spot Stephanie and Nadine at my locker. Stephanie leans and blows a huge pink bubble with her gum and Nadine just stands silently next to her, like a dangerous blond tree. In my head, I run through a checklist of items in my locker that I might need to take home: science book, math workbook, home economics sewing project, Austen, three dirty pairs of gym shorts. Stephanie sees me approaching and an evil smile spreads across her face. In the interest of personal safety, I'm about to decide I can get away without turning in my math workbook tomorrow. I've got a solid C in there, so exchanging my nonexistent math career for my life seems like a fair trade. But then Stephanie notices something behind me and elbows Nadine, who follows her gaze. She looks back at her master, who pushes herself from my locker and turns and walks, so Nadine follows her off down the hall, and away from me.

The threat now mysteriously gone, I kneel in front of my locker and work the combination. As I pull out my math workbook (might as well keep up my grade in that class while I can, never know when Stephanie might feel the need to terrorize me again and jeopardize my average standing) I see Mavis out of the corner of my eye. She is strutting by me on my right, and as she passes she looks at me and winks, then speeds up and after Stephanie and Nadine.

I'm only thirteen. I haven't seen very much in my life and I know even less. But I have noticed that sometimes—maybe because of fear and adrenaline, or maybe just because even at my age I am occasionally aware of the importance of an event or a time—reality seems to slow down, like the exciting sequences in *The Bionic Woman*. It is in this slow motion that I watch as Mavis gains on Stephanie and Nadine. In high-waisted bell-bottom jeans that are so long they drag on the floor (even with her platforms), she is strutting up to the two girls with wide, confident steps. Her midriff is bare beneath her knit crop top, and huge, gold hoops swing from her ears like perches I've seen in parrot cages.

I close my locker and stand, but I can't leave. I can't take my eyes off the scene playing out not thirty feet from me, near Mrs. Blankenship's home economics classroom. Mavis has sidled up to Nadine and she's saying something in her ear. Even from this distance I can see Nadine's brown eyebrows rise. Then Mavis turns to Stephanie and says something else, something that makes Stephanie, who I believed to be inhuman, look very human and very afraid.

The year we met, Mavis was kicked out of our art class for calling Mr. Ankeny a racist dickhead because he wouldn't let her sculpt a ceramic bust of Isaac Hayes. Mr. Ankeny didn't understand why Mavis was so upset, but I did. Art is a reflection of oneself and one's experience. My dad taught me that. How would old, white Mr. Ankeny know anything about a teenaged black girl and her experience?

After class that day, I went up to her in the hall and told her that I kind of knew how she felt. I explained that I would have reacted the same way if Mr. Ankeny had refused to let me immortalize Andy Gibb in clay. She just laughed and asked me to sit with her at lunch and we have been friends ever since. And as I watch her now, her hoops swinging and her magnificent jeans dragging, I hope and pray that she will always be my friend. And that someday, when she needs a favor, I can help her the way she's helped me.

Chapter 27

WHEN TEA REALLY ISN'T FOR EVERYTHING

My afternoon walks home from the bus stop always seem like punishment for something. If my day was good, trudging up the hill to our house is a complete buzz-kill. If my day was horrid, then the quarter-mile, thirty-five-degree trek is even worse. We live at the very end of Desert Shadows drive. The winding street begins all the way down at the bottom of a hill, where our housing development reaches out to the rest of the "civilization" that is Kingman, by way of Southwest Third Street, where the school bus routinely collects and deposits me and the eternally conjoined make-out couple, Cliff Barret and Diane Rimerez.

It is cooler today, cooler than it has been in months, a reminder that eventually this part of northern Arizona will live up to its name and get cold. Some winters it even snows here. Snow on cactuses is weird and incongruent, but then again very little in this town makes much sense. I'm dragging myself up my street and am gratefully about to the crest the hill where my home and a snack and reruns of *Gilligan's Island* await, when I spot the big, black car in front of Nina's house. It looks like one I've seen before, but it's hard to be sure. Every car I've ever seen in front of her place has been big and black. It must be the desired vehicle for real estate professionals.

As I pass, I glance into Nina's front window. This is impolite, I know, but I can't help myself. Nina is the most interesting grown-up I've ever met, and since she already leaves her drapes open all the time (at least during the day), looking into her window is like tuning in to a fantastic television show staring my favorite, glamorous, international jewel thief. My mother would say I'm being nosey. But the goings-on inside Nina's house rival any in our neighborhood at any time of day, and as a member of this community I feel it is my duty to stay informed.

There is glare from the setting sun on Nina's living room window but I can see enough, or maybe too much. Inside, Nina is arguing with a man. He looks like a man I've seen coming out of her house before, the one with the dark, shiny hair. Nina appears to be doing most of the talking, but now and then he says something back to her. In front of her yard, I stop walking and go straight to gawking. Through the glass, I can hear Nina's voice. Her words aren't quite intelligible, but the tone is unmistakable; she's upset, and she's crying. She reaches up and grabs the man's suit jacket sleeve, but he pushes her hand away and disappears from the window. My feet are stuck to the asphalt under my sandals, and even though I know I'm being rude, and I should turn around right this second and leave, I can't. I'm worried, really worried. I wonder if I should go get my mom, but then the front door swings open and the man steps out and strides quickly down the walkway to the black car. Behind him, Nina appears in the doorway.

"Wait!" she calls out to him. It is just after four p.m. Nina is still in her robe, the same one I've seen her in before. It's lavender and ruffle-y and underneath it is a matching, and very revealing, nightgown. Through the lace, I can see the outline of a nipple and I'm embarrassed for her.

"Wait," she says again, this time quieter and choked off by a sob. She wipes her nose on the sleeve of her robe only a millisecond before she sees me standing in the street staring at her. She sniffs and smiles, trying unsuccessfully to pull on the Nina-Reynolds-Realtor suit.

"Hey, kid!" she says.

"Are you okay?" I ask her. Asking someone if they're okay when it is clear that they are not is always so stupid. But then again, so is stating the obvious and just making everything more uncomfortable. Nina sniffs again and slips her forefingers under her eyes to remove mascara-damaging tears. It is a noble effort on her part, but it is too late. She is a beautiful racoon in a negligée.

"Oh, sure," she says. "Just having a tough day. I'm alright, though. How was your day?"

"Not too bad," I tell her.

"Still going to the dance with that guy?"

"Yup," I say, "Ethan, and the dance is on Friday."

Nina's eyes are drier now and she studies me for a moment. "Did you tell him about your new business?" she asks. I shake my head.

"He wouldn't like it. I know it," I admit, feeling almost ashamed to tell her.

"Well," she begins, "if he doesn't like it, tell him to go screw himself, okay? You're a woman. We have to watch out for ourselves and for our bottom line. I mean, who else is going to, right?" She rubs at her eyes again and lets out a little laugh that sounds more like a cry.

"Want me to come in and make some tea for you?" I ask.

"Oh, no. That's sweet of you, kid, it really is. But I think today might just call for vodka, you know?" She is definitely beginning to cry again. I want to help her, but I haven't learned how to help women like her with things like this, yet. There are no classes at my school that teach you how to handle this kind of situation, and my mom never cries. She just fumes and goes to her bedroom.

"You have a good time on Friday, though, okay?" Nina says, sniffing.

"Okay," I tell her. "I'll give you all the details on Sunday. We could have High Tea again," I suggest. I want to give her something to look forward to. Sometimes when I'm upset about something it helps to think of things I want to do in the immediate future.

"That sounds perfect," she answers, "I can't wait." Nina is holding the door frame with both of her hands, as if she's bracing for an earthquake, and several fresh tears zip unchecked down her cheeks. With my presence on the street in front of her yard, I am torturing this woman. I know she wants to run into her house and cry, but I don't want her to go. I am afraid (needlessly, I tell myself) for her. Like my new friend holding onto her doorway for dear life, I know something is coming, something bad. I push down the undefinable fear.

"Will you be okay?" I ask honestly, earnestly.

"Oh, sure!" Nina promises, liberating one of her hands from the door jamb, so that it can swipe at the air in front of her in protest. "I'll be fine!" Even from here I can see that two of her long, perfect fingernails are broken, their edges jagged and sharp. As if reading my mind, she suddenly looks down at her fingers. "Looks like it's time for a new manicure." Her mouth laughs. Her eyes don't.

S. J. Coffey

"We could do that on Sunday," I say. "My Aunt Marnie gave me a manicure kit and, like, fifteen bottles of polish."

"You know, I think that sounds like a terrific plan, kid," she says, smiling. "Tea and manicures on Sunday it is, then!"

I nod and head across the street to my house.

"Hey, Melanie?" Nina calls out, so I stop and turn back around.

"Yeah?"

"Do something for me, would you?" she asks.

"Sure," I say, "anything."

Nina is leaning in her doorway now, one hand still on the frame. "Please just always remember to be yourself, okay?"

I nod, and she continues, "It's all anyone can really ever ask of you. They can take everything from you, but even when you don't have anything left, you'll still have that—yourself, who you know you are inside, you know?" I nod silently and just smile, lost for what else to say as time hangs heavy between us. Then abruptly Nina laughs and gives me a wan smile, then goes in and disappears into her home, closing the door behind her.

―――――――◇―――――――

In addition to the deluxe manicure set my Aunt Marnie gave me for Easter this year (she gave Steven a Swiss Army knife, my mom was horrified) she also gave me my own overnight bag. She said it was for trips down to Phoenix to visit her but since my mother says an unsupervised stay with my Aunt Marnie will happen "when hell freezes over," I'm going to make use of it to transport all my dance-related accoutrements to Anna's house this evening. I'm already wearing my new suit and it took me two difficult hours with my Easy Curl 2000 to transform my head from a blond afterthought into something resembling a hairstyle. I was going for a smooth, longer Toni Tennille but several locks of my hair are, like me, uninterested in conforming. So what I ended up with was more of an unruly Kate Jackson. I'm not averse to looking like the brainier of Charlie's Angels so I've decided to embrace the look.

With my suit I'm wearing my clogs, at least for now. My mother does not know about my platforms and they are tucked at the bottom of my overnight bag, where they will stay until I am safely out of mothering range. Leslie and I are meeting at Anna's house for dinner and pre-dance primping and concealing of my black eye, which I'm currently examining in the mirror over my dresser. It is better, less purple and more swamp green, and Anna assures me that with the proper spackling, it can be covered, so I'm hopeful.

There's a little tap at my door only seconds before it opens, and my mom steps in. "Ready to go to Anna's?" she asks, smiling.

"Yep!" I tell her, patting my bulging overnight bag as I plop onto my bed. My mom has something in her hand. She sits down next to me and gives me a tube of lipstick. It is heavier than one would think a tube of lipstick would be. The case is thick and squarish, with two interlocking Cs on its side. I pop the lid off and screw up the color. It is a frosty light pink. My mother smiles excitedly.

"It's Chanel. I only use it for special occasions," she says. The color is pretty, but it reminds me of Stephanie Harris; pale and pink and dangerous.

"It's really pretty, Mom," I tell her, "but I was going to

wear the lip gloss Nina gave me." I pull the bright, berry-colored bottle from my suit jacket pocket and show it to my mother, who frowns.

"Oh, honey, no. That color is way too bright for you. And glosses like that are so garish and cheap looking."

I am disappointed in my mom's quick dismissal of a lip color I was certain I was born to wear, but I don't want to hurt her feelings. "Nina gave it to me," I say quietly. Shirley sighs and makes the face people make when they learn something they've known all along.

"Oh, well," she says, "that explains it."

I want to tell her that it does not explain it. She doesn't know Nina like I do, and Nina's choice in lipsticks doesn't explain anything.

"I like this color," I say, looking at the gloss in my other hand. "It's pretty and sets off my suit."

"I know, Mel, but it's too old for you. You need something more understated."

"Understated?" I attempt to clarify.

"Oh, yes," my mom says, patting my knee for emphasis, "when in doubt, always go with understated. You don't want to be the girl at the party whose lipstick veritably screams, 'look at me', do you?"

I shrug. Maybe she has a point. "Are you sure?"

"Absolutely," she says, "the most beautiful woman in the room is always the one who's elegant and understated. Calling attention to yourself is never attractive." She takes the lipstick from me. "Here," she says, "let's try it." She turns my head toward her and gently applies the color to my lips. It is smooth and silky but tastes weird. "There, take a look," she says, grabbing a hand mirror off my dresser and holding it in front of my face.

In the mirror is a girl I know is me, but she doesn't quite look like me, especially not with these strange lips that are the color of the inside of an anemic seashell. But it doesn't look terrible and maybe my mom is right. Being understated does sound way cooler.

"See," my mom says, her face in the circle of glass next to mine, "gorgeous."

I nod, and she runs a soft thumb under my eye and frowns. "That Ms. Fitzmaker, I should really have a talk with her. Letting you get hit like that."

"It wasn't her fault, Mom," I say, laughing a little. "I kind of did it to myself."

"I suppose so," she concurs, smiling. I place Nina's little bottle of gloss on my dresser, and my mother—now secure in the knowledge that her daughter won't make a cosmetic spectacle of herself in public—hugs me.

"Alright," she says, "let's get you to Anna's so you guys can get to work on that bruise. You sure you have everything you need? You can borrow anything of mine you'd like."

"That's okay. Anna says her mom's got all kinds of cover-up and stuff."

"Hmm, well," my mother says, "Jean has had her share of skin problems, that's for sure. She would certainly know how to cover a blemish or two."

While my mother waits, and I gather up the rest of my things, I wonder if what she just said about Anna's mom was a compliment or an insult, and decide, as I follow her out the door, that it was probably a little of both.

Chapter 28

SLOW DANCING TO SOFT ROCK ON THE DECK OF THE TITANIC

Anna's mom drives a steel-grey seventy-seven Mercedes wagon. It's very fancy and she's very attached to it. I know this because every time she gives me a ride somewhere she says, "Melanie, dear, remember to respect the interior," so I am always careful to make sure my shoes are clean before I step inside the pristine, Prussian sanctuary of her car. Once, in the drive-through line of the Tastee-Freez with Anna and her little brother Toby, Anna's mother Jean had passed back my swirled cone and repeated, as usual, "respect the interior." I had, of course, done as she asked and kept all traces of my ice cream confined to the front of my rainbow T-shirt, but while we were making our way back home, and Toby-the-tyrant (as Anna likes to call her little brother) was quiet for a minute, the multi-layered-ness of Jean's comment came to me. For her, "respect the interior" clearly meant that she wished I would not get ice cream, or anything else sticky, on the upholstery of her fine new automobile. But, I reasoned that day as I crunched through my cone, it could also be a kind of personal mantra. An order to protect one's own internal life, one's soul, if say one participated in that particular spiritual maintenance plan.

Tonight, Toby-the-tyrant is back at Anna's house plopped in front of the TV catching up on his cartoon relatives with his dad, and Anna's mom is playing chauffer to us girls. Anna, rightfully, rides shotgun and Leslie and I are in the back seat. Per my dad's strident instructions, I'm wearing my seatbelt. Leslie is not.

"It will wrinkle my dress," she says, smoothing the fabric of her pink floral granny dress. This prompts Anna to weigh in from the front seat.

"Yeah, well, flying into the back of my seat at fifty miles an hour will wrinkle your face."

"Anna's right, Leslie," Jean agrees with her daughter, "buckle up. I don't want to have to explain to your father that you died a bloody death on the road because you didn't want to go to the dance in a wrinkled dress." Obviously Anna inherited her affection for blunt, unnerving commentary from her mother—a woman who, despite never having had a job in law enforcement, could tell you exactly how and where you could lose your life to violent crime. Her collection of books on criminal behavior and institutional punishment is bigger than Anna's. Leslie and I exchange raised eyebrows and, as ordered, Leslie pulls her seatbelt over her dress and buckles.

I look into Jean's rearview mirror. Thanks to Anna's skill with a cover stick and powder, my bruise is all but invisible. We're almost to the school and I can hardly breathe. I hope Ethan likes my suit. I hope Stephanie Harris doesn't show up. I hope I don't fall off my shoes. I look down at my feet. My new platforms are strapped tight over my suntan-colored sandalfoot pantyhose. (I got my first pair this past summer and quickly learned what a vaginal yeast infection was.) Before we left Anna's house, I practiced walking in the shoes for another fifteen minutes or so while Anna and I waited for Leslie to apply yet another coat of mascara. Leslie will now be attending the dance with two pet tarantulas where her eyes should be. She looks pretty, though. And Anna is smart in her taupe, three-piece lady leisure suit, complete with insanely pointy collars. I'd say that all in all we're a pretty foxy trio.

I remind myself to breathe as Anna's mom pilots her Mercedes up to the curb in front of the junior high's gymnasium doors.

"Alright," Jean instructs, "you girls be careful, stay together, have a good time, and I'll be here to pick you up at ten thirty, okay?"

"Will do, Ma," Anna says, opening her door. Leslie and I thank her for the ride and step out, and as Jean's car pulls away we all look at the front doors of the gym, then at each other, and then Anna breaks the silence in her usual delicate way. "Alight you two. Let's get this over with." She sighs like a prisoner going to the scaffold and heads for the gymnasium doors.

"Ready?" Leslie says, giggling. I nod that I am and we follow our stolid leader into the gym.

———————◇———————

The inside of the gym/lunchroom/athletic torture palace looks amazing. The lights are dim and most of the wooden bleachers have been pulled out for seating. Above center court a large, mirrored ball casts tiny dots of light all over the room and everyone in it, which, at this point, is about a third of the student population. Leslie and Anna and I are a little early since Anna's mom wanted to get back in time to read to Toby before he goes to bed.

"What should we do first?" Leslie asks, bouncing. I survey the room for my date.

"I don't think Ethan's here yet," I announce.

Leslie touches my arm reassuringly. "Don't worry, Mel, he'll be here soon."

Anna is less encouraging. "If he doesn't show can we go home soon? My feet already hurt."

Leslie socks her in the shoulder. "No! We're not going home early! We're waiting for Ethan and we're going to have fun, okay?"

"Jeez, okay," Anna concedes, rubbing her arm, "you don't have to get all physical about it."

"Okay, then," Leslie says, nodding resolutely, "Mel and I are going to go get some punch. Maybe you should go sit down for a minute and change your attitude."

"Okay, feisty-pants, relax," Anna retorts. "What's gotten into you?" She gives me a look and then parks herself on a nearby bleacher as I follow Leslie to the refreshment table.

We get in line behind three other kids. "What if he doesn't show?" I ask Leslie, who just smiles.

"He'll show, Mel. I know it. I'm usually right about most things, aren't I?"

This is a hard one to answer. Yes, Leslie is usually right about things but that's only because most of her predictions could honestly go either way. Last week, when we were going to take our lunches outside and eat on the grass, she predicted that it would only rain if we wished it wouldn't. Her theory was that, if we hoped for one thing, the opposite would come true. So, we joined hands over our brown bags and wished for it to rain. Fifteen minutes later, it did just that. Our lunches ruined, and Anna and her hardline science and reality stuff once again validated, Anna informed Leslie that she would no longer be allowed to make group decisions. This seemed unfair to me, since the governance of our group was, and should be, a democratic process wherein all three of us have a say. I said that very thing to Anna who, at length, agreed and said that Leslie could have her one-third vote status restored on the condition that—should she be the deciding vote in a decision involving flooding and other life-and-death decisions—her vote could be overruled in favor of public safety.

When it is finally our turn at the punch bowl, Leslie orders three cups and takes six cookies and we carry our spoils back to the bench where Anna sits waiting, one loafer off, and rubbing her toes.

"Took you guys long enough," she gripes, taking her cup of punch.

"You're grumpy," Leslie says, pouting as she sits down on the bleacher just above and behind Anna.

"I'm sorry," she says, "I'm just not good at this social stuff."

"Well, it's not really my specialty either," I tell her as I sit down next to her, glad to be safely off my feet. "I'm just hoping to get through the evening without seriously injuring and/or embarrassing myself." I take a sip of punch and look over at the door. "Where is he?" I wonder aloud.

"Hey, if Carnac the Magnificent back there is to be believed," Anna says, gesturing in Leslie's direction, "Ethan will show up if you just tell yourself he won't."

"Okay, fine," I say, "he's not going to show, then, so what? I'll still get to have a sleepover with my two best friends, and that's okay with me." I smile at Leslie and Anna.

"That's the spirit!" bounces Leslie.

"Oh, good grief," Anna says, looking at the gymnasium doors, where Ethan is walking in. My heart jumps in my chest. He's here.

Next to me, Anna turns around and frowns at Leslie. "How do you do that?" she asks.

Leslie shrugs. "I don't know. It's a gift. Besides, it's science. You almost never get what you ask for and you almost always get what you don't ask for."

"That's not science," Anna says, turning back around, "I don't know what that is, but it's definitely not science."

"Whatever," Leslie says and then fusses with my hair. "Go talk to him, Mel!"

I am so nervous, and I don't know if my legs will work but I stand and start moving them anyway. "Wish me luck, guys," I say, as I walk, heel, toe, heel toe, carefully across the gym floor. Behind me Leslie calls out.

"Go get 'em, Mel! Break a leg!"

"Seriously, goofy?" Anna says, blunting the moment. "Break a leg? Have you seen her shoes? You are dangerously tempting fate there."

"I thought you didn't believe in fate," Leslie counters.

"I don't," says Anna.

"Then why did you just tell me not to say break a leg?"

"Because it just, you know," Anna stammers, "seems reckless given the situation."

"So, you do believe in fate?" Leslie asks, smugly.

"I don't believe in fate, but you just shouldn't go looking for trouble by saying stuff like that, that's all."

"You mean, don't tempt fate then?" Leslie frowns.

"Right," Anna says, "don't tempt fate."

"How can you tempt something you don't believe in, then?" Leslie, in her own convoluted way, is soundly making

S. J. Coffey

her point, but I'm not listening anymore. Across the room, while a slow Bee Gees song plays, Ethan smiles and begins walking toward me. Like Mavis and the other myth worthy people in my head, Ethan seems to move in slow motion. His silky, red shirt is two buttons undone and as he walks, his gaze never leaving mine, he tosses his head to the right a little, flipping his smooth, black hair out of the way of his cool, green eyes.

Just in time, I step over a stray power cord leading to the deejay's table and manage to make it to Ethan without falling on my face right in front of him.

"Hey," he says, coming out of slow motion and into my reality.

"Hey," I answer.

"You look amazing," he tells me.

"Thank you, so do you." For fifteen seconds neither one of us can seem to come up with anything else to say. But then, like a sparkling disco angel, Mavis saunters up.

"Hey, little buddy!" she says, laying out her palm for me like a life preserver.

"Hey, Mavis!" I slap my hand into hers and she gives me the once over.

"Damn. You are lookin' sassy, this evening!"

"You're looking pretty disco-rific yourself, there," I tell her.

"Well," she answers, fluffing her hair, "I do like to dress for a party."

"This is Ethan," I say, touching Ethan's sleeve lightly. Mavis eyes him thoughtfully.

"You're in my algebra class, right?" she asks.

"Yeah, I think I've seen you in there," he confirms.

"Well," Mavis laughs, "I don't always get to class, so you probably haven't seen me there, much."

"Nice to meet you, Mavis," Ethan says, all formal.

"Are they here?" I ask Mavis.

"Is who here?" Mavis looks confused and I'm regretting asking her in front of Ethan but then she catches on. "Oh!" she says, smiling conspiratorially. "Nope, I haven't seen either of those two."

"Haven't seen who?" Ethan asks.

"Oh, nobody," I cover. "Just some girls who aren't my biggest fans."

Ethan frowns a little but then seems to drop the matter as Mavis turns to go. "Listen, I got an appointment under the bleachers, if you know what I mean," she laughs. "But you two have fun now."

"I need to ask Mavis about a science thing," I tell Ethan. "I'll be right back, okay?" He nods, so I hurry after Mavis.

"Did you get my drawing back from Stephanie?" I whisper. Mavis slows and turns to me, shaking her head.

"She said she didn't have it. She was worried her momma would find it, so she flushed it, I guess."

"Do you believe her?" I ask.

"About as much as I believe any cracker-bitch like her. Now stop worrying, okay?" she says, nudging me. "Stephanie Harris isn't gonna do nothin' tonight but paint her toes and sulk, trust me."

"Okay, if you say so."

"I do say so. Now go and have fun with that boy!" she orders.

"Thanks, Mavis."

"Think nothin' of it, little buddy," she says, before turning and heading off into the growing cluster of teenagers in the center of the gym.

I walk back over to Ethan. "Sorry to run off, there."

"Did you get the science thing straightened out?"

"Um, yes I did, all straightened out," I say. "The problem in question has been solved. Absolutely. All taken care of." A slow song starts and boys and girls pair up here and there and walk out to center court.

"Good song," I say, trying not to fall off my shoes.

"Yeah, it is," Ethan agrees. "You want to dance?" he says, putting his hand out to me. Nothing verbal is coming to me, so I just nod and take his hand and follow him out into the turning, light-speckled crowd.

———◇———

"It's only September. Why is it so damned cold already?" Stephine wonders, wishing she'd brought a sweater as she and Nadine walk up to the gym doors.

"You sure we should be here?" Nadine asks. "Mavis told us not to come."

Stephanie takes a deep, irritated breath. "Listen, Nadine, I'm the only reason anyone in this school has been paying any attention to you at all lately," she says, her voice icy. "Without me, you'd still be doing nothing on Friday nights but sitting at home watching *Wheel of Fortune* with your drunk-ass daddy."

Nadine is not happy to hear this truth, and she is wounded. But she says nothing as Stephanie pulls open the gymnasium door. "Now do your job and protect me from that negra bitch, before I find myself a new best friend."

Stephanie gives her one last bone-chilling glare and goes inside. And because she has no choice, and because Stephanie is right about her dad, Nadine follows her inside.

———◇———

Beneath the smooth fabric of his shirt, I can hear Ethan's heartbeat. Mine is a bird on espresso but his is rhythmic and slow. He can't possibly feel like I do, not with a heart rate like that. My head is on his chest. It would be on his shoulder, but he is significantly taller than me so my ear is now just to the right of his heart. Lub dub, lub dub, lub dub.

"Why are you here with me?" I ask as we turn to the music.

"Because I like you," he says, chuckling.

I pull away and look up at him. "I like you, too," I say. "But you could be with anybody. The queen of the school herself tried to put a hit on me so she could be with you tonight."

Ethan frowns. "Who, Stephanie?"

"That's the one," I answer, trying not to look afraid. "She attempted to have Nadine Melnick turn me into a paraplegic."

"Oh," Ethan says, "that's who you and Mavis were talking about earlier. Boy, I knew she was bad news, but…"

"But she's gorgeous and graceful and has that accent," I say, cutting him off, "and every guy in the school wants her."

Ethan drops his eyes on mine as another slow song begins to play. "Stephanie is not the girl for me," he says, effortlessly turning me to the beat of this new song. "And the only thing she ever reads is the back of a hair color box. Now, are we going to talk through this song, too?" I shake my head and put my ear back over his heart as we turn and turn and turn.

--------◇--------

Near the refreshment table, Anna and Leslie watch Melanie and Ethan dance.

S. J. Coffey

"Oh," croons Leslie, "look at them."

"Yeah," Anna agrees. Despite herself, she is moved too. She does not like dances and she would prefer to be at home watching PBS with her dad. But, she decides, the sight of her friend, so happy at last, is definitely worth missing the NewsHour for. She's just thinking that maybe coming to the dance with her friends was a good idea when Dennis and Sean blunder up.

"Would you two ladies care to take a spin around the dance floor?" Dennis asks in his best used car salesman voice.

"Have you both bathed recently?" Anna asks. Sean nods enthusiastically.

"I took a bath before I came here tonight. Used my mom's bubble stuff and everything."

Anna turns her attention to Dennis. "And what about you?" she asks, crossing her arms over her chest. "When was the last time your hide got personal with soap and water?"

This is a tough one for Dennis, who looks thoughtfully at the ceiling and strokes his beard, or rather his chin where his beard would be if he had a beard yet. "Um, yesterday?"

"That'll do, I guess," Anna pronounces, taking his arm and offering him to Leslie as if he's a horse just days from the glue factory.

"How come I get the dirty one?" Leslie protests, as Anna grabs Sean's chubby hand and leads him in the direction of the dance floor. "Round one, dirty one, what's the difference?"

"Well, smell, for one thing," Leslie says, scowling as she follows Dennis, who is suddenly offended. "Hey, I used my brother's Jovan Musk," he corrects, pulling Leslie into his clutches. "I smell great."

---⋄---

Over behind a large speaker, like a leopard in the brush, Stephine stands next to Nadine and watches Leslie and Anna dance awkwardly (and in her opinion stupidly) with stooges One and Two. She moves her eyes over the rest of the turning couples and spots Melanie Chaffee dancing with Ethan. *Look at her,* she thinks, *she's a foot shorter than he is, the little weirdo.* Her eyes narrow and plans form in her head. She turns and looks behind her, where Nadine practices being invisible. "Find Mavis," she hisses. "Now." Nadine says nothing and hurries off to do her master's bidding.

---⋄---

The song is ending. I wish it wasn't. I wish it would go on forever and ever, but I have to pee, and soon. I pull myself from Ethan's warm, thumping chest and look up at him. "Um," I begin, elegantly as always, "I need to go to the restroom."

Ethan laughs. "Yeah, I need to hit the can too."

While his delivery is not entirely gentlemanly, I do not care, because he's smiling down at me. "Meet me over on the bleachers in five?" he requests.

"Okay," I nod, and pull myself away from him.

"Next dance is mine, alright?" he says, smiling as he turns and strides effortlessly through the moving amoebas of adolescents.

Since the girls' locker and rest room is on the opposite side of the gym, I turn and run-walk toward the door which is, thankfully, not far away.

---⋄---

Stephanie leans against the wall just outside of the boys' locker room, waiting. She does not mind waiting, not for things as important as Ethan Wilde. When she sent Nadine off to deal with that black girl, she saw Ethan go into the restroom. First, she thought about lurking outside the girls' restroom in wait for that little weirdo, but then she decided on another plan, a better plan.

Ethan can't resist her, anyone with eyes would know that. She looks amazing tonight. Her hair is perfect, her makeup is perfect (thank God that pimple on her nose finally popped, rendering itself so much easier to conceal with makeup) and her outfit, as always, is perfect. She's wearing the jeans she knows Ethan loves, her cutest tiny top and her highest platform sandals, the ones that make her almost as tall as he is. Everything is perfect, and Stephanie knows, standing there outside the boys' room, within urinal-cake smelling distance, that it's going to be a perfect night. It will be the night when Ethan finally sees reason and admits that he is in love with her too. He will tell her that on the dance floor as they turn to an Eagles ballad, and they we be together forever.

She's imagining the perfect, cathedral-length veil for her wedding dress when he comes out of the restroom drying his hands on the sides of his corduroys.

"Oh, hey," Ethan says, stopping short when Stephanie steps in front of him.

"Gonna save a dance for me?" she purrs, running a hand down his arm. She is surprised when he jerks away.

"I'm here with Melanie, Steph. You know that," he tells her frankly, flatly. She is not listening.

"Oh, I thought maybe we could just have one little ol' dance. One little dance couldn't hurt, now could it?"

Ethan begins walking away from her. "I told you I was going with Melanie. I'm sorry."

Stephanie follows him. "Now, what in the world could you see in that silly little thing?"

"Stephanie, listen," Ethan says, looking so serious but so cute, "you're beautiful and all, but she's just more my kind of girl, you know?"

"And what kind of girl is that?" Stephanie asks as if she cares.

"The nice kind, okay?" Ethan explains. "She's polite and funny and she reads, and she doesn't dress, well, like you dress." It is hard for Stephanie not to eye roll. She is getting just so annoyed. She wants to do damage, lots of damage.

"Guess little Miss Melanie Chaffee does all kinds of things I don't, hmm?" she says, running her fingertips back up Ethan's arm with one hand and pulling that little troll's drawing out of her pocket with the other. She hands it to him.

"Looks like she's quite the artist," she says, smiling cat–canary.

Ethan slowly unfolds the small, toothy piece of paper and looks at the image for more than a few moments. "How do you know she drew this?" he asks, finally.

"I watched her scribble the nasty little thing up, right there in front of me at choir practice, in church! Can you believe it?" Stephanie can't help herself and begins laughing, not giggling, but full on laughing, Disney villain style. She likes the sound, the way it rings in her head like bells. *Yes,* she thinks, *I like it very much.*

"Still think your Melanie is a 'nice' girl?" she asks, still laughing.

S. J. Coffey

But, frustratingly, Ethan doesn't answer. He just bolts off, taking that dopey girl's drawing with him. *Why, oh why,* Stephanie thinks, *Does nothing ever go my way?* Now she will have to come up with a whole new plan, bother.

———◇———

I must have come out of the bathroom before Ethan because I don't see him anywhere, so I climb up a few bleacher levels for a better view and to find a seat. Then I see him, weaving his way through the packs of kids towards me. He looks up and sees me, so I smile but he does not smile back. A knot of fear forms in my gut as I watch Ethan grow closer. He looks angry and upset. And when he gets to the bleachers and begins climbing up to me, my heart beats ten beats faster with each step he takes.

"Hey," I say, when gets up to my level.

"Hey," he replies, quiet and not smiling.

"Are you okay?" I ask, and then, when he shows me a piece of paper—a piece of paper like my kind of paper—I know why he isn't smiling.

"Is this yours?" he asks. "Did you draw it?"

"Where did you get that?"

"Is it yours?" he presses.

"Would it matter if it was?" I ask, already knowing that it matters.

"Yes," Ethan says. "It matters. It matters a lot," he stands there, the drawing, my drawing, dangling from his fingers. On the paper, I can see the curve of a breast and a lock of curly hair. "It's really good," he admits.

"I'd say thanks, but I don't think that was a compliment." I'm nauseous. I want to throw up.

"I think I'm just gonna head home, okay?" he tells me. Parts of me are breaking inside. I can hear cracks and pops and groans from every cell in my body.

"Not impressed with my entrepreneurial skills, huh?" I joke, idiotically.

"God, Melanie," Ethan says, loud and scary, "how could you even look at stuff like that, let alone *draw* it?"

"I don't know," I say, not lying.

"Jeez, Mel, you're a *girl*," he nearly spits the word at me.

"You got me there," I say. "I am, in fact, a girl."

He looks sickened and turns to go. "Yeah, but I didn't think you were *that* kind of girl."

If my butt was made of super glue it could not have been more stuck to that bench. I am incapable of moving. All I can do is watch as Ethan lopes down the bleachers, two at a time. He is in such a hurry to get away from me. I am immobilized, but then I think of the one thing that will get me off that bench in a shot. "My drawing!" I squeal aloud, not caring who hears me. I have to get it back, so I hop up and, teetering on my shoes, I pick my way down the bleachers and onto the floor and then I take off running after Ethan.

———◇———

Stephanie has caught him, for now at least. Ethan was just opening the gymnasium door when she saw him. He's standing in front of her now. He is angry with her, but he'll get over it, especially now that the little weirdo is most likely out of the way.

"How's your little artist girlfriend doing?" she asks him, eyelashes fluttering. Ethan stabs the drawing at her.

"Here, take this thing. I don't want it."

Stephanie pushes the drawing down into the bottom of her front jeans' pocket and touches Ethan's cheek. "I'm sorry if I upset you. I didn't want to, but I thought you should know." Part of what she just said is true. Stephanie didn't want to upset Ethan, she loves Ethan. She belongs with him. The other part, however, is not true. She did not think he should know. The less Ethan Wilde knows, the better. But telling him was necessary, really. There was no other way to make him see that he is hers. The completeness, the spherical perfectness of her life would be impossible without him. There is no queen without a king, right? Because if there's one thing in this world that Stephanie Harris knows, it is that she is a queen, and not just any queen, she is a queen who is meant to rule.

———◇———

I can see her there, Stephanie, not twenty feet from me. She's talking to Ethan near the exit door. I run up just in time to watch as he gives her the drawing, my drawing. The one that will end everything. I turn and run, dodging kids and teachers as tears make my vision a mottled watercolor. And this time, I don't see the power cord to the deejay's table, and the heel of my right platform sandal comes down on it and twists sideways. A sickening pop makes its way from my ankle to my ears and I'm face down on the gymnasium floor.

My ankle is screaming, and I choke back sobs as a warm, soft hand touches me gently on the shoulder.

"Melanie?" a tinkly voice asks. "Are you okay?" My hands feel the grit of the floor and I smell lavender and roses and look up. Above me, his face full of concern and his corn-silk-fringed blue eyes blinking, is Smiling Alan—

AKA (in what I now know is a very cruel world) Fat Alan. He is not smiling now. "Are you okay?" he asks me again. I nod and push myself up off the floor. Alan offers a fluffy hand and I take it, gratefully, and pull myself to an unsteady standing position. My ankle hurts.

"Thank you, Alan," I say. "Could you maybe help me get to the restroom?"

"Of course," he says, letting me lean on his arm. "You went down like a sack of flour. I heard something crack, too. Is your foot broken?"

"I don't think so. I can walk on it and wiggle my toes."

"Oh, that's good," Alan says, sounding relieved. "My mom's a nurse and she says that as long as you can wiggle your toes there's probably nothing broken."

I wonder, absurdly, if this general rule of thumb regarding broken bones applies to all the parts of the human body. I imagine that if you broke your arm in three places you could probably wiggle your toes just fine and still be in need of serious medical attention.

Hobbling along next to Alan, holding onto his padded forearm beneath a pressed and starched sleeve, I can think of only the sanctuary of the girls' locker room. I glance over at Alan, who smiles at me. "You're doing just fine," he encourages, "almost there."

"I'm glad you were here," I tell him. "Do you think anyone else saw me fall?"

"Maybe a few kids, but nobody seemed to care much," he says. I am relieved to hear that I didn't cause a huge spectacle, and that most likely Ethan and Stephanie did not see my literal downfall, but it is a little disturbing to hear that no one else cared. Still, I am, and will always be, indebted to Alan Bomart.

At the door to the girls' locker room, I grab a hold of the door handle and release Alan's arm. "Will you be okay?" he asks.

"I think so," I say. Alan pulls a folded handkerchief from his shirt pocket and carefully blots at my cheeks. "You've got a little mascara, here," he says, smiling warmly. "There, that's better." He hands me the soft, flowery-scented cloth. "You can keep it," he says. "I've got lots of them." I take the gift and hope that Alan doesn't have a surplus of handkerchiefs because he needs them. I can think of few things more heartbreaking than gentle Smiling Alan in tears.

"Would you mind finding Anna and Leslie for me?" I ask.

"Sure, I know Anna. She's in my advanced chem class."

"Thank you, Alan, for everything, for helping me," I say, trying to smile as fresh tears form.

"Any time, Melanie," he says. "I'll see you on the bus."

I nod. "I'll save you a seat."

Alan smiles and, as if sensing my need to escape, waddles gracefully out into the crowd.

Inside the girls' locker room, I make my way to a bench between the banks of lockers. Flinching in pain I sit down and let the tears flow unabated down my face and onto the lap of my lemon-yellow skirt, staining it with bumble bee smudges of black mascara.

Chapter 29

NEW FRIENDS
BEARING COOKIES

The meeting is about to start, and Shirley is starving. After dropping Melanie at Anna's house, she had to stop by the store and then get home to make a quick dinner for Dan and Steven. They were perfectly happy with burgers and frozen crinkle fries in front of the TV, but she hadn't had a chance to eat something herself before she had to leave for the meeting. Hitching up her shoulder bag, she makes her way through the maze of chairs and gossiping ladies, over to the refreshment table in hopes of a cookie to tide her over.

At the table, Mrs. Magnussen is arranging plates of relief. "Need any help?" Shirley asks, her motives not entirely altruistic.

"Oh, no, dear. I think I've got it all under control," the tiny, round, pink confection of a woman says.

"Any more news about those drawings?" Shirley eyes a plate of large, chocolate chip cookies and wonders if it would be rude to take two.

"Not yet," Patty Magnussen says, brushing non-existent crumbs from her dress. "But I've been praying to Our Lord danged near every hour to show us the light on this. And I just know He'll come through for His flock any time now."

"Well, that's good news then," Shirley says, smiling. She reaches for a cookie, only to have Mrs. Magnussen tap her outstretched hand, ever so gently, with a puffed, marshmallow finger.

"Ah, ah!" she scolds, causing Shirley to retract her hand in surprise. "Not yet! These are for *after* the meeting," she explains, as though the grown woman in front of her is a kindergartener. "Elsewise, they'll all be long gone before I even say a word!" she says, smiling sweetly. "You understand."

"Oh, of course," Shirley says, embarrassed and humiliated. "I understand completely." Simmering, she turns and looks for a seat.

In the second to last row of the chairs, Shirley spots Amelia Jackson sitting on the center aisle. Amelia is staring straight ahead as she tucks an errant hair into the tight bun at the back of her neck. Feeling Shirley's eyes on her, she looks up, then smiles and pats the empty chair next to her. Grateful for the friendly face, Shirley weaves through the chairs toward her. She takes the seat next to Amelia, who is now munching happily on a cookie.

"Hey, how'd you get one of those?" she asks. "I almost lost an arm trying to get one."

Amelia smiles wickedly. "I took it while she wasn't looking. She was busy lecturing some poor lady about the evils of sin."

"What's a sin is that awful dress," Shirley says, making Amelia laugh.

"You got that right. Woman looks like a damned birthday cake exploded." She extends her hand. "Amelia Jackson, we talked the other night."

Shirley takes her hand and shakes. "I'm Shirley, Melanie's mom."

"I know." Amelia finishes her cookie, then pulls another one out of her purse and hands it to Shirley.

"Oh, thank you!" she says, thrilled by the treat. "You're a lifesaver."

"You're very welcome," says Amelia. "These things are torture. I only manage to drag myself here for the cookies."

Shirley laughs and breaks off bite-sized pieces of cookie. "Thank you for having Melanie over for dinner, and for dropping her home."

"Of course, it was no trouble at all. She helped me with dishes and cleanup more than Mavis ever does. She's a sweet little church mouse. Funny, too."

"Church mouse?" Shirley says, confused.

"Well, she just seemed like such a quiet little thing when I met her," Amelia says, smiling. "But she's not, is she?"

"No," Shirley laughs, "she isn't. She talks a lot about Mavis. She's been a good friend to Mel, I think."

"And your girl's been a hell of a friend to my Mavis, too."

"You're with Morris and Tate, right?" Shirley asks.

"Mmm hmm. I'm a legal secretary there. I came up here from Phoenix for that job. Put the kids through a lot but I love it. My boss is a little too friendly sometimes but I can manage him."

Shirley smiles, jealous. "I was in law school fifteen years ago, and then Steven happened."

"I was first year when Jamal showed up. Put a stop to school in a hurry."

"Kids have a way of changing plans for us, don't they?" Shirley says and Amelia nods.

"They're worth it though. Don't know what I'd do without those two."

"Yes, they are," Shirley says in agreement, just as Mrs.

Magnussen totters up to the podium, hat in hand.

"Oh, no," Amelia says, letting out a low whistle, "here we go."

Up on the stage, Patty sets her pink pillbox hat up on top of her hairdo and pushes it into place. The small, round hat is dotted with tiny, floating white feathers that look an awful lot like birthday candles. Unable to help herself, Amelia lets out a giggle and hearing her Shirley begins to laugh too, neither one of them caring much when three or four ladies in their vicinity shoot hostile glares their way.

———◇———

I am alone in the girl's locker room and then they are there. Leslie sits down next to me and Anna crouches on the floor in front of my assaulted ankle. "Whoa, this thing is swelling up like crazy," she says, unbuckling my sandal and gently pulling it off.

"He knows," I manage to push out.

"Who knows?" Leslie says, frowning.

"Ethan, goofy. Did he see one?" Anna asks, and I nod.

"Stephanie showed him the one I lost in choir practice." The tears are here again but it doesn't matter, my face is a mess. Everything is a mess.

"I'm so sorry, Mel," Leslie says, wrapping her long arms around me.

"We gotta get this thing up," announces Anna, referring to my bloated ankle. She takes my other sandal off and pulls me up. "Come on. Upsy-daisy, kid."

Anna is in fact two months younger than me, but her parental demeanor in this terrible situation is welcome. I let her and Leslie hold me up, and with my sandals looped over my wrists we make our way to the door and, hopefully, the end of this nightmare.

But when we walk out of the girls' room, Stephanie is waiting. She pushes herself from the wall she's been holding up and walks slowly over, one foot crossing over the other, supermodel-runway style.

"Aw," she tortures, looking down at my foot, "what's the matter?"

"Excuse us, please," Anna says, trying to push past. But behind Stephanie stands Nadine, who does not look happy to be here. We are trapped.

"Did Ethan leave already? And what happened to your foot? Did you fall off of your shoes?" Stephanie asks, holding back a giggle. "Oh, now, that *is* a shame. But since I told you to stay away from him and you didn't, I guess you got what you deserved, didn't you?"

So many questions I can't, and don't want to, answer. I can't seem to form words, but Anna can. "Move it, you underfed Barbie," she says, trying again to push past our tormenter.

"My word," Stephanie taunts. "You are a *manly* girl, aren't you? You gonna beat us up?"

"Violence is the solution of inferior minds," Anna replies, her voice full of dignity and strength. "Now get out of our way before I go find Mavis."

It is weird sometimes the way things work out. As far as I can tell, life is mostly a puzzle with pieces that don't go together, but occasionally things seem to click as if they had been planned. My Aunt Marnie calls this serendipity but tonight, as I feel Mavis's arm fall around my shoulder, I'm just going to call it a Godsend.

"Better listen to the nerd, bitch," Mavis says from behind me.

Stephanie glowers at Mavis then turns to Nadine. "I told you to take care of her," she bristles.

Leslie hugs Mavis. "I knew you'd come!" she squeals. Mavis smiles and gently extricates herself from her fan's rabid grip.

"Nah, it looks like the bookworm here has got the situation under control."

Stephanie applies a counterfeit smile for Mavis. "Evening, Mavis," she says, stepping back just enough to let the four of us pass. I can't speak, and I don't want to, but as I hobble by on the arms of my friends, I look up at Nadine. Her mouth is set stone and her eyes are hard, but something sits behind them. It is my feeling that she is not what she seems or what people think she is. She is still terrifying. I do not wish to be alone with her, but she is not evil. She is not like Stephanie, I'm sure of it.

Finally, we are beyond the reach of Stephanie and the door is in sight. But Anna, feeling the need for closure of the moment, turns to Stephanie and flashes a smile. "Hey, Stephanie," she says, painting a verbal target on her own back, "the bathroom's free if you need to purge."

———◇———

Shirley is tired, hungry and so over listening to Patty Magnussen. And now, because of this mess with some kid manufacturing their own pornography, tonight's usually dull, but usually brief, PTA meeting has dragged on for more than two hours.

"Ladies, please!" tiny, round Patty shout-sings from the podium. "This is quite worrisome, but we cannot all talk at once!"

Shirley has to smile to herself. For once that little pink menace is being outtalked. Most meetings, she's the loudest (and highest pitched) voice in the room, but tonight her words are being soundly run over by those in the audience.

"My Jimmy had three of them in his sock drawer. Three!" Laura Swanson hollers from the back left.

"And Joseph and Alan had five each!" Mary Farnsworth chimes in.

Laura Swanson is in tortured, motherly tears. "Jimmy is only twelve! What kind of monster would provide a twelve-year-old child with material like that?"

Up front, Mrs. Magnussen is conciliatory but firm. "Now, Laura, we know that boys will be boys, don't we? They can't help the way they are any more than girls can change themselves. The Lord, in all his wisdom, made them that way. We are *all* God's children."

There is rumbling and nodding of agreement in the audience, but Shirley, her eyes filled with frustration and confusion, just looks over at Amelia, who shrugs and whispers, "No offence, but you white ladies sure do like to get worked up over things."

"I wish I could dispute your assessment," Shirley whispers back.

Amelia lets out a quiet giggle, then pulls another cookie from her purse, breaks it in two and gives half to Shirley, who smiles gratefully.

At the podium, Mrs. Magnussen continues to try and contain her PTA meeting, which has become a sack of ferrets.

"Ladies!" she shouts. "Ladies, please! I promise you, as Jesus is my witness, we will find the pervert who is producing and distributing this evil smut and degrading the souls of our fine young men and boys!"

Anna's bed is soft, but so firm and supportive underneath.

Kind of the opposite of Anna, really, when you think about it. I'm resting in Anna's room, my foot propped on a pillow and buried in a hand towel filled with ice. Anna's refrigerator has an ice maker. It is a luxury I had never experienced until I stayed over at her house for the first time back in the sixth grade. At the time, I had never seen ice cubes like that. At my house, our ice supply was misshapen and often unreliable, as I was fond of picking individual cubes from the trays when I was too lazy to just crack the whole tray and refill it. Strangely, this habit infuriates my dad, who is rarely ruffled by anything. I've only seen him yell about two things: messing with his paints and unauthorized ice cube removal. This is interesting to me because it tells me that 1) my dad has a variable threshold for irritation, and 2) the destruction and/or enhancement of someone else's personal expression is on a par with half empty ice cube trays.

"Leslie's dad is coming to pick her up soon. My mom says he'll run you home, too." Anna's voice sounds sad. She sits down on the bed next to me. Leslie is in the bathroom picking flakes of mascara out of her eyes and for the moment we're alone.

"I'm sorry I ruined the whole night," I tell her.

"You didn't ruin anything," she says, lifting the towel and examining my ankle, which is beginning to change colors. "I've had enough of goofy Leslie to last me at least a week. I'm happy to read for a bit and then hit the hay."

"Oh, yeah?" I answer, trying to joke. "Need some quality time with your boyfriend, Jack?"

"Ha ha, very funny," Anna deadpans. "I'm not reading about the rippers anymore. There are some more recent murders over in California I'm trying to figure out."

"Figure out?" This new information about my curious buddy and her hobbies is disturbing, but I'm currently too heartbroken to care.

"It's just, you know," she continues, "I like puzzles."

"Yeah, puzzles with bodies," I say, managing a chuckle.

"What can I tell you, games are more interesting when the stakes are higher. Besides, unlike you two idiots, I'm not distracted by boys," she explains.

The second part of what she just said is obviously confusing, but it is the first part I'm stuck on. "Higher stakes?" I ask, frowning. Anna is about to answer when her bedroom door pops open and Toby-the-tyrant frog hops into the room.

"Ribbit!" he yells. "I'm a frog! See? Ribbit, ribbit!"

"Yeah, and I'm a French chef, you little beast. You might want to get the heck out of my room." Anna's vague, if not very cultured threat is lost on her little brother.

"Leslie's dad's here!" Toby shouts. I am upset and in pain and this kid only has one volume setting. I want to go home.

"Thank you, idiot. Now get out," Anna commands, and for once Toby obeys and ribbits his way out of the room, slamming the door behind him.

Anna picks up my overnight bag from the floor and stuffs my things in it, topping the rumpled mess with my new and very treacherous shoes.

"Those things should come with a warning label," Anna says, speaking the utter truth. "Are you gonna be okay?" she asks.

"I think so. I just want to get in bed and disappear."

"Well, don't disappear for too long. I can't manage Leslie by myself, you know," she says smiling wryly.

I nod anemically and Anna heads for the door. "I'll go see if goofy has finally flushed herself, then let's gets you home."

Chapter 30

EVIL PRINCESS
STEPHANIE VS. THE
MOHAVE COUNTY PTA

F or some reason, over the past twenty minutes Shirley has grown increasingly anxious. It is past nine thirty, the meeting has not ended and at least seven suburban mothers are now standing, and some of them are yelling. Up front, Mrs. Magnussen struggles for control.

"Now, everyone!" she calls out. "Just calm down! We'll get to the bottom of this, but we all just need to stop shouting over each other and sit down!"

No one listens. In Shirley's head, all their voices seem to be melding into each other. *This is what a mob sounds like*, she thinks.

Next to her, Amelia watches Mrs. Magnussen and frowns, the little W between her eyes, deep. But then Patty begins to sing, and the W defers to the three lines of surprise forming on Amelia's forehead. "What in the hell..." she says, low and in Shirley's direction.

"Is she *singing*?" Shirley asks, and Mrs. Magnussen, as if in response to the question, pushes a huge, warbling mezzo soprano out of her squat, fuchsia-covered body. It is a hymn, one that Shirley has heard before, but never quite like this.

Each note seems higher than the next until Patty drops it, like an anchor over a ship's deck, inexplicably three or four octaves. The effect is unsettling, unprecedented and, Shirley reasons, unwelcome.

"Damn," Amelia says, covering her ears with her long, graceful fingers capped by long nails painted a tasteful nude color, "is that woman singing or trying to attract every tomcat in the entire town?"

Shirley feels a little punchy and can't for the life of her suppress a laugh. "I have no idea," she sputters. But Mrs. Magnussen's novel plan appears to be working. Shouts and calls to get local law enforcement involved in the search for the mysterious analog pornographer give way to gasps and quiet whispers as the ladies, one by one, find their seats beneath their skirts and sit down.

Order, at least for the moment, restored, Patty finishes her song, capping the bizarre performance with her arms outstretched and her eyes cast heavenward. "Amen," she concludes, "and thank you, Jesus." She wraps her arms around herself as if her Lord and Savior himself is standing behind her and holding her in a warm (and of course platonic) embrace.

Shirley peeks over at Amelia only to find her new friend's eyes wide, looking back at her, and without warning she lets out a snorting giggle. Amelia claps a hand over Shirley's. "Oh my God, stop," she whispers, stifling her own giggles, "you're killing me!" Several ladies in front of them turn and glare and a "Shhhh!" emits from somewhere in a back row.

"Alrighty, then," Mrs. Magnussen says softly. "That's better. Now, I suggest that we all just take a moment for prayer." She interlaces her plump fingers together under her nose and addresses the Infinite. "Dear Lord Jesus, we ask that you give us patience during this trying time. And that you help us find this boy who is committing these awful infractions against you and your young people…"

Behind her, Shirley hears the push bar on the heavy rear door clunk, just before the door opens, and like everyone else in the room she turns to see whose heels are clicking into the room as Patty Magnussen drones on.

"Lord Jesus, help us find this boy who is drawing these craven images and help *us* to help *him*. He is a sinner and he needs your grace…"

A young woman's voice is laughing, loud and clear and from deep inside her chest. "Boy!" the young woman's voice calls out, interrupting Patty's carefully crafted prayer, "who said anything about a *boy*?"

Shirley watches as a tall, slim teenaged girl with long, flipped, blond hair strides up the center aisle in tight, wide-leg jeans and very high platform sandals.

"Who the hell is *that*?" Amelia whispers to Shirley, who just shakes her head and watches as this young woman pulls every eye, and every molecule of oxygen in the room, to herself.

"Trust me, ladies," she says, her voice bouncing off the flat, painted brick walls. "it wasn't any *boy*." She stops in the middle of the aisle and looks up at Patty Magnussen. "Evening, Mrs. Magnussen," she says, a smile tugging at the corners of her mouth.

"Stephanie, what are you doing here? Shouldn't you be at the dance?" Patty asks.

"Got bored," Stephanie says, sighing dramatically and slapping her hands on the sides of her thighs.

Mrs. Magnussen frowns down at the woman and looks a little…is that surprise, or fear in her eyes? "Miss Harris, do you have information on this matter?" she asks. "If so then we should perhaps speak privately."

"Oh," Stephanie scoffs, "now why would we need to go to all that trouble?" She begins turning in slow circles in the center of the aisle. "I have a feelin' the person who can help us with this might just be sittin' right here, in this very room." She smiles and continues to turn, her gaze the burning candle at the top of an undernourished lighthouse. "A little bird told me Mrs. Chaffee attends these meetings." Now, Captain Stephanie holds her hand above her eyes, shielding them from some invisible glare as she mock searches the audience for her prey. "Where, oh where are you, Mrs. Chaffee?"

A few feet away and one seat from the center aisle, Shirley pulls courage from deep in her empty belly and stands. She is numb. And afraid of this lithe, frightening young woman. But as if called by a demon, she stands anyway. And as she does, she feels a hand on hers and looks down to see Amelia Jackson squeezing her fingers. Amelia gives her an encouraging nod and releases her hand, so Shirley speaks. "I'm Shirley Chaffee. Can I help you?"

"Mrs. Chaffee," Patty Magnussen says from atop her perch, "did your son Steven have anything to do with this?"

"I don't believe so, no," Shirley says, her voice strong and steady. The words are barely out of her mouth before the laughter starts again, Stephanie Harris's laughter. The sound is sharp and hurts Shirley's ears. She worries she's getting another migraine.

"That's because it wasn't your *son* who drew those dirty pictures, lady, it was your *daughter*!" Stephanie almost screams the last word, before bursting into more peals of jagged laughter that land on the gasps and whispers of the women in the hall. Shirley's ears ring and she's sure she's getting a migraine as Stephanie saunters over, unfolding a small piece of good quality drawing paper as she nears her. Finally within striking distance, Stephanie deploys her weapon and shoves the paper almost under Shirley's nose.

"Here ya go, ma'am. I believe this belongs to Melanie. I imagine she might like to have it back, don't you think?" the cat says, spitting yellow feathers.

The room is dead silent now and, floating and feeling unreal Shirley reaches out and takes the drawing. It is her daughter's work, she knows that, but she has to stare at it for a few seconds because she feels like she's dreaming all of this, every bit of it, even the cookies. Then, on automatic pilot, she picks up her purse, skootches carefully in front of Amelia, who offers a gentle smile, then Shirley steps into the aisle and walks slowly to the door.

Behind her, Amelia gathers her things and stands as every last white lady watches her. "You know," she begins, closing her eyes for a moment for strength, "my daughter told me all about you." She opens her eyes and drops them on Stephanie. "And I told her to just hold her tongue, leave you alone, stay out of trouble with white folks like you."

Only feet from Amelia, in the center of the aisle, Stephanie pops a hip and crosses her arms over her C cups. "Well, she *didn't* leave me alone, lady. I should call the cops on both of you. She *threatened* me," she huffs.

"And with good reason, from what I've seen here tonight," Amelia says, seeming more tired than angry. "Hurting another woman hurts all of us, don't you know that? None of us are gonna get anywhere in this world if we keep drag-gin' each other down, no matter what color we are." Amelia takes a breath and exhales, long and loud, then turns and clacks to the door on her boots.

Burning holes in Amelia's back with her eyes, Stephanie seethes. And if Mrs. Caruthers, who heard it from Betty Zohler, who heard it from Vi Davidson who was sitting behind Amelia Jackson that very evening is right, Amelia could be heard saying, just under her breath as she pushed open the heavy exit door, "Nasty White Bitch."

Outside, in the dark parking lot of the Mohave County Parks and Recreation Center, Shirley rests her hot back against the cold metal of the driver's side door of the Suburban. In the light of the only streetlamp she stares down at the drawing. Her daughter's drawing. She hears shoes crunching towards her in the dark, on the asphalt, but she doesn't bother to push her car keys between her fingers or even look up. She can't take her eyes from the chubby, naked woman on the paper in her hand.

"You okay?" Amelia asks as she walks up and parks her hip against the huge vehicle's wheel well. "Some car you got here," she says, putting a cigarette to her lips. "Somethin' happens to y'all's house, all four of you could probably live in this thing." She laughs and lights up, then takes a long drag and offers the smoke to Shirley, who shakes her head.

"I can't believe this," Shirley says.

"Lil church mouse has got quite a pair, I guess," Amelia says, exhaling a plume of smoke and laughing at the same time.

Shirley looks up at the stars. "Yeah, I guess she does. Don't know where she got them, sure wasn't from me."

"Aw, now," Amelia replies, elbowing her new friend, "you don't give yourself enough credit," she jabs the business end of her cigarette at the rec center door. "Looked plenty tough in there, just now."

Shirley allows herself to smile a little. "You think so?"

"Sure do," Amelia says, crushing the butt under the toe of her boot. "Buy you a drink? I know I could sure use one."

"I should get home and talk to Dan about this," Shirley answers. "Rain check soon?"

"Absolutely, anytime," Amelia says, smiling. Then she reaches into her purse and pulls out another one of Mrs. Magnussen's contraband cookies and hands it to Shirley, who frowns, laughs and takes it.

"How many of those have you got in there?"

"As many as I need to get through two hours of that horseshit," Amelia answers, looking back at the rec center.

"Thank you," Shirley says as she opens the heavy car door and climbs in.

"Good lord," Amelia exclaims, laughing, "that thing come with an elevator?"

"Oh, it's Dan's," Shirley explains, pushing her key into the ignition.

"Well," Amelia admonishes, "tell *Dan* to get you a car you can't fall out of. You're gonna break your damned neck one of these days."

"You know what?" Shirley says, rolling down her window and pulling her door closed. "I think I will. I hate this thing." She puts the truck into drive.

"Go easy on the lil church mouse, okay?" Amelia asks. "It isn't easy being a girl."

Shirley nods. "Call me about that drink," she says, pulling away.

Watching her go, Amelia takes another cookie out of her bag and bites into it.

"Mmm hmm," she says to no one, as she heads to her own car a few spaces away. "That lil pink lady is mean as hell, but she does make a very tasty cookie."

Chapter 31

THE FOOTWEAR
RECKONING

Like a contestant in an unintentional sack race, I'm leaning on Anna as we step-drag our way to my front door. My ankle is huge and my suntan, sandalfoot nylons are a torn wad of uselessness in my overnight bag, which swings awkwardly from Anna's shoulder. My left foot is housed securely in last season's clog shoe, but my destroyed right foot is naked and obvious.

I grab hold of my front door handle and take my bag from Anna, who asks, "Want me to come in with you?"

"No," I tell her, "you're my friend, I'm not going to inflict that on you. You've put up with enough from me already."

"Well, it wasn't a great night, but you have to admit it was pretty interesting. I mean, from an sociological viewpoint," she says, turning my tragedy into a soft science experiment.

I try to laugh a little. "Super, I'm glad it was fun for somebody."

Anna doesn't answer me. Instead she hugs me. Which is weird, because aside from a smack on the back of someone's head to make a point, Anna doesn't like to touch other people, let alone hug them. Her embrace is awkward and fervent and for a second I can't breathe.

"It'll be okay," she says in my ear. "These things always pass." Then, as if I'd just delivered a silent but deadly fart, she pulls herself from me and hurries down the walkway to where her mom's Mercedes waits in the drive.

Anna's sage words, while comforting in the long run, aren't doing anything for me right now. And if it weren't fifty degrees out tonight, and my ankle wasn't a mangled mess, I'd head for the hills and hide out in the desert all night with the other wretched, unwanted creatures. But then I decide that, in addition to being poisonous and pointy, the desert's nocturnal inhabitants might not want me in their environs, any more than my parents are going to want me in theirs once they find out what I did. And I know they'll find out soon. Hell hath no fury like a wronged Stephanie Harris. This town is small, and her influence is wide. My life is over, but I need ice and my bed, so I push the door handle and hobble inside.

"Melanie JoAnne?" my mother calls out before I've even shut the front door. She's using my middle name. That is a bad thing.

"Yeah?" I say, holding onto the wall as I hop down the hall.

"Come sit down please," she says. But when I come around the corner to the living room, and she takes in my mascara-stained face and my battered ankle, her voice softens. "Good lord, honey, what happened?" she asks, rushing over to take my bag and help me down into the living room.

"I tripped and twisted it," I tell her as she helps me sit down on the sofa.

"You sure did," she says, pulling my foot up onto the couch to examine it. "Dan," she says, turning her attention to my dad, who's in his chair on the other side of the room, hiding behind a copy of *Woodworking Today*, "would you please go get some ice? There's an ice bag in the hall closet."

"Sure thing," he says, standing. "Wow," he exclaims, just noticing my injury. "What in the hell happened, MellyBean? Are you okay?"

I nod because I cannot form words just yet. "I'll get that ice," he says, rushing out of the room.

"I'm glad you came home," my mother says, running her soft fingers over my ankle. "This looks like a bad sprain." She prods the offended thing here and there and moves my foot in little circles. "I don't think anything is broken but you're going to need to rest it for a few days. Good thing it's the weekend. You should be able to walk on it okay by Monday, so you shouldn't have to miss any school."

Fantastic, can this night get any worse? The thought had barely formed in my head before I realized I shouldn't have even thought it, because a millisecond later she said it. "Honey, we have to talk."

I'm pretty sure no good conversation has ever started with "Honey, we have to talk." Certainly not for the recipient of the statement, anyway.

"Can't I just go to bed?" I beg, hoping to postpone this discussion until tomorrow or never, whichever comes first. "My ankle really hurts," I say, laying it on thick in hopes of a pity pardon.

"I'll give you some aspirin. That should help with the pain and the swelling, so you can sleep," she says, not answering my question. And if she thinks I'm going to sleep much tonight, maybe it's possible she doesn't know what I did.

She pulls a piece of paper from her skirt pocket. "We need to talk about *this*."

With the fine-tuned timing of someone who's lived with my mother for the past sixteen years, my dad drops soundlessly into the living room and hands my mom the ice pack. He sits down on the coffee table across from me and ruffles my hair. "How'd you wipe out, kiddo?" he asks, chuckling and unaware that this has just become a chuckle-free zone.

"I tripped over a power cord, I think." I'm not lying. *At least not yet*, I think as I adjust the cold bag on my ankle.

"We should talk to the school," my dad says. "They have to be more careful about that kind of stuff."

"I'll call Principal Naylor on Monday," my mom answers, still looking at the drawing in her hands. Then she looks up at me in a way I know (even at thirteen years old) that I will never forget, and asks me a question I never wanted to answer. "Why, Melanie JoAnne? Why have you been drawing these?"

"Darling," my father addresses my mother gently, using a pet name I've rarely heard him use on her, "why don't we talk about this tomorrow, like we'd planned? Mel's tired and that thing's got to hurt like hell."

"No," she says, cutting him off, "if any of us are going to get any sleep at all tonight, we need to get this over with, right here, right now."

My mother is angry. Not "pick up your socks" angry, or even "Dan and his damned gravel" angry. She's silent angry. Her voice is low and measured and scary. "Do you have any idea what I went through tonight because of this?" she says, giving the paper a shake. She unfolds the drawing and shows it to me. It's the one of the chubby lady. The one Stephanie had.

"How did you get that?" I ask.

"Shouldn't I be the one asking the questions, here?" My mom says, as what simmers inside her reaches a rolling boil.

Sensing the growing danger inside his wife, my dad jumps in. "Your mom had a bit of a situation this evening at the PTA meeting," he says.

"I can explain," I begin. "I wanted to…" But I realize then that I am not entirely certain why I've been making drawings of naked women to sell to adolescent boys. I wanted the money, and the shoes, for sure, but there was something else I wanted, too. I just haven't been able to verbalize it yet.

"How did you even know how to draw stuff like this?" my mom asks. "When have I ever let you see women in this way?" Her eyes lock on mine. I drop my gaze to my mascara-stained lap. I want to tell her *she* taught me how to look at women this way. I want to tell her every time we ate grilled cheese sandwiches and tomato soup and watched her soap operas and their accompanying coffee advertisements, she taught me. But I don't think she'll understand. So for the moment I just tell her the outer truth, the one she's asked me for.

"I'm good at anatomy," I tell her. "I really just needed to look at a few photos and magazines and stuff to get the hang of it."

My mom frowns. "What photos?" she asks. "Where did you get them?"

I glance over at my dad. It's a knee-jerk, or more properly, a neck-jerk, reaction that I don't have time to censor. For his sake I wish I did, because my mother looks over at my dad in a way I have never seen her look at him. It is a facial cocktail of sadness and fury that makes me suck in a breath of air and feel instantaneous regret.

"Dan," she begins, cocking her head the same way I've seen a coyote do just before it pounces on an unsuspecting jackrabbit, "are you still getting those m*agazines?*"

"I like the articles?" my dad answers, shrugging and offering a smile, instead of a steak, to the dangerous beast in front of him. He's hoping humor will save him from this one but when he looks over at me, we both know we're toast.

"Good lord, Dan!" my mother yells, standing and starting to pace. "How did she find them?"

"It's not his fault. I took them. And I had to look pretty hard, too. He did a really good job of hiding them," I say, coming to my dad's rescue. But now my mom's eyes are back on me.

"What on God's green earth were you thinking, Melanie?"

"Look in my bag," I tell her. I could just start explaining the whole sorted thing, but now seems like a good time for visual aids and a moment for contemplation.

My mom reaches down, picks up my overnight bag and puts it on the coffee table in front of her. It's too stuffed with torn pantyhose and dashed hopes to close so she sees them right away: the platforms. Frowning, she reaches in and takes one out. "Where did you get these?" she asks me.

"At Babbitts," I answer, truthfully.

"I know where you got them. I've seen these there. I meant, where did you get the money for them? They were expensive." I don't have time to answer her because my mother isn't dumb and she puts everything together right there in front of me in just under ten seconds. "Oh my God," she says, her eyebrows running for her hairline, "you bought these with the money you made from selling those pictures, didn't you?"

I want to answer her, but I can't really think of any words that work in this particular circumstance, so I just continue to study my own lap.

"How could you do this to me, Melanie? How? Do you know what I had to go through tonight at the PTA meeting? That young woman was awful, just awful."

"What young woman?" I ask. My mother shakes her head as if she could make herself wake up from this nightmare. "Stephanie Harris."

"Oh," I say, nodding. "She must have gone over there after the dance."

"She marched into the meeting and gave me this," she says, shaking the beleaguered chubby lady again, "right in front of everyone. It was horrid. If Amelia Harris hadn't been there, I don't know what I would have done."

"Mavis's mom was there?" I ask but my mother doesn't answer.

With her arms crossed tight over her chest, she wears a groove in our mushroom-colored, high-low shag. "I just don't know how, or why, you would do this to me." She stops mid-pace and glowers down at me.

I am tired, my ankle is throbbing and I want to go to bed and hide, and she won't let me. Frustration and pain push new tears from my eyes. "I did it because of *you*," I say, matching her glare for glare. "You wouldn't buy them for me, so I bought them myself, with the money *I* earned!" I push myself up from the sofa, my ice pack clunking onto the floor. "And you know what else?" I challenge, my eyes on hers as my father watches impotently. "I liked doing the drawings and selling them. I did! For the first time boys were looking at *me* and wanting something only *I* could give them. I wasn't just weird Melanie Chaffee anymore. I was special. I was *smart*." With the back of a fist, I swipe angry tears from my cheek.

"Of course you're smart, honey," my dad says, reaching for a hand I won't let him have. "And why would you think you're not special?"

"You took money for that filth, Mel," my mother says to the carpet. "How could you?"

"I didn't just do it for the money," I tell her, standing on the tiptoes of my pounding right foot because it hurts too much to put it flat on the floor. "I did it because *I'm* the best artist in school, that's why. And I'm at least smart enough to know how to make my one and only talent pay."

"Oh, *that* makes me feel *so* much better," she says sarcastically. "Melanie"—her eyes find mine again from across the expanse of living room between us—"what's gotten into you? I taught you to be a lady, to have dignity. This isn't like you." She sinks into her rocking chair and looks up at me. "You aren't that kind of girl."

And then I can't help it, it just pops out. I laugh, sad and sardonic. "You know," I say swiping at more tears, "that is the second time someone has said that to me tonight." I turn and grab the wall behind me for support. My dad pops up and tries to help, but I pull my arm away. I don't want, or deserve, anyone's help. I know that, but just in case I haven't properly ruined everyone's night effectively enough, I turn to shoot a few more nails at my mother before I go. "I don't know what kind of girl I am, yet. But I know one thing's for sure, and that's that you don't know anything at all about me. And you know what else?" I say, driving a nail deep. "I *liked* doing those pictures! And I *liked* taking money for them. And why not? Sex sells, right Mom?"

I have gone too far, and I know it. My mother is quiet, and her eyes are damp. She doesn't say anything to me, so I turn and limp out of room and down the hall to the sanctuary of my room. Behind me, I can hear my dad say to my mother, his voice full of apology and padded, hopeful humor, "I really do like the articles."

Chapter 32

DEATH OF
A SALESWOMAN

t is just past four on Saturday afternoon, but my room is still very dark. It is dark because I am dark, inside and out. There is sun and warmth outside. I'm sure it's a lovely day but I wouldn't know. My lime-green checkered curtains are drawn tight against the Arizona sun and my soul is deep within the confines of my head, which is a swirling vortex of regret and wishful thinking.

I'm lying on my back, on my bed in the gloom, staring up at the ceiling. Our house, like lots of houses around here, has what my mother calls popcorn ceilings. It's some sort of bumpy stuff that helps absorb sound better than a regular smooth ceiling, I guess. I have been staring at it since I woke up this morning around ten, when my mom came in to check on me. I didn't talk to her. I haven't talked to anyone since last night. She asked me if I was hungry. I just pulled the covers up over my head.

My ankle doesn't hurt as much but it's still fat, and now it has purple and blue patches all over the outside of it, especially along the edges of my instep. It looks weird. I don't care. I don't care about anything. Or at least I'm trying not to. I'm hoping I can get out of school on Monday, because after all my foot is clearly a mess. What better, more obvious excuse is there?

I can't see him. I just can't. If I see Ethan Wilde I will die. No ifs, ands, buts or anything else about it. I'll drop dead right there in the hallway near the door to Mr. Ottopopy's advanced algebra class. It seems fitting that my life would end there, outside of a mathematics classroom. The epitaph on my tombstone would read: "HERE LIES MELANIE JOANNE CHAFFEE, A LOVELY YOUNG WOMAN CUT DOWN IN HER PRIME BY HUBRIS AND QUADRATIC EQUATIONS."

I'm deciding what outfit to wear for my funeral's open casket service when there is a knock at my door. "Nobody's home!" I call out to nobody. I pull in a deep breath, sigh loud and long, and wonder if my mom would let me wear my platforms if I were dead. I don't think she would. My ankle is proof that those things are dangerous.

There it is again, the knocking. "What?" I shout at the universe. The universe doesn't listen or care but the door opens and apparently my brother does. He steps in carefully, like the floor is covered in broken bottles.

"How're you doing?" he asks, sitting down at the foot of my bed.

"My life is over," I answer. "Other than that I'm great."

"Your life isn't over, spaz," he says, patting my ankle.

"Ow!" I squeal, all dramatic.

"Oh, sorry," Steven says, retracting his hand. "Still hurts a lot, huh?"

I nod but it's not my ankle that hurts the most right now. "Did Mom and Dad tell you? About my hobby?" I ask.

"Selling dirty pictures on the junior high school black market? Very nice," he says, grinning. "You're gonna be a legend in this town. High school kids are even talking about you."

"They are?" I ask, sitting up and putting my pillow in my lap.

"I was at the Circle K a little bit ago and ran into Howie James, Alison Kingston and the Belmont twins and all they could talk about was *my* crazy sister, the porn dealer." He laughs and pulls five Pixy Stix—two grape and three lemon-lime (my favorite)—out of his shirt pocket and hands them to me. "Here," he says, "I picked these up for you."

"You didn't have to do that," I tell him as I tear open a grape one and pour some of the sweet–sour powder onto my tongue. It tastes delicious. "Thank you, though," I say and stick out my very purple tongue.

"Nice. Now your tongue matches your ankle," Steven says, touching my foot gently. "You probably won't even have to go to school on Monday, lucky dog."

"I will if Mom has her way," I tell him.

"I don't know. That thing looks pretty bad." He examines my ankle more closely and whistles. "That's a lot of black and blue. I'm sorry that happened to you, sis," he says kindly.

"It's my own fault," I say, shrugging. It's quiet for a moment and I think he's about to say something else nice, and I'm hoping he doesn't because nice Steven is just weird. But then, in the distance, we hear something. A siren. No, wait, three or more sirens. Steven frowns and gets up and goes to the window. The sirens are getting louder and closer, so I slide off my bed and limp over to the window too.

"Did you set something on fire again?" I ask my brother.

"Ha ha, very funny," he deadpans.

As we watch, out in the street, two Kingman P.D. cruisers and three sheriffs' cars pull up in front of Nina's home.

Under my thighs, the brick of the front retaining wall is warm, almost hot. I'm thinking it feels nice. Then I'm thinking that's insane, and why would I care how nice the warm brick feels on my backside, when something terrible has happened. Nina's front door is open, and I feel invaded for her. Policemen and sheriff's deputies mill about and go in and out of Nina's home. From across the street I can see that there are dirty boot and shoeprints on the carpet in Nina's living room.

Steven is sitting next to me and I am so glad for it. We haven't said anything to each other for the entire twenty minutes we've been sitting here watching.

"Where's Nina?" I ask, finally.

"I don't know, Mel," he says, his voice low and solemn.

"I'm worried," I confess.

Steven nods and touches my hand. "It'll be okay," he tells me. But I don't believe him. There are cops everywhere and Nina is nowhere in sight. Something is very, very wrong.

We are quiet for a few more minutes, and then Steven turns and looks down the street, our street. "Oh, man," he says, and I follow his gaze to an ambulance rolling up the street. It is not speeding. Its lights are not flashing, and there are no more sirens.

"Oh no," Steven says, wiping a bead of sweat from under the bridge of his glasses, "they're not using their lights or sirens."

"What does that mean?" I ask, feeling five years old and lost. I look at my brother, who looks back at me and says nothing. His face tells me all I need—but don't want—to know. Nina is dead.

We are silent, there, sitting on the warm, lumpy brick wall watching. Two men dressed all in white step out of the ambulance and stroll to the back of the van, where they pull out a gurney. Absurdly, some small, unused part of my brain is wondering (while I watch the men steady the slim bed on its fold-out wheels) what linen company makes the narrow little fitted sheets that go over the gurney's skinny, shallow mattress? Is it Sears? Or maybe JCPenney's, where my mom gets all our bedsheets?

The men shove the gurney into Nina's front door and disappear. Do hospitals have to have gurney sheets made special for them? The sun is hot and hurts my ankle. It is throbbing. I want to cry but I don't. And if hospitals have to have their gurney sheets made special, do they have the cases for their tiny, gurney-sized pillows specially made, too? Oh, God, one of the men in white is backing out of the front door. He is holding something heavy, something that looks like the end of a gurney. I've never seen tiny pillowcases in Babbitt's, either. I wonder if my Aunt Marnie knows where to get them.

Nina is there, on the gurney, under a sheet. It is a regular sheet—a white one the same size as the one on my bed, but mine is lime green. This sheet floats around the sides of the gurney, making the person under it look like a sleeping ghost. They wheel the sheet-ghost on the gurney out of the front door, clunking the wheels down hard on her walkway, once, twice. "Don't hurt her," I tell the men in white. "Please don't hurt her."

They are wheeling her down the walkway when I get a glimpse, quick and sure, of a head of very red, short hair. The man in white who has to back his way all the way to the ambulance tugs on the sheet, covering her hair. Nina's

S. J. Coffey

hair. She is an anonymous, horizontal ghost again, but I know it's her, even if they don't.

"Why did they do that to her?" I ask, blaming everyone and no one. My face is hot, and my eyes are stinging. I squeeze my lids together and try to hold back what I cannot hide.

I hear my brother say, "I don't think they did anything, Mel." I don't open my eyes. I don't want to watch anymore. I don't want to see them put her in the van. I don't want to see them take her away. But it doesn't matter, I can hear them. The van's engine turns over and I hear the road under its wheels crunch as the van pulls away. And when I open my eyes, I am just in time to see it roll down the street, turn and vanish. The vision is—and I imagine will always be, for the rest of my life— viewed from behind the veil of tears that have collected in my eyes and are now slipping down my cheeks, one after the other.

"Do you think she did it?" I ask Steven. "Do you think she killed herself?"

"I don't know," he answers, giving me no answers.

"She wouldn't have killed herself, Steven. I knew her. She wouldn't have done that."

"Did you really know her, though, Mel? Did you? You only hung out with her a few times, right? How can you know anybody that quick?"

"I did know her," I protest as sobs threaten in the back of my throat. "At least I felt like I did." Steven scoots over and pulls me under his arm and—as if given permission by my brother's act of kindness toward his little sister—I break into choking, gasping sobs and turn my face to his musty, worn T-shirt.

"She was so familiar to me," I whisper between gulps of air. "It was like she knew me already. Like she knew what it's like to be me. Like she understood me."

"I understand you, sis," Steven says, holding me tight.

"No, you don't. Not like she does." I stop, realizing my error in tense. "Did," I correct, and weep. There are tears on my Disney *Aristocats* pajama bottoms now. I have been in my pajamas all day.

"Well," my brother says, "maybe I don't understand you *all* the time." He looks down at me and smiles. "And as for Ethan Wilde, he's a dork if he can't see how amazing you are. I'd like to see him run a successful publishing company from his bedroom." He laughs a little and squeezes me hard. I hear rocks being crushed and rearranged behind me. Someone is ruining Dad's yard again.

"Steven," my mother says as she steps up onto the wall, "your dad needs your help in the backyard."

He opens his mouth to object, but then his eyes commune with my mom's and he just nods and slips down off the wall. "Tell your father that dinner is in an hour," she calls after him as he trudges around the front wall and in the direction of the backyard.

Delicately, and with great care, my mother lowers herself onto the wall and sits down next to me. She brushes more dirt off her hands than is actually on them, then rests her eyes on me. They are brown and soft. "Are you okay?" she asks me. I nod, and she pulls a tissue from her pocket and hands it to me. I blow and wipe my nose while the same department of my brain that was concerned with gurney sheets now sets to work on the question of why mothers always seem to have tissues on hand.

"She was still in her nightgown," my mom says, now staring at Nina's house, where half a dozen cops and deputies still shuffle about, chatting. One of them has a cup of coffee and he's laughing. I recognize the cup. It is one of six I saw dangling from one of those wrought iron cup trees everyone has these days. The tree was on her kitchen counter. The cup is orange with tiny green frogs. It's a nice cup. It is Nina's cup and he is using it without asking. I want to kick him where Steven has always told me to kick boys who upset or hurt me.

"Where did they find her?" I ask. "Do you know?"

"Mmm hmm," my mom begins, still staring at the men on Nina's doorstep. "I spoke with Mavis's mom a few minutes ago. Her firm has connections in the Sheriff's Department."

"What happened to her?" I beg, "Please tell me."

"Well," she says, taking a deep breath, "they found her in her car. It was still running, and the garage door was jammed. They couldn't open it."

"What does that mean?" I ask, but I know the answer. Two years ago, after we'd first moved here, my pet hamster Beady Eyes got sick. Without any obvious cause, he had stopped eating and had quickly grown thin. His breathing was labored, and he never left the toilet paper bed he built in the corner of his cage. My dad explained to me that he was suffering and needed to be put down. I asked him if we would have to take him to the vet for that, but dad said that he could do it himself. I didn't watch the gruesome proceedings but from what Steven told me, my father had simply put Beady Eyes in one of the small, brown paper bags my mom uses for packing Steven's lunch every day, and then held it over the exhaust pipe of our idling Suburban.

"Is it like what Dad did to Beady Eyes?" I ask.

"Kind of," my mom explains. "But she did it to herself—at least that's what they're saying."

"Who says that?" I sniff.

"The men in the Sheriff's Department, I guess," she answers.

"Do you think she killed herself, Mom?" I ask as puddles form in my lower eyelids again.

My mother is quiet for a moment. We watch the uniformed men in Nina's yard laugh and elbow each other and walk in and out of Nina's front door.

"They got her carpet all dirty," I say quiet and low.

My mother sits up straighter and folds her hands in her lap, Sunday church style. "Nina wasn't wearing a speck of makeup when she passed, no jewelry either," she says, turning to me. Her eyes are on mine and she is telling me something, something big and important, without any words at all.

"But I've never seen Nina even step out and get her paper off her doorstep without a full face of makeup on, and eyelashes, too," I say, puzzled. "Why would she…" I've run out of words and reasons, so I look to my mom, but she's just sitting there, watching the men pack up their things and get into their cars.

But I'm not looking at them, I'm looking at her. My mother's eyes are so pretty and round, with lashes that flare out a little at the corners. There are soft crinkles around them now that weren't there last year, and the powdered skin in front of her ears is starting to pull down, as if it has become too heavy. And at her forehead, tiny colonies of silver hairs have begun to replace the brown ones that used to live there. Men use lots of words to describe women—

beautiful, gorgeous, sexy, ravishing. My mother is all of those things, I am sure, but I would never use those words to describe her. My mother is lovely, just *lovely*. I reach over and take one of her smooth, velvety hands and hold it in both of mine.

"I know one thing," she says, breaking the hot stillness of the afternoon, "Nina was not the kind of woman to willingly take her last breath without looking her best."

"Do you think they'll do an investigation, or an autopsy?" I ask.

My mother lets out a little, sardonic laugh and her voice is different when she speaks. It is harder and unlike any voice I have ever heard her use. "Now why in the world would they want to waste county money on something as silly as a dead hooker from Las Vegas?" She turns and looks at me and despite her little laugh there is no frivolity in her face. She looks dead serious and angry as hell. I am scared of her and in awe of her all at the same time. "It's an open and shut case, right?" she concludes.

"Was Nina really just a prostitute?" I ask, trying not to cry again. My mother's eyes look damp and shiny, but she doesn't cry.

"Maybe she was and maybe she wasn't," she says. "But no woman is all one thing, Melanie. Remember that. We all play lots of roles in our lives. It's how we survive."

"Would Nina have mattered more if she *was* just a real estate lady?" I ask.

"To the people in this town?" she says. "Probably. But she wasn't just a realtor or even a prostitute to you, was she?"

I shake my head and don't try to stop the tears this time. My mother pulls me close and rocks back and forth, back and forth.

"I guess I have some work to do," she says into my hair. "I need to get to know my own daughter a little better, don't I?"

"I'm sorry I embarrassed you, Mom."

"I'm sorry, too, honey," she whispers. "For so many things."

We sit in the quiet. The sun is sliding toward the hills and I can hear a woodpecker assaulting a barrel cactus somewhere. It taps, my mother rocks me and I cry for all I have lost and for what I expect she has lost, too. I feel her breathe against me and smell her perfume, flowery and light. Then she gives me another squeeze, and smiles. "Come on," she says, suddenly chipper, "let's go make those boys some dinner." I nod limply as she pulls herself up onto the wall and stands, offering me a hand. I let her pull me up and lead me across the gravel. My dad's going to have to rake the whole thing again tomorrow.

"Hey, Mom," I say, blotting my eyes with the exhausted tissue. "Do you love him? Dad, I mean?"

She stops in front of our door and looks right into me. "Of course I do. I love your father with all my heart. How could I not?" she asks, smiling and brushing the backs of her fingers along my cheek. "He gave me you." Then my mother turns and pushes the door open and holds a hand out to help me inside, but before I go in I turn and look one last time at the house that belonged to my friend.

Across the street, I notice something I hadn't been able to see before when all the men were in the way of Nina's living room window. Today was bright and sunny, and it still will be for at least another half an hour or so. But despite the warm sun of the day Nina's drapes are shut tight.

The way I see it, it doesn't matter if Nina had sex for money or not. Men profit from women and their bodies all the time, and often without our permission. *Good for Nina*, I think as I turn and follow my mom into our house. *She beat them to it.*

Chapter 33

CONSEQUENCES, TIME SERVED AND PENAL LABOR

Principal Naylor is nice. Usually, I like him, and he seems okay with me, too. He's got to be younger than my dad and he's cute in a beefy, cuddly way. And I like the way his dark brown eyes always look like they're smiling, even when his face isn't. He is looking at me now from behind his wire-rimmed glasses. He's not smiling but I know he wishes he could. His eyes leave mine and look to my right, where my mom sits next me. My dad is on my other side, and next to him sits Mrs. Magnussen, stubby legs and pink orthopedic loafers dangling an inch above the floor. Principal Naylor's eyes track over to her. Her mouth is open—it's always open—and she's about to say something, but Principal Naylor cuts her off. "Really, Patty," he says, adjusting in the creaky, ancient chair behind his desk, "you don't have to be here."

"Oh but I do, Principal Naylor! I do!" Mrs. Magnussen bubbles. "As president of the PTA it is my most solemn duty."

"Uh huh." Principal Naylor looks annoyed, the way my dad looks when my mother talks about dresses.

"Okay listen, Melanie," he says, turning to me, "this is pretty damned serious."

"Principal, please! Watch your language!" Mrs. Magnussen interrupts, scooting forward just enough to let her tiny feet make contact with the floor. Mr. Naylor doesn't answer her, he just keeps looking at me. Behind him, through his office window, I can see the telltale rust-colored cloud of a dust storm approaching from the west.

"If you were an adult"—the principal frowns at me—"you could do real prison time for distributing pornography."

"But she's a thirteen-year-old girl!" my dad says, defending me. My mother is quiet. She hasn't said anything since I was called to the principal's office after lunch period and I found her sitting here with my dad and Mrs. Magnussen.

My mom didn't make me go to school yesterday, or the day before, because my ankle still looked so gross, but this morning she said I had to "face the music," and wrapped my ankle in an elastic bandage, handed me lunch money and told me to go get in the car. She drove me to school, and as we pulled out of our driveway and passed Nina's house, she reached over and gave my hand a gentle pat with hers. I did not cry, but I wanted to.

Almost nobody has talked to me the whole morning, and my teachers have avoided eye contact with me entirely. Mr. Greely, my science teacher, was the one exception. When I walked in and sat down at my lab table, he had handed me back my test on the nervous system from last week and said, "Good job, Ms. Chaffee. Best score in the class. You're a gifted anatomist."

Mavis, having somewhere more entertaining to be, was not there. But Dennis had answered Mr. Greely's compliment with a hearty, "I'll say!" from the back of the room. Then he and Sean and Joe had clapped in solidarity for a solid fifteen seconds, before Mr. Greely told them to settle down, and that the three of them had the lowest test scores, and maybe they could learn a thing or two from me. As I looked down at the giant red A emblazoned on my paper, I thought that those three had learned too much from me already.

"I'm only going to suspend Melanie for a week," Principal Naylor is saying to my father, who puts an arm around me and squeezes my shoulder.

"That seems fair," my dad says. But, predictably, Mrs. Magnussen doesn't agree.

"Suspended!" she barks out like a Pekingese puppy after the mailman. "Why, Miss Chaffee should be expelled!" she cries, popping out of her chair and stomping one of her miniature feet soundlessly on the carpeted office floor. "This is an outrage!" she sputters on. "Principal Naylor, I really must object!"

On the other side of me, in her chair, my mother finally speaks. "Sit down, Patty," she says, sounding tired.

"I will not!" Mrs. Magnussen spits back and, chubby fists on chubby hips, she scowls at Mr. Naylor. "Principal?" Her voice goes up at the end of Mr. Naylor's title but she's not asking him anything, she's telling. "You have to do something!" she rants. "Someone has to stand up for our Lord, for morality, for decency!" She punctuates that last word with a fat finger jabbed heavenward at the florescent light panels above her as her fluffy bosom heaves in distress.

From the direction of my mother, I hear the soft zip of nylon over nylon as she uncrosses her suntan-pantyhosed legs. "Patty," she says, slow and vibrating, "sit *down*."

I lean forward in my chair between my parents and look over at Mrs. Magnussen and then back over at my mother, who is transferring her handbag from her lap—where it has been sitting, coveted, beneath her hands—to the floor at the side of her chair.

Principal Naylor leans back in his noisy desk chair and says nothing as my mother stands. She takes a breath and smooths the front of her navy poly-blend skirt imprinted with tiny red anchors, then turns hard aport and drops her eyes on her diminutive opponent.

"Mrs. Magnussen," she begins, squaring her beige, cashmere shoulders, "I am a lady. I learned how to be one from my mother. She was not the kindest woman, but she was always a lady—genteel, well-mannered, a wizard with a Jell-O mold. But dammit, she never put up with smug, self-righteous…bitches like you!"

Mrs. Magnussen's fuchsia lips open and close twice before expelling a response. "Why! Mrs. Chaffee! I am *appalled!*"

"It's Shirley, Patty," my mom answers, collecting herself a little, "and I'm pretty appalled myself. I'm appalled that you're even in this room right now. You don't belong here. This is a *public* school and as stated in the United States Constitution, it is part of the *state*, and therefore it is *separate* from the church, any church, including the United Methodist Church of Kingman, Arizona, where *we* will no longer be attending services."

My mother pauses for breath and I seize an opportunity for important clarification. "What about the choir?" I ask, quietly.

"Especially the choir!" my mom spouts, winding up again as Patty Magnussen just looks up, her pink mouth a perfect O.

"Patty Magnussen," my Mom says, bringing it home, "you are *not* a teacher. You are *not* a secretary. Hell, you're not even a janitor in this school. You're a choir director and I have it on good authority that your perfect little nephew Benjamin bought eight drawings from my daughter, eight!"

"Actually," I correct, "it was nine."

"Nine?" she asks me, eyebrows up, before turning her attention back to Mrs. Magnussen. "Why are you still here!"

"Well!" the Reverend Magnussen begins solidly, before coming up empty and turning to Mr. Naylor. "Principal?" she implores, neutered and small.

"You should go, Patty," the principal says, reengaging.

Patty Magnussen huffs and with great difficulty bends over and gathers her purse and her bible, then waddles to the door behind us. She turns and points accusingly at Mr. Naylor as she opens the door. "I would have thought better of you, Principal," she says, stepping through the doorway, "you're a *Christian* man!"

Mr. Naylor drops forward in his desk chair and rests his interlaced hands on the blotter. "Yeah, that's what my wife tells me," he answers, giving my dad a wink. I can't help but giggle as the tiny pink menace huffs out the door, slamming it soundly behind her.

Next to me, my mother slowly sits back down. Principal Naylor smiles at me and smacks his palms onto the desk. "Okay, Melanie," he says with finality, "finish out the day today, and then I don't want to see you again until a week from now, okay?"

"Okay," I say, relieved too soon.

"And while you're out," he says, dropping the hammer, "I want you to write an essay."

"What?" I protest.

"Melanie JoAnne," my mom says, her hand on my knee.

"No less than five pages," Mr. Naylor continues, "outlining your business model and how it could be adapted to a more…*legal* format, maybe poetry or something."

"Never gonna sell," I state truthfully.

"Melanie!" my mom nearly shouts, then she stands again and takes my arm and pulls me up. "Come along, dear," she says flatly.

"She'll have the paper to you by next Wednesday, Principal Naylor," she tells the man who just ruined my life for the next week.

"I have no doubt," he says, smiling and rising to shake my dad's hand as he follows me and my mom out.

"Oh," he adds suddenly, "and Melanie?"

"Yeah?"

"Single spaced."

"Gah!" I exclaim. "Seriously?"

My mom is nearly pushing me through the door but I'm not having it. Today has been hard enough already, and this guy is making it way worse.

"Fine!" I concede. "But someday, if you ever need a job, don't come crawling to me, buddy. I will NOT be hiring you!"

As my mom and dad sandwich and escort me out of the office and into the hall, I'm pretty sure—before the door shuts behind me—that I can hear Principal Naylor laughing and laughing and laughing. Jerk. He's not that cute.

Chapter 34

DUST STORM SURVIVAL AND PENGUIN DANCING IN THE GRAVEL ZEN GARDEN

The wind still pushes at the windshield and the air around them is still rust red, but it is clearing. Shirley's hands rest on her handbag as she looks out the window of the Suburban and Dan drives up the street to their house. A pair of aluminum chairs with yellow webbing bounce down the street toward them.

"There go the Hudsons' lawn chairs again," says Dan, deftly dodging chair number two. "We get these damned dust storms every other month," he continues, "you'd think they'd remember to take their outdoor furniture in. It's pretty hard to miss the red cloud ten miles out."

"I hate this car," Shirley says, still staring out her window.

"What?" Dan's confused.

"The Suburban," Shirley clarifies. "I hate it."

"You hate it?" Dan asks. "Why? I mean, we've had it for over three years and you're just now telling me you hate it?"

"You said you wanted to get a truck. This isn't a truck, it's a shipping container on wheels. I don't like it." Because they are pulling into their driveway, Shirley takes her sunglasses off and slips them into her purse. Dan cuts the engine and the two sit in silence while the wind winds down outside. Shirley leans forward and looks up at the sky. Through the gritty air, the sun is just visible again. "Oh good," she says, "it's almost over."

Dan's more interested in the lifeless, black vinyl cover to their gas BBQ grill that's now hanging, just out of reach, from the garage roof. "Aw, hell," he says, "now I have to drag out the damned ladder and get that thing again."

"See," Shirley points out, "we didn't know this dust storm was coming any sooner than the Hudsons did. Storms happen and sometimes you don't have time to prepare. That's just the way it is."

Over in the driver's seat, Dan watches her. "You were pretty impressive in there today, Sweet," he says, smiling and using a pet name for Shirley he never uses anymore. "Sure gave ol' Mrs. Magnussen the what for." He chuckles and pulls his keys from the ignition.

"Just sticking up for my own daughter," she says. "For once."

"What are you talking about?" Dan asks. "You always defend the kids. You're a great mom."

Shirley doesn't answer, instead she opens her door and steps out into the waning dust storm.

"Shirley," Dan starts, but then opens his own door when she slams hers shut. "Shirley!" he calls out again as he hurries around the massive front end of the Suburban to his wife, who's standing on the walkway in front of the gravel yard, staring up at the sky.

"Look," she says, sensing him by her side. She points up at the sky where swirling dust alternately obscures and then reveals patches of blue sky and dark, rolling rain clouds. "Rain is coming."

Dan nods, and then says something Shirley does not expect, and doesn't even know quite yet that she wants. "I think you should go back to school."

Shirley pulls her eyes from the sky and looks over at her husband, who looks different in this strange, orange and blue light. "You do?" she asks.

"Yeah, I do," Dan says, smiling. "The kids are older and doing fine."

"Fine?" Shirley interrupts, laughing. "Were you in the same meeting in the principal's office that I was just in?"

Dan begins laughing, too. His overgrown brown hair whips around his face in the wind and Shirley reminds herself to make him an appointment at the barbershop tomorrow. "Our girl is something, isn't she?" he says, stepping closer to his wife.

"That she is, I guess," Shirley answers, smiling.

"She'll be okay, honey," Dan says, pulling her into his arms. "We'll all be okay. You should finish. You've only got, what, two more years left?"

"About that, I think," Shirley says, feeling Dan's still-strong arms under her hands.

"Then go back. The kids and I will be alright. I'll help out more, I promise. UNLV's got a decent law program, I think. You could commute on your class days, maybe stay overnight in Vegas when you have exams and stuff."

"So theoretically, then, *you're* going to cook the kids' dinner, do the laundry, go to PTA meetings and everything? You saw what Patty Magnussen is like in there. She's awful!" Shirley can't help herself and bursts into giggles.

"Hey," Dan insists, "I can handle Patty Magnussen."

"No one can 'handle' Patty Magnussen," Shirley contradicts, pulling herself away and heading down the walkway toward the front door.

"Okay," Dan concedes, following her, "so maybe I won't 'handle' her, but I can certainly deal with her, and the school principals and the teachers and coaches and stuff, too." He catches up with his wife and takes her hand near the front door. "I'll do whatever it takes, Shirley, I promise." His eyes settle on hers.

"Really?" Shirley says. She knows he's telling the truth. She knows he'll do what he says he'll do. Daniel Chaffee's word has always been his bond. There is no man in the world more loyal and honest than her husband. That is why she married him. It is also sometimes why she wishes she hadn't. He is so good, so steadfast, and when she's feeling low and wishing for a different life, he seems so boring. But he isn't boring, she knows that. Instead, she realizes, looking up into the hazel eyes she fell in love with all the way back in college, the same eyes her daughter inherited, it is her life that has become boring.

Then, wordlessly, Dan does the strangest thing. He steps back a little and drops a hand to her waist. He takes her hands, one and then the other, and puts them around his neck.

"What's this?" Shirley asks.

"Something your daughter taught me," he answers. Then he begins to turn, penguin-style, like Melanie showed him more than a week ago, when Nina across the street was alive and he hadn't yet known what his clever little girl was up to.

"Are we *dancing*?" Shirley asks, pulling back a little and eyeing Dan playfully. "Since when do you dance?"

Dan begins to hum a song Shirley hasn't heard in years. It is a respectable rendition of The Percy Faith Orchestra's "Theme from A Summer Place".

"We went to this movie on our first date," Shirley says, feeling Dan nod against her neck. "You hated this movie."

Dan pulls back and smiles at her. "Yeah, but I liked you," he says, looking at his wife. The sky has grown dark over them and far away, thunder complains. But Dan pulls his wife close, and resumes humming and slowly turning her as huge Arizona raindrops begin to fall, leaving dark, nickel-sized dots on the dusty walkway and gravel yard.

Shirley lets herself settle into the arms of this man she's known longer than anyone except her parents and her sisters. Her hair is getting wet and her husband's feet are a little unsteady as they dance, but the air around them feels electric and smells of damp earth and peppery, crisp creosote leaves. Shirley turns her face into her husband's neck and adds his familiar scent to Arizona's petrichor, and for a moment there is nothing else, until her heel slips off the walkway and she steps into the gravel.

"Are you okay?" Dan asks, holding her up in his arms.

"I'm fine," Shirley answers, steadying herself and smiling up at him. "But oh no," she teases, "look what I did!" She steps back and takes his hands in hers and pulls him into the tiny rocks, laughing and leaving divot after destructive divot.

"Oh, yeah, great, thanks," Dan laughs.

Unsuccessfully suppressing a fit of giggles, Shirley reaches down and scoops up a handful of gravel and throws it at him. "Hey!" he calls out over the growing din of the rain and thunder. "You throw like a girl!"

Shirley, her hair a mess of wet, permed ringlets, takes off running across the rocks, stopping only to grab more gravel to pelt her husband with. For a moment, Dan just stands there laughing and dodging rocks from his precious yard, but then he takes off after her, carelessly and happily tromping through the stones until he catches her, giggling and panting.

"I love you, Shirley Chaffee," he says, holding her tight in the middle of the yard, in the middle of the relentless desert rain.

"I love you," Shirley answers as Dan smudges water from her cheek with his thumbs.

"I'll buy you a new car," he tells her as lightning in the sky behind her haloes her head. "Anything you want under two thousand dollars."

"And gets good gas mileage," Shirley adds, laughing too.

"Yes," her husband agrees, "with good gas mileage." Then, holding her face, he kisses her hard. And for the first time in a long time, Shirley Chaffee thinks about the future, her future, and smiles against her husband's warm, familiar lips.

Chapter 35

ENEMIES, FRIENDS AND MENSTRUAL MEDITATIONS IN THE BOYS' ROOM

I think my stupid period is starting. I was sitting there in health class, which is my last class of the day thank goodness, and I felt it—the weird twinge just above my pubic bone that feels like gas but definitely is not gas. And like I've done every month since last July, I kept ignoring the feeling and telling myself it was just my Cheerios duking it out with the disturbing chicken and noodles concoction I inflicted on my lower GI in the lunchroom today.

I'm wondering if Leslie, who is fidgeting in the desk next to mine and who also ate the same dangerous poultry-related mess I ate, is having similar tummy troubles, so I pass her a note that reads: "Do you have the farts? My stomach is going nuts and I don't know if it's from what we had for lunch or if my period is just starting."

If I had been smart, and not in pain, I would have remembered not to use the word "fart" in the note because Leslie, who spends the bulk of her time with her brothers, finds all things flatulent, hilarious. So only seconds after she reads my note, she gets an unfortunate case of the giggles, causing Ms. Fitzmaker—who has only just begun to expound on the mind-blowing, hydraulic machinery of the penis—to swivel her head, and home in on my buddy like a hungry barn owl on a mouse.

"Leslie?" she asks, adjusting the whistle around her neck and strolling down the aisle between Leslie and me. "Do you have something you'd like to share with the class?"

"No," Leslie stammers, still suppressing giggles. Leslie is beyond me. How could any girl find a note about farts and period cramps more fascinating, not to mention funnier, than a lecture about boy parts? Ms. Fitzmaker stops in front of Leslie and puts her hand out. Leslie hands the note over. Traitor.

I was under the incorrect assumption that—after being suspended and given a very unwanted (and I think unwarranted) essay assignment—today could not get any worse. But, given the events of the past week, I should have known better.

Leslie looks over at me and mouths the words, "I'm sorry" as our P.E. teacher and current professor in the embarrassing arts reads the note to herself, then smiles and hands it back to me. "Wait a few minutes then ask to go to the restroom, Melanie," she whispers. "I'll give you the hall pass." She turns and walks back up to the front of the classroom and a few minutes later, as instructed, I request the hall pass and hurry out of the room.

The halls are empty and the laminated piece of cardstock with the words HALL PASS written on it in black marker feels sticky in my hand. I try not to wonder why, as I round the corner at the end of the hall near the restrooms and run into Stephanie Harris.

"Well, looky here!" she exclaims, smiling at me in a way that makes me very uncomfortable. "If it isn't lil Melanie the weirdo. Good thing I'm the hall monitor today, or I would have missed seein' you."

I step to the left and try to go around her, but she moves and blocks my way. "Wanna know something?" she asks.

"Not really," I answer, "but I bet you're going to tell me, anyway."

"Mavis is in my English class and guess what? She wasn't there today."

"Well," I tell her, feeling my lower belly begin to cramp in earnest, "Mavis kind of makes her own schedule."

Stephanie lets me walk past her but follows. "Why are you even bugging me?" I ask her, as she catches up and ambles along beside me as if we're the best of friends. "You got what you wanted, Stephanie. Ethan won't have anything to do with me, now."

"I know"—she mock pouts—"such a shame. Guess he didn't wanna be seen with a slutty *pornographer.*"

"They're just pictures," I say, stopping in front of the restrooms. "Why should you care?" And then I do something I would never have done a month ago. I give Stephanie Harris the snotty once over. I cross my arms, stick out a foot and run my eyes over her, Farrah-flip to platform sandals. "Besides," I say, sticking my chin out just a little, "from the looks of you, I'd say there's a strong possibility that a career in my fine industry is in your very near future."

Stephanie smiles and looks away, the way people, girls and boys, do when they've been burned and need a second to formulate a comeback.

"You know," she begins, "I hear you walk home every day all by yourself."

This is true. I do walk home most days. I could take the bus, but as long as the weather isn't too bad, I like to walk and think. But today, because of my ankle, I'll be taking the bus.

"Is our chat over?" I ask her. "Because I've really got to pee."

"Well, isn't that just a coincidence. I was about to go powder my nose myself. I'll come with you," she says, walking over to the girls' room and pulling open the door. "After you," the spider says to the fly.

I cannot be alone with her, not now. My stomach is killing me, and I'll be lucky if I haven't ruined my Wednesday underwear already. I need to be alone.

"You know, Steph," I announce, looking over at the boys' room door to the left, "I don't know if it's the overpowering stench of urine or the dozens of wads of toilet paper stuck to the ceiling, but lately I find I'm more comfortable in the boys' room." I walk over and open the boys' restroom door. "Care to join me?" I ask. I'm gambling on the premise that, despite her very dirty dealings in all things junior high school, Stephanie Harris would not be caught dead coming out of the boys' bathroom. It is a perilous wager, for sure, but I'm fresh out of options.

"Fine," she says, flipping her hair and confirming my suspicions about her vanity, "we can finish this later. Maybe, I'll just walk you home in a bit. Then we can have a *real* girl chat." She gives me another sickening smile and slides into the girls' room, the heavy door closing behind her.

The inside of the boys' bathroom isn't as bad as I'd imagined. It is smelly, but there's less garbage on the floor than in the girls' room, which is encouraging. I look under all the stall doors and, finding them all gratefully empty I zip into one and check out the lady situation.

It has started. My Wednesday undies are ruined, and I am without anything, not even a panty liner. Employing an emergency tactic my mother taught me, I carefully roll toilet paper into a makeshift pad, then stand and tuck it into my underwear, feeling especially grateful that I wore dark blue jeans to school today. Had I been wearing my snow-white Dittos as I'd planned, I would be in even more trouble. For once, I am glad my mom hasn't done the laundry yet.

I step out of the stall and wash my hands in front of the mirror. I can take the bus home today to avoid Stephanie, and I can take it home tomorrow, and the day after that, and the week after that, but she will always be waiting, ready to pounce. I stare up into my own eyes and wonder what Nina would tell me to do.

Steven was right, I didn't know her very well, but I knew her enough to know that she would never let a woman like Stephanie push her around. I reach into my right front pocket and pull out the lip gloss she gave me. I unscrew the cap and slide some on my lips. I try to look tough. I look ridiculous. My training bra is showing through my worn-out favorite T-shirt (with three cute bunnies on it), and I want to cry but I won't, so I stuff the gloss back into my pocket just as the bathroom door opens and Alan Bomart lumbers in. As always, he is smiling.

"Hey, Melanie. What're you doing in here? The girls' toilets all clogged up again?"

"Something like that," I say, trying not to look upset. But Alan, in addition to his ever-present good nature, is very intuitive.

"Are you okay?" he asks, leaning against the sink next to me.

"I'm not sure," I say, trying to laugh. "I think Stephanie Harris intends to rearrange my face after school today."

"Oh, dear," he says, frowning. "Maybe you should take the bus with me."

"I can't," I tell him, only just now deciding what I have to do. "I haven't seen Nadine Melnick today. Stephanie will be alone, so this is probably the best time to stand up to her. Besides, I'm already suspended for a week, so I'll have time to heal before I have to come back to school." I laugh for real this time because, although terrifying and true, this last fact is funny.

"Are you sure, Mel?" Alan asks, eyes wide. "She has really long fingernails, sharp too."

"I'm sure," I tell him, and I am.

"I'll walk home with you," Alan says, bouncing both of his chins resolutely for emphasis. "My house isn't far from yours."

I should tell him no, but I don't. "Are you sure you want to put yourself on Stephanie Harris's radar? She's not an enemy you want to have, trust me."

Alan just smiles sadly. "What's another one to someone like me?"

"Alright," I say, "you can be my second, then."

At the old-timey dueling reference, Alan bounces again and rubs his round hands together. "Excellent, m'lady," he says, bowing gallantly. "I am at your service."

I smile and laugh. "I'll see you after school then, by the field, okay?"

Alan nods eagerly. "Of course."

"I better go," I say, opening the restroom door. "Thank you, Alan." But before I leave I turn to him one more time. "Oh, hey, Sir Galahad?"

"Yes, m'lady?" Alan smiles back.

"Bring bandages."

Chapter 36

DUELING FOR HONOR IN THE MIDDLE SCHOOL CLOVER PATCH

As promised, my loyal second, Alan, is waiting when I walk out of the rear doors of the main school building. Since I'm suspended for the next week, I've got a stack of books, topped with my Jane Austen, in my arms. It has been raining and the clean smell of wet dirt and creosote hits my nose and clears my head.

"Maybe she won't show," Alan offers.

"I don't know," I say, limping slightly on my sore, but wrapped and functional ankle, "I kind of hope she does."

"You do?" Alan asks, as we cross the track and step onto the grassy field. "You *want* to fight that crazy girl?"

I don't *want* to do anything involving Stephane Harris, right now, or ever. What I *want* to do is ride the bus home in a safe (if not loud and stinky) environment, and eat cheese crackers in front of an episode of *The Brady Bunch* I've seen five times already.

"I don't want to fight her or anybody else," I explain to Alan as we walk. "But I don't want to spend the rest of the year living in fear of her and her goon, Nadine, either." The charming and formidable Ms. Melnick's name is still on my lips when there she is, not fifty yards ahead of us, a teenaged monolith alone in the middle of the field.

"Oh God, what's that?" Alan says, stopping.

"That," I say, breathing deep and wishing to be teleported elsewhere, "is Nadine Melnick."

"I heard she shot her own dog," Alan says, low and reverent.

"That's the rumor," I answer. My eyes have locked with Nadine's and she begins to slowly walk toward us.

"What should we do?" Alan's asks.

"You should go get on the bus, Alan," I say, turning to him. "This isn't your fight and there's no use in both of us getting creamed. I didn't know she would be here too."

"I could go get help," he suggests.

"No," I tell him for his own good. "Most of the teachers have left already, but if you hurry you can still make the bus."

"No, I'm staying with you." Alan is resolute, so I nod and watch as Nadine gets closer and closer. She is within ten feet of us when I smell Love's Baby Soft cologne and Aquanet hairspray, and I hear that voice, slow and syrupy, behind me.

"Pretty day isn't it?" Stephanie asks, as she sidles up next to me.

I look over at Alan and whisper. "Okay," I instruct, feeling my stomach flip, "now you can go get help."

Alan's chins jiggle and he turns and runs back toward the school.

"Oh, now," Stephanie condescends, "where's your little fat friend goin'?"

"He's not fat," I tell her. "And his name is Alan."

"Oh, yeah," Stephanie says, tapping her chin with a pointy, pink nail, "Fat Alan, that's what they call him."

I would defend my friend's honor more, here, but Nadine is now directly in front of me.

"Hey, Nadine!" I say, cheerful in the face of destruction. "So, what's it going to be today? A broken jaw? Or maybe you could just make my left eye match my right one. I'm suspended all next week so the sky's the limit, injury wise." I manage to get out an authentic, if not terrified laugh before Stephanie cuts me off.

"Ugh!" she groans, and pulls me around to face her. "Shut up! What did Ethan ever see in a little chatterbox whore like you?" She steps back fifteen feet or so and addresses her henchwoman. "Nadine, do your job."

But Nadine's not moving. She just stands there staring at me.

"Go on, you big dummy!" Stephanie commands.

Seeming to obey her master, Nadine steps closer to me and takes my arm.

"Hey, so," I negotiate, "it would be great if you didn't actually kill me. My brother's birthday is next week and I kind of need to be there."

I've now resigned myself to injury and possible hospitalization. Earlier, I thought that maybe with the right conditions I might be able to best Stephanie in an actual fight. I've fought with my brother enough times to know how to wound another human, and Stephanie—while a perfect specimen of current female attractiveness standards—is pretty wimpy. Her arms are about as big around as cardboard toilet paper rolls. And I know she doesn't have any brothers, which makes her a lightweight in my book. But Nadine Melnick is another story entirely. She's so scary she even has her own mythical backstory.

Nadine stands, oak-tree sturdy, behind me with one

hand on my left arm and a thick forearm across my training bra. I can feel her chest rise and drop against my back and her breath smells like spearmint gum.

"She wasn't in Georgia all summer, like she told everyone," Nadine whispers in my ear. "She was down in Phoenix. Her mom got her a nose job for her birthday."

Then it dawns on me. I've noticed Stephanie has looked especially perfect this year.

"That was only two months ago," Nadine continues as I watch Stephanie cross her arms and pop a hip, obviously impatient to watch me get killed.

"Um," I ask Nadine, whispering and feeling absurd, "do you always update your victims on your friend's most recent cosmetic surgeries?"

"Nadine!" Stephanie calls out. "Stop talking and just do it already!"

Nadine ignores her boss and, thankfully, elaborates. "Stephanie's nose hasn't *healed* all the way, yet." After this cryptic statement, I feel Nadine's python-like arm loosen, and as she steps back, she says, this time loud enough for Stephanie to hear, "And she is *not* my friend."

"Nadine!" Stephanie screeches. "What in the hell are you talking about?"

It seems I've found myself in the middle of some sort of junior high school girl mutiny. I turn around and look at Nadine, who taps a stubby, almost nail-less forefinger on her nose and nods as she looks at Stephanie.

Now I'm not always the sparkliest chip in the mirror ball, but I do know how to dance when the music starts, and just now, looking at Nadine, I suddenly know exactly what tune she's playing.

Huffing and puffing, Alan Bomart runs. Generally, he does not run. His grandmother sees to that. She says he has asthma but he's not sure she's correct. He's read all the books on the subject and his symptoms just don't match up. Still, it is nice to be able to skip running laps during gym class and read books. Alan likes books.

Far on the edge of the field, Alan spots three boys rolling in the grass, the regular sized one and the chubbier one are mercilessly tickling the skinny one.

"Call uncle!" the chubby one yells.

Alan recognizes them. He has seen his new friend, the Lady Melanie, conversing with them near her locker in the hall a few times. They are not the crusaders, or even the cavalry, that his lady requires, but they will have to do. So Sir Alan the Stout runs, jiggling and reluctant, to enlist his new support troops.

———◇———

"Do you think you get to be my friend for *nothing*!" Stephanie screams at the silent, stoic Nadine.

I set my books down on the grass. The way is clear, and I know what to do. I just really don't want to do it. I can send my brother howling to his room with a good four finger scratch, but I've never fought anyone before. I really don't know how.

"Nadine!" Stephanie's hands are on her boney hips and she's glowering at her underling in a way that would wither most girls, but Nadine's not budging. She just continues to stand behind me, arms crossed and huge, sneakered feet planted.

"Nadine," Stephanie pronounces, exhaling an audible huff, "I hope you know that *we* are no longer friends."

"Not a problem," Nadine answers, and I wonder what universe I just dropped into.

———◇———

"Maybe I'll go out for volleyball this year," Leslie announces, sitting next to Anna on the bus.

"Aren't you already in every sport this school offers?" Anna says, not looking up from her copy of Tolstoy's *Crime and Punishment*. "What're you trying to do, win the decathlon or something?"

"They don't have a decathlon for girls." Leslie frowns. "Just a pentathlon."

"Really?" Anna says, looking up. "That seems stupid."

A grimy hand smacks the window next to Leslie, who squeals and jumps.

"Oh, for chrissakes," Anna says, leaning over Leslie and looking out the smudged window. "What do those idiots want, now?" She pushes the window down and addresses the stooges, plus one, standing outside in the parking lot.

"What do you clowns want?" Anna calls out.

"It's Mel!" Sean shouts up to the girls. "Come quick!"

Anna stands. "Come on, goofy!" she says, and grabs Leslie's sleeve and pulls.

———◇———

Nadine behind me, and Stephanie in front of me, I give negotiations one last ditch effort.

"You know, Steph, I'm still cool with skipping the blood and beating thing if you are. I mean, we can just agree to disagree, right?" It is a lame argument, I know, but now, even though Nadine seems to have inexplicably switched teams, I'm suddenly gripped with fear. I am afraid of Stephanie Harris. She hates me, and violence fueled by hate tends to result in blood, and in this case, specifically my blood. Now, in the moment, I do not want to do this.

"You'd like that wouldn't you?" Stephanie is walking towards me. I want to run, now, immediately.

"Actually," I say, trying to laugh and sound casual, "that would be great."

Then, as if she flew, Stephanie is close, only inches from my face. "Oh, I bet you'd just *love* to run away, wouldn't you?" She is so close I can see the thick, peachy concealer under her eyes and on the blemishes on her cheeks and chin. There are way more of them than I thought she had, and they are artfully covered. If she weren't about to kill me, I would ask Stephanie Harris for makeup tips.

"I can let you go, you know," Stephanie says, her eyes on mine and her stale breath my breath. "That would probably be the best thing, wouldn't it?" she asks, I assume, hypothetically. "Then we could just leave each other alone and you could run off with your loser friends and that *nigger* girl, Mavis."

Until those words, *that* word, left Stephanie's perfect, glossed lips, I would have been grateful to run away, to go home and hide for the next seven days. But things are different now.

"Take that back," I order.

"I could," Stephanie says, then she shoves me, hard. Her hands hit my shoulders like swinging two-by-fours and I'm nearly knocked off my feet. "But I won't," she concludes, poking a fingernail into my chest. "I"—poke—"don't"—poke—"have to."

I am mad, madder than I've ever been, even at Steven. I shove Stephanie back as hard as I can, and she stumbles, several times, almost falling off her shoes. Her face is different, now. She is shocked and so am I.

"Well," she says, laughing, "look at the little weirdo."

"Yeah," I say, stepping up to her, "look at me." I swing once. She dodges easily, still laughing. Twice. She's laughing harder. But the third swing, like a cliché punch, lands soundly on Stephanie's perfect square jaw and she's not laughing anymore, but I am in serious pain. "Oh, my God!" I exclaim, pulling my throbbing hand protectively to my chest. "Your face is so *hard!*" I am hoping her face hurts as much as my hand when, surprisingly, Stephanie slams all one hundred pounds of herself into my upper body, instantly dropping me to the ground.

———⬦———

I can see them all above me while she lands one punch after another. My arms are up and I'm trying to protect my head, but I can see kids, a lot of kids, gathering in an unorganized circle around the two of us while Stephanie destroys me. The grass is wet and cold from the rain earlier and the back of my bunny shirt is soaked. I'm going to die here, on the athletic field of Kingman Junior High School. Irony definitely has it in for me.

———⬦———

Alan gasps when he spots the pack of kids in the middle of the field where he left Melanie a minute ago. There must be at least thirty of them. They are cheering and yelling, and he can't see her anywhere. He turns to the others and addresses Anna, who's followed by Leslie, Sean Mendoza,

Joe Thomasson and Dennis Franklin (a kid who has tried to extort test answers from Alan in their American history class, more than once).

"Melanie must be in real trouble," he tells Anna.

"You guys go ahead," Anna says, then she peels off to the left. "I'll try to find Mavis."

When they reach the crowd, Alan, Leslie and the stooges push through the kids and into the center of the ring, where they find Stephanie and Melanie rolling around on the grass. Melanie's only visible cheek is smeared in blood, her blood, and Leslie gasps, "Hurry, Mavis."

———————◇———————

No one has seen Mavis Jackson all day, but Anna knows where to find her. Breathing hard, she runs up to the bleachers on the far edge of the field and yells, as loud as she can, "Mavis!" It is silent except for the distant hollering and whistling coming from the fight in the center of the field, but Anna smiles with relief when she sees movement beneath the metal slats. "Hurry!" she calls out again as Mavis, holding a bleacher for balance, stoops and steps out from under the bleachers.

"What is it?" Mavis asks as a handsome boy Anna has never seen before follows her out from underneath the bleachers.

Anna wants to ask who the young man is but there isn't time. "This way," she says, turning and running back toward the crowd. "Mel's in trouble!"

Leaving the young man fixing his hair and straightening his clothes behind her, Mavis takes off after Anna. "How did you know where to find me?" Mavis asks as they run.

"Seriously?" Anna replies, breathless, as Mavis laughs and follows her.

Stephanie is on top of me. I would not have thought she would feel so heavy, but I am immobilized by her weight. I push her away enough to punch her in the side of her left breast, but it does not feel like human tissue and sort of bounces back. I am just realizing that Stephanie Harris stuffs when she lands a solid punch to my left ribs. It is agony and for a second I can't breathe, but then Stephanie laughs and takes a moment to gloat, so I seize the opportunity and ram my knee into her gut. She lets out a grunting noise and I skootch out from under her and stand. To my left, I can see Alan and Leslie and the stooges watching.

"Get her, Mel!" I hear Dennis call out above the cacophony of cheering and yelling. *Wonderful*, I think, wobbling. *Now I have an audience.*

"Out of the way!" Anna yells, as she pushes through the pack of adolescents between her and the friend she would kill for. "Move it!"

"Nice work, bookworm," Mavis calls out from behind her as she follows. "You're a feisty one!"

"Come on," Anna says, reaching back and grabbing Mavis's arm, "we have to help her!" She spots Leslie and the boys ahead of her and pushes up to the front of the interior circle of the crowd.

Leslie throws her arms around Mavis. "Thank God!" she squeals. "You have to help her!" She turns and looks into the ten-foot grass arena where Melanie stands, unsteady, as Stephanie Harris pushes herself up from the ground, holding her belly. The left side of Melanie's face is bloody, and her lip is split, but Stephanie doesn't look great either. An ugly bruise is forming on her jaw and while she's not bleeding, her perfect hair is matted with Melanie's blood.

"Help her!" Anna pleads to Mavis.

"Hold on," Mavis says, the little W crinkling between her brows, "give her a minute."

In front of me, and swaying like me, Stephanie holds her stomach. She looks terrible, all covered in my blood like that. And even though I want to fall down, I sense my opponent is significantly weakened, so I charge at her with everything I've got. I can feel her under me as we fall, and when we hit the earth one of her ribs smashes into mine and we both scream in pain. And then somehow, as soon as I feel wet grass beneath the back of my hands, I am on my back and Stephanie is on top of me again. Her experience in hand-to-hand combat clearly outweighs mine and I wonder—as I lie there and she punches me on the side of my head (again)—just what other skills this southern belle must have picked up during her years in Georgia.

But Stephanie is tired. I can hear her breathing hard as she pushes herself onto her knees and tries to catch her breath. So I push up too and, aiming for her temple like she just did to me, I punch her as hard as I can, and she falls to the side.

Cheers erupt and I can hear Mavis and Anna and Leslie in the crowd.

"Nice work!" Mavis calls out.

"Yay, Mel!" Leslie hollers.

"Someone should call an ambulance," Anna says.

S. J. Coffey

But I don't need an ambulance. I feel great. I sit up and smile up at my friends. I can taste blood. It is salty and sweet. I won. I kicked Stephanie Harris's butt. They are all smiling down at me—Leslie and Anna and Mavis and the stooges. But then Anna is not smiling and I know, as I take my eyes away from them and look over to where Stephanie was, but isn't anymore. I know. I know, just before I feel my back hit the ground, hard, that I have made a terrible miscalculation and, like so many underdogs before me, I have underestimated my enemy. And now I am going to pay.

Stephanie leans down. "What're you gonna do now, you little weirdo?" she whispers into my ear. I want to give her an answer. I wish I could, but I am finding all of sudden that I can't breathe, and I realize, with horror, that Stephanie's slim, manicured hands are around my neck and they are squeezing, tighter and tighter and tighter.

Anna sees it first. The others are still cheering and jumping and acting like idiots, but Anna is watching as Stephanie Harris pushes herself up onto her hands and knees and like a tarantula, scrambles over and climbs onto Melanie, shoving her back down onto the ground and wrapping her hands around Mel's neck.

"Mavis!" she screams to the tall, young woman next to her. "Do something!"

Mavis looks across the tiny arena to where Nadine stands— arms still crossed, watching the fight—and their eyes meet. Mavis looks down at the struggling pair on the ground, then back up at Nadine, and Anna watches in awe as the two titans exchange nods and come to some sort of taciturn agreement. Then Mavis steps forward. And so does Nadine.

There are times in a girl's life when brute force fails and one must resort to more tactical measures. I believe this might be one of those times.

I am looking up at Stephanie. Her face is above mine and she is grinning like a ghastly clown with aqua blue eye shadow, but around her there's an aura of scintillating, jagged speckles of light. She is a glorious, monstrous Madonna. I think I might be dying. I hope I am not because if I am, I am in hell, because Stephanie Harris has to be one of the devil's angels.

There are no more strategies, honest or not, to deploy now. Subterfuge is the only option and—relying on last year's beginning acting class with Mrs. Abigail Madole—I take it. I close my eyes and go limp, utterly and completely limp.

———◇———

Anna is horrified and watches, helpless, as Melanie stops moving. Beside her, Leslie gasps and the crowd's cheering diminishes and gives way to mutters and murmurs of concern.

"Mel!" Mavis screams, and Anna watches as Mavis and Nadine run, slow motion, to Melanie and Stephanie.

"You killed her, you crazy bitch!" Mavis is yelling, as she and Nadine each take an arm and try to pull Stephanie from Mel. "Get off of her!"

Then Stephanie's face shifts and the mask of hostility and rage slips off. "I didn't mean to," she stammers, "I…"

———◇———

S. J. Coffey

I can hear Stephanie and Mavis. Mavis is next to me. "Mel! Mel!" she's calling. "Wake up, lil buddy!" It is funny how fast you can think when things are going wrong, when your body and your brain are full of adrenaline and fear.

Like Lazarus, I *could* sit up now. Mavis is here and I know I am safe, but I can still feel Stephanie's weight on me. She is sitting on my stomach like I'm a good thoroughbred horse. I bet she's had English riding lessons. I want English riding lessons. I like horses.

No, I'm not going to end this yet. Not this way. Not with Stephanie's heavy one hundred (possibly one hundred and two) pounds of weight still on me. She thinks she won. I should do something fast. Mavis will pull Stephanie off me any second and I'll lose my chance to end this war with the perfect Barbie girl for good.

"I'm sorry," Stephanie is saying. "I didn't mean to kill her." I can feel her weight shifting, I have to act, and now. So I do.

———————◇———————

Tears are forming in Anna's eyes and she cannot move. She's not even sure she is breathing. Next to her, Leslie's hands are clasped in front of her lips and she is repeating over and over, "Please be okay. Please be okay. Please be okay." Anna knows Leslie's mantra will not save her friend, but inside the safety of her mind she is reciting it too. *Please be okay. Please…*

On the ground, Mavis is next to Melanie, and Nadine is standing over Stephanie, who has pulled her hands from Mel's neck and is muttering something as she moves to get off her victim.

Anna is staring at what she is coming to believe is her friend's corpse, when Melanie sits bolt upright and slams her forehead into Stephanie's nose.

———⋄———

Her nose—Stephanie's brand-new, absolutely perfect nose— is spraying blood all over my faded bunny shirt.

Above me, as the crowd erupts in cheers and whistles, Stephanie hops off me and clamps her hands over her gushing nose. "Look what you did! Look!" she is screaming. I'm looking alright. I'm watching her bleed and I'm telling myself I should care about her destroyed nose, but I don't. Mavis is hugging me and Anna is hugging Mavis and Leslie's arms are around all of us and she is crying.

"Oh, Mel!" she says. "We thought you were dead!"

"She wasn't dead," Mavis says, laughing and putting her hand out to me. "She was just playin' possum, weren't you lil buddy?"

I nod and slap my hand on hers and she pulls me up. I am woozy, but I smile and I watch Stephanie, still holding her nose and sobbing, as the crowd parts for her and she runs off towards the school. I assume she's going in search of her dignity and the school nurse. I hope for her sake she can still access both.

The crowd of kids thins and Mavis drops an arm around me and squeezes me gently. "Damn," she says with a whistle. "You got a hard head."

"Yeah, Mel," Anna says, swabbing at her eyes and sniffing. "Very strategic, had me fooled for sure."

"Are you *crying*?" I ask her.

"She is!" Leslie bounces.

"Well I thought you were dead, Mel!" Anna says. "You

scared me silly!"

I realize now that my strategy, while effective, may not have been the best for everyone. "I'm sorry, you guys," I say. "I was kind of out of options."

"It certainly looked like it," Alan says, walking up with my books in his arms. "I was about to call an ambulance." I am so happy to see his sweet, round face, I could cry.

"Thank you, Alan," I tell him. "You're an excellent second and a true hero indeed."

Behind Alan, Dennis, Sean and Joe walk over. "Way to go, Chaffee!" Dennis says, slapping my back a little too hard.

"Ow," I let out.

"Sorry 'bout that, Mel," Dennis says.

"That was amazing!" Sean chimes in, thankfully without touching me.

"Truly stellar effort, Melanie," Joe says quietly, giving me a shy smile.

I reach for my books, but Alan pulls them away. "No, m'lady," he says, bowing gallantly. "I shall carry your load for you today." Then he reaches in his pocket, pulls out a rumpled bandage, and hands it to me.

Alan's show of chivalry prompts bursts of laughter and teasing from the stooges. "M'lady!" Dennis scoffs. "Is that what we're calling you now, Mel?"

"Yeah," Sean adds, "Melanie's no lady!"

Joe is silent but Alan, as usual, comes to my defense. "Now, gentlemen," he says, taking on a decidedly Elizabethan air. "Ms. Melanie, here, is most certainly a lady," he explains, "and as such, we must look after her."

"Look after her?" Mavis says, laughing. "It sure didn't look like she needed any lookin' after a minute ago."

"Got that right," says Nadine.

I remember. "Oh, Mavis, this is Nadine."

The two titans exchange a quick look and then laugh. "We know each other," Mavis says.

"Yeah," Nadine concurs. "We met when she threatened me."

"Sorry about that," Mavis concedes.

"Come on," Anna says. "Let's go call Mel's mom. She's going to need a ride home today, I think."

"I can walk," I protest as we all head across the field in the direction of the school's main office.

"Sweetie have you seen your face?" Leslie says, mocking me.

Anna looks at the tall girl standing next to her. "Mavis," she says, "you are a true friend to our Melanie, here."

"Thank you," Mavis replies. She looks at me and winks. "Mel's easy to be friends with."

"And," continues Anna, "I would like to just say that I am sorry I misjudged you because you're a disadvantaged negro."

"A what!" Mavis pops back. "Girl, we have got to get you educated. Negro. What's wrong with you?"

"I have issues," Anna admits blandly.

"And do I seem *disadvantaged* to you? I mean, come on, look at these threads."

"You always dress amazing, Mavis," Leslie flatters.

"Thank you," Mavis replies, turning to Anna. "Damn skippy, you got issues."

Anna shrugs. "What can I say? My parents are Republican."

And as we walk together, all of us, I am hurt but happy. And I know now—and I imagine I will remember later in my life—that I am walking with the best friends I will ever have.

Epilogue

It is the second Friday after the Wednesday that changed my life, and I am sitting again (finally) at my lab desk in science class with Mavis. It has only been a week and two days, but everything is different. I am different. Mr. Greely's backside is not different, though. It is still perfect, and I have to look up at it again while he writes tomorrow's homework assignment on the board.

I am finishing a drawing of the human skeletal system while Mavis picks purple polish off her thumbnail and watches.

"Femur, right?" she asks, correctly.

"Very good," I say.

Mr. Greely turns from the board. "Don't forget, guys. Your skeletal system diagrams are due on Monday."

"Copy yours?" Mavis asks.

"Sure thing," I say, and hand her the drawing.

"Thanks," she says, standing only seconds before the bell rings. I don't know how she does that. Like her, it's a fantastic mystery.

"What're you up to this weekend?" she asks as we make our way to the classroom door.

"Sleepover at my place tomorrow night," I tell her. "You want to come? I'll tell my mom to get real Coke," I say, teasing.

"Okay," she says, "I'd like that."

"Do you have a sleeping bag?"

The little W appears between her eyes. "Do look like I got a damned sleepin' bag?"

"You can borrow mine." I laugh. "I'll use my brother Steven's. I'm immune to his germs."

———◇———

When I follow Mavis out of the science room and into the hall, Ethan Wilde is leaning against some lockers. My eyes land on his and Mavis gives me a nudge.

"Go talk to that boy, would you?" she says. "He's been moping around here all week. It's getting on my nerves."

I nod and she smiles and puts her palm out, so I slap her five before she struts off down the hall.

Ethan pushes away from the lockers and walks toward me, so I meet him in the middle of the hallway. It's just before the first lunch period, so kids stream past us in both directions. But we are still just standing there looking at each other.

"I wanted to tell you," he begins. "I'm sorry. I shouldn't have left you at the dance like that."

"No sweat," I tell him, and it isn't.

"So," he says, shifting, "do you want to go to the movies tomorrow? You know, as long as you're not drawing those pictures anymore. I mean, I'm sure you're not doing them anymore. I don't know why I'm asking. I know you're really not that kind of girl."

I don't know how to answer Ethan any other way than with a question. And like lots of the questions I seem to have for boys, I'm fairly certain I already know the answer.

"What if I *was* still doing those drawings?" I ask, my eyes never leaving his, even though he can't seem to keep them on me, now. "Would you still want to be with me?"

I already know the answer, even though Ethan doesn't say it. In fact, he doesn't say anything. He just looks away from me and then back at his feet, as if they're interesting in some way. They are not. He is not.

"I'm sorry," I tell him as I look down the hall to where Anna and Leslie stand talking to Alan, who smiles at me, as always. "I already have plans tomorrow night." Ethan looks confused. I would say I feel bad for him, but I don't. He has Stephanie, although I think she's still down in Phoenix getting her nose fixed, poor thing.

I turn to go, but before I do, I look at silent Ethan. "And you know what else?" I say. "I think I *am* that kind of girl."

In front of me, Anna and Leslie and Alan wait near the library and wave. And as I walk, Mavis, and then Nadine, catch up. And behind me is every boy who ever told me not to do something.

Just before we get to the library, I spot Dennis and Sean and Joe talking to a pack of boys. Dennis takes a few bills from one of them, then spots me and gives me a nod. I nod back and smile. *And as for my career in smut peddling,* I think as I get to the library and hug my friends, *I may be just a little too young for retirement.*

THE END

Author Bio

S.J. Coffey is an award-winning screen and fiction writer living and working in Portland, Oregon, with her fiancé Mark and their weight-challenged tabby, Mow Mow. (Feel free to visit Mow Mow's Instagram @fatcatmowmow. She's utterly shameless and will probably follow you if you have food.)

Ms. Coffey's next book, *Firebug*, a young adult suspense-romance about a charismatic high school arsonist, will be in print, e-book and audiobook early next year. Find updates at http://www.sjcoffey.com.